A HAUNTING NOTE

A HAUNTING NOTE

*Music of the Uncanny and Inexplicable
in Classic Speculative Fiction*

Edited by
Chad Arment

COACHWHIP PUBLICATIONS
GREENVILLE, OHIO

A Haunting Note (anthology)
© 2024 Coachwhip Publications edition

Cover: Violin © Nikkytok
CoachwhipBooks.com

ISBN 1-61646-596-4
ISBN-13 978-1-61646-596-4

Contents

The Old Nurse's Story

ELIZABETH GASKELL

(1852)

You know, my dears, that your mother was an orphan, and an only child; and I dare say you have heard that your grandfather was a clergyman up in Westmorland, where I come from. I was just a girl in the village school, when, one day, your grandmother came in to ask the mistress if there was any scholar there who would do for a nurse-maid; and mighty proud I was, I can tell ye, when the mistress called me up, and spoke to my being a good girl at my needle, and a steady honest girl, and one whose parents were very respectable, though they might be poor. I thought I should like nothing better than to serve the pretty young lady, who was blushing as deep as I was, as she spoke of the coming baby, and what I should have to do with it. However, I see you don't care so much for this part of my story, as for what you think is to come, so I'll tell you at once. I was engaged and settled at the parsonage before Miss Rosamond (that was the baby, who is now your mother) was born. To be sure, I had little enough to do with her when she came, for she was never out of her mother's arms, and slept by her all night long; and proud enough was I sometimes when missis trusted her to me. There never was such a baby before or since, though you've all of you been fine enough in your turns; but for sweet, winning ways, you've none of you come up to your mother. She took after her mother, who was a real lady born; a

7

Miss Furnivall, a granddaughter of Lord Furnivall's, in Northumberland. I believe she had neither brother nor sister, and had been brought up in my lord's family till she had married your grandfather, who was just a curate, son to a shopkeeper in Carlisle—but a clever, fine gentleman as ever was—and one who was a right-down hard worker in his parish, which was very wide, and scattered all abroad over the Westmorland Fells. When your mother, little Miss Rosamond, was about four or five years old, both her parents died in a fortnight—one after the other. Ah! that was a sad time. My pretty young mistress and me was looking for another baby, when my master came home from one of his long rides, wet, and tired, and took the fever he died of; and then she never held up her head again, but just lived to see her dead baby, and have it laid on her breast before she sighed away her life. My mistress had asked me, on her death-bed, never to leave Miss Rosamond; but if she had never spoken a word, I would have gone with the little child to the end of the world.

The next thing, and before we had well stilled our sobs, the executors and guardians came to settle the affairs. They were my poor young mistress's own cousin, Lord Furnivall, and Mr. Esthwaite, my master's brother, a shopkeeper in Manchester; not so well-to-do then as he was afterwards, and with a large family rising about him. Well! I don't know if it were their settling, or because of a letter my mistress wrote on her death-bed to her cousin, my lord; but somehow it was settled that Miss Rosamond and me were to go to Furnivall Manor House, in Northumberland, and my lord spoke as if it had been her mother's wish that she should live with his family, and as if he had no objections, for that one or two more or less could make no difference in so grand a household. So though that was not the way in which I should have wished the coming of my bright and pretty pet to have been looked at—who was like a sunbeam in any family, be it never so grand—I was well pleased that all the folks in the Dale should stare and admire, when they heard I was going to be young lady's maid at my Lord Furnivall's at Furnivall Manor.

But I made a mistake in thinking we were to go and live where my lord did. It turned out that the family had left Furnivall Manor House fifty years or more. I could not hear that my poor young mistress had ever been there, though she had been brought up in the family; and I was sorry for that, for I should have liked Miss Rosamond's youth to have passed where her mother's had been.

My lord's gentleman, from whom I asked so many questions as I durst, said that the Manor House was at the foot of the Cumberland Fells, and a very grand place; that an old Miss Furnivall, a great-aunt of my lord's, lived there, with only a few servants; but that it was a very healthy place, and my lord had thought that it would suit Miss Rosamond very well for a few years, and that her being there might perhaps amuse his old aunt.

I was bidden by my lord to have Miss Rosamond's things ready by a certain day. He was a stern proud man, as they say all the Lords Furnivall were; and he never spoke a word more than was necessary. Folk did say he had loved my young mistress; but that, because she knew that his father would object, she would never listen to him, and married Mr. Esthwaite; but I don't know. He never married, at any rate. But he never took much notice of Miss Rosamond; which I thought he might have done if he had cared for her dead mother. He sent his gentleman with us to the Manor House, telling him to join him at Newcastle that same evening; so there was no great length of time for him to make us known to all the strangers before he, too, shook us off; and we were left, two lonely young things (I was not eighteen), in the great old Manor House. It seems like yesterday that we drove there. We had left our own dear parsonage very early, and we had both cried as if our hearts would break, though we were travelling in my lord's carriage, which I thought so much of once. And now it was long past noon on a September day, and we

stopped to change horses for the last time at a little smoky
town, all full of colliers and miners. Miss Rosamond had
fallen asleep, but Mr. Henry told me to waken her, that
she might see the park and the Manor House as we drove
up. I thought it rather a pity; but I did what he bade me,
for fear he should complain of me to my lord. We had left
all signs of a town, or even a village, and were then inside
the gates of a large wild park—not like the parks here in
the north, but with rocks, and the noise of running water,
and gnarled thorn-trees, and old oaks, all white and peeled
with age.

The road went up about two miles, and then we saw
a great and stately house, with many trees close around
it, so close that in some places their branches dragged
against the walls when the wind blew; and some hung
broken down; for no one seemed to take much charge of
the place;—to lop the wood, or to keep the moss-covered
carriage-way in order. Only in front of the house all was
clear. The great oval drive was without a weed; and neither tree nor creeper was allowed to grow over the long,
many-windowed front; at both sides of which a wing pro-
jected, which were each the ends of other side fronts; for
the house, although it was so desolate, was even grander
than I expected. Behind it rose the Fells, which seemed
unenclosed and bare enough; and on the left hand of the
house, as you stood facing it, was a little, old-fashioned
flower-garden, as I found out afterwards. A door opened
out upon it from the west front; it had been scooped out
of the thick dark wood for some old Lady Furnivall; but
the branches of the great forest trees had grown and over-
shadowed it again, and there were very few flowers that
would live there at that time.

When we drove up to the great front entrance, and
went into the hall, I thought we should be lost—it was
so large, and vast, and grand. There was a chandelier all
of bronze, hung down from the middle of the ceiling;
and I had never seen one before, and looked at it all in

amaze. Then, at one end of the hall, was a great fire-place, as large as the sides of the houses in my country, with massy andirons and dogs to hold the wood; and by it were heavy old-fashioned sofas. At the opposite end of the hall, to the left as you went in—on the western side—was an organ built into the wall, and so large that it filled up the best part of that end. Beyond it, on the same side, was a door; and opposite, on each side of the fire-place, were also doors leading to the east front; but those I never went through as long as I stayed in the house, so I can't tell you what lay beyond.

The afternoon was closing in, and the hall, which had no fire lighted in it, looked dark and gloomy, but we did not stay there a moment. The old servant, who had opened the door for us, bowed to Mr. Henry, and took us in through the door at the further side of the great organ, and led us through several smaller halls and passages into the west drawing-room, where he said that Miss Furnivall was sitting. Poor little Miss Rosamond held very tight to me, as if she were scared and lost in that great place, and as for myself, I was not much better. The west drawing-room was very cheerful-looking, with a warm fire in it, and plenty of good, comfortable furniture about. Miss Furnivall was an old lady not far from eighty, I should think, but I do not know. She was thin and tall, and had a face as full of fine wrinkles as if they had been drawn all over it with a needle's point. Her eyes were very watchful, to make up, I suppose, for her being so deaf as to be obliged to use a trumpet. Sitting with her, working at the same great piece of tapestry, was Mrs. Stark, her maid and companion, and almost as old as she was. She had lived with Miss Furnivall ever since they were both young, and now she seemed more like a friend than a servant; she looked so cold and grey, and stony as if she had never loved or cared for any one; and I don't suppose she did care for any one, except her mistress; and, owing to the great deafness of the latter, Mrs. Stark treated her very much as if she were a child. Mr. Henry gave some message from my lord, and then he bowed goodbye to us all—taking no notice of my sweet little Miss Rosamond's outstretched hand—and left us standing there, being looked at by the two old ladies through their spectacles.

I was right glad when they rung for the old footman who had shown us in at first, and told him to take us to our rooms. So we went out of that great drawing-room, and into another sitting-room, and out of that, and then up a great flight of stairs, and along a broad gallery—which was something like a library, having books all down one side, and windows and writing-tables all down the other—till we came to our rooms, which I was not sorry to hear were just over the kitchens; for I began to think I should be lost in that wilderness of a house. There was an old nursery that had been used for all the little lords and ladies long ago, with a pleasant fire burning in the grate, and the kettle boiling on the hob, and tea-things spread out on the table; and out of that room was the night-nursery, with a little crib for Miss Rosamond close to my bed. And old James called up Dorothy, his wife, to bid us welcome; and both he and she were so hospitable and kind, that by and by Miss Rosamond and me felt quite at home; and by the time tea was over, she was sitting on Dorothy's knee, and chattering away as fast as her little tongue could go. I soon found out that Dorothy was from Westmorland, and that bound her and me together, as it were; and I would never wish to meet with kinder people than were old James and his wife. James had lived pretty nearly all his life in my lord's family, and thought there was no one so grand as they. He even looked down a lit-tle on his wife; because, till he had married her, she had never lived in any but a farmer's household. But he was very fond of her, as well he might be. They had one ser-vant under them, to do all the rough work. Agnes they called her; and she and me, and James and Dorothy, with Miss Furnivall and Mrs. Stark, made up the family; always

remembering my sweet little Miss Rosamond! I used to
wonder what they had done before she came, they thought
so much of her now. Kitchen and drawing-room, it was
all the same. The hard, sad Miss Furnivall, and the cold
Mrs. Stark, looked pleased when she came fluttering in
like a bird, playing and pranking hither and thither, with
a continual murmur, and pretty prattle of gladness. I am
sure, they were sorry many a time when she flitted away
into the kitchen, though they were too proud to ask her
to stay with them, and were a little surprised at her taste;
though to be sure, as Mrs. Stark said, it was not to be
wondered at, I remembering what stock her father had
come of. The great, old rambling house was a famous place
for little Miss Rosamond. She made expeditions all over
it, with me at her heels; all, except the east wing, which
was never opened, and whither we never thought of going.
But in the western and northern part was many a pleasant
room; full of things that were curiosities to us, though
they might not have been to people who had seen more.
The windows were darkened by the sweeping boughs of the
trees, and the ivy which had overgrown them: but, in the
green gloom, we could manage to see old China jars and
caned ivory boxes, and great heavy books, and, above all,
the old pictures!

Once, I remember, my darling would have Dorothy go
with us to tell us who they all were; for they were all portraits of some of my lord's family, though Dorothy could
not tell us the names of every one. We had gone through
most of the rooms, when we came to the old state drawing-room over the hall, and there was a picture of Miss
Furnivall; or, as she was called in those days, Miss Grace,
for she was the younger sister. Such a beauty she must
have been! but with such a set, proud look, and such scorn
looking out of her handsome eyes, with her eyebrows just
a little raised, as if she were wondering how any one could
have the impertinence to look at her; and her lip curled
at us, as we stood there gazing. She had a dress on, the

like of which I had never seen before, but it was all the
fashion when she was young: a hat of some soft white stuff
like beaver, pulled a little over her brows, and a beautiful
plume of feathers sweeping round it on one side; and her
gown of blue satin was open in front to a quilted white
stomacher.

"Well, to be sure!" said I, when I had gazed my fill.
"Flesh is grass, they do say; but who would have thought
that Miss Furnivall had been such an out-and-out beauty,
to see her now?"

"Yes," said Dorothy. "Folks change sadly. But if what
my master's father used to say was true, Miss Furnivall,
the elder sister, was handsomer than Miss Grace. Her picture is here somewhere; but, if I show it you, you must
never let on, even to James, that you have seen it. Can the
little lady hold her tongue, think you?" asked she.

I was not so sure, for she was such a little sweet, bold,
open-spoken child, so I set her to hide herself; and then I
helped Dorothy to turn a great picture, that leaned with
its face towards the wall, and was not hung up as the others
were. To be sure, it beat Miss Grace for beauty; and, I
think, for scornful pride, too, though in that matter it
might be hard to choose. I could have looked at it an hour,
but Dorothy seemed half frightened at having shown it
to me, and hurried it back again, and bade me run and
find Miss Rosamond, for that there were some ugly places
about the house, where she should like ill for the child to
go. I was a brave, high-spirited girl, and thought little of
what the old woman said, for I liked hide-and-seek as well
as any child in the parish; so off I ran to find my little one.

As winter drew on, and the days grew shorter, I was
sometimes almost certain that I heard a noise as if some
one was playing on the great organ in the hall. I did not
hear it every evening; but, certainly, I did very often; usually when I was sitting with Miss Rosamond, after I had
put her to bed, and keeping quite still and silent in the
bedroom. Then I used to hear it booming and swelling

away in the distance. The first night, when I went down to my supper, I asked Dorothy who had been playing music, and James said very shortly that I was a gowk to take the wind soughing among the trees for music: but I saw Dorothy look at him very fearfully, and Bossy, the kitchen-maid, said something beneath her breath, and went quite white. I saw they did not like my question, so I held my peace till I was with Dorothy alone, when I knew I could get a good deal out of her. So, the next day, I watched my time, and I coaxed and asked her who it was that played the organ: for I knew that it was the organ and not the wind well enough, for all I had kept silence before James. But Dorothy had had her lesson, I'll warrant, and never a word could I get from her. So then I tried Bessy, though I had always held my head rather above her, as I was evened to James and Dorothy, and she was little better than their servant. So she said I must never, never tell; and if I ever told, I was never to say *she* had told me; but it was a very strange noise, and she had heard it many a time, but most of all on winter nights, and before storms; and folks did say, it was the old lord playing on the great organ in the hall, just as he used to do when he was alive; but who the old lord was, or why he played, and why he played on stormy winter evenings in particular, she either could not or would not tell me. Well! I told you I had a brave heart; and I thought it was rather pleasant to have that grand music rolling about the house, let who would be the player; for now it rose above the great gusts of wind, and wailed and triumphed just like a living creature, and then it fell to a softness most complete; only it was always music and tunes, so it was nonsense to call it the wind. I thought at first that it might be Miss Furnivall who played, unknown to Bossy; but one day when I was in the hall by myself, I opened the organ and peeped all about it and around it, as I had done to the organ in Crosthwaite Church once before, and I saw it was all broken and destroyed inside, though it looked so brave and fine; and then, though it

was noonday, my flesh began to creep a little, and I shut
it up, and run away pretty quickly to my own bright nursery; and I did not like hearing the music for some time
after that, any more than James and Dorothy did. All this
time Miss Rosamond was making herself more and more
beloved. The old ladies liked her to dine with them at
their early dinner; James stood behind Miss Furnivall's
chair, and I behind Miss Rosamond's all in state; and, after
dinner, she would play about in a corner of the great drawing-room, as still as any mouse, while Miss Furnivall slept,
and I had my dinner in the kitchen. But she was glad
enough to come to me in the nursery afterwards; for, as
she said, Miss Furnivall was so sad, and Mrs. Stark so dull;
but she and I were merry enough; and, by-and-by, I got
not to care for that weird rolling music, which did one no
harm, if we did not know where it came from.

That winter was very cold. In the middle of October
the frosts began, and lasted many, many weeks. I remember, one day at dinner, Miss Furnivall lifted up her sad,
heavy eyes, and said to Mrs. Stark, "I am afraid we shall
have a terrible winter," in a strange kind of meaning way.
But Mrs. Stark pretended not to hear, and talked very loud
of something else. My little lady and I did not care for the
frost; not we! As long as it was dry we climbed up the steep
brows, behind the house, and went up on the Fells, which
were bleak, and bare enough, and there we ran races in the
fresh, sharp air; and once we came down by a new path
that took us past the two old gnarled holly-trees, which
grew about halfway down by the east side of the house.
But the days grew shorter and shorter; and the old lord,
if it was he, played more and more stormily and sadly on
the great organ. One Sunday afternoon—it must have been
towards the end of November—I asked Dorothy to take
charge of little Missey when she came out of the drawing-
room, after Miss Furnivall had had her nap; for it was too
cold to take her with me to church, and yet I wanted to
go. And Dorothy was glad enough to promise, and was so

fond of the child that all seemed well; and Bessy and I set off very briskly, though the sky hung heavy and black over the white earth, as if the night had never fully gone away; and the air, though still, was very biting and keen.

"We shall have a fall of snow," said Bessy to me. And sure enough, even while we were in church, it came down thick, in great large flakes, so thick it almost darkened the windows. It had stopped snowing before we came out, but it lay soft, thick and deep beneath our feet, as we tramped home. Before we got to the hall the moon rose, and I think it was lighter then—what with the moon, and what with the white dazzling snow—than it had been when we went to church, between two and three o'clock. I have not told you that Miss Furnivall and Mrs. Stark never went to church: they used to read the prayers together, in their quiet gloomy way; they seemed to feel the Sunday very long without their tapestry-work to be busy at. So when I went to Dorothy in the kitchen, to fetch Miss Rosamond and take her upstairs with me, I did not much wonder when the old woman told me that the ladies had kept the child with them, and that she had never come to the kitchen, as I had bidden her, when she was tired of behaving pretty in the drawing-room. So I took off my things and went to find her, and bring her to her supper in the nursery. But when I went into the best drawing-room there sat the two old ladies, very still and quiet, dropping out a word now and then but looking as if nothing so bright and merry as Miss Rosamond had ever been near them. Still I thought she might be hiding from me; it was one of her pretty ways; and that she had persuaded them to look as if they knew nothing about her; so I went softly peeping under this sofa, and behind that chair, making believe I was sadly frightened at not finding her.

"What's the matter, Hester?" said Mrs. Stark, sharply. I don't know if Miss Furnivall had seen me, for, as I told you, she was very deaf, and she sat quite still, idly staring into the fire, with her hopeless face. "I'm only looking for my little Rosy-Posy," replied I, still thinking that the child was there, and near me, though I could not see her.

"Miss Rosamond is not here," said Mrs. Stark. "She went away more than an hour ago to find Dorothy."

And she too turned and went on looking into the fire.

My heart sank at this, and I began to wish I had never left my darling. I went back to Dorothy and told her. James was gone out for the day, but she and me and Bessy took lights and went up into the nursery first, and then we roamed over the great large house, calling and entreating Miss Rosamond to come out of her hiding-place, and not frighten us to death in that way. But there was no answer; no sound.

"Oh!" said I at last, "Can she have got into the east wing and hidden there?"

But Dorothy said it was not possible, for that she herself had never been there; that the doors were always locked, and my lord's steward had the keys, she believed; at any rate, neither she nor James had ever seen them: so I said I would go back, and see if, after all, she was not hidden in the drawing-room, unknown to the old ladies; and if I found her there, I said, I would whip her well for the fright she had given me; but I never meant to do it. Well, I went back to the west drawing-room, and I told Mrs. Stark we could not find her anywhere, and asked for leave to look all about the furniture there, for I thought now, that she might have fallen asleep in some warm hidden corner; but no! we looked—Miss Furnivall got up and looked, trembling all over—and she was nowhere there; then we set off again, every one in the house, and looked in all the places we had searched before, but we could not find her. Miss Furnivall shivered and shook so much that Mrs. Stark took her back into the warm drawing-room; but not before they had made me promise to bring her to them when she was found. Well-a-day! I began to think she never would be found, when I bethought me to look out into the great front court, all covered with snow. I was

upstairs when I looked out; but it was such clear moonlight, I could see, quite plain, two little footprints, which
might be traced from the hall door, and round the corner of the east wing. I don't know how I got down, but I
tugged open the great, stiff hall door; and, throwing the
skirt of my gown over my head for a cloak, I ran out. I
turned the east corner, and there a black shadow fell on
the snow; but when I came again into the moonlight, there
were the little footmarks going up—up to the Fells. It
was bitter cold; so cold that the air almost took the skin
off my face as I ran, but I ran on, crying to think how
my poor little darling must be perished, and frightened.
I was within sight of the holly-trees when I saw a shepherd coming down the hill, bearing something in his arms
wrapped in his maud. He shouted to me, and asked me if
I had lost a bairn; and, when I could not speak for crying,
he bore towards me, and I saw my wee bairnie lying still,
and white, and stiff, in his arms, as if she had been dead.
He told me he had been up the Fells to gather in his sheep,
before the deep cold of night came on, and that under the
holly-trees (black marks on the hill-side, where no other
bush was for miles around) he had found my little lady
my lamb—my queen—my darling stiff and cold, in the
terrible sleep which is frost-begotten. Oh! the joy, and
the tears of having her in my arms once again! for I would
not let him carry her; but took her, maud and all, into my
own arms, and held her near my own warm neck and heart,
and felt the life stealing slowly back again into her little
gentle limbs. But she was still insensible when we reached
the hall, and I had no breath for speech. We went in by
the kitchen door.

"Bring the warming-pan," said I; and I carried her upstairs and began undressing her by the nursery fire, which
Bessy had kept up. I called my little lammie all the sweet
and playful names I could think of—even while my eyes
were blinded by my tears; and at last, oh! at length she
opened her large blue eyes. Then I put her into her warm

bed, and sent Dorothy down to tell Miss Furnivall that all
was well; and I made up my mind to sit by my darling's
bedside the live-long night. She fell away into a soft sleep
as soon as her pretty head had touched the pillow, and I
watched by her until morning light; when she wakened up
bright and clear—or so I thought at first—and, my dears,
so I think now.

She said that she had fancied that she should like to go
to Dorothy, for that both the old ladies were asleep, and
it was very dull in the drawing-room; and that, as she was
going through the west lobby, she saw the snow through
the high window falling—falling—soft and steady; but she
wanted to see it lying pretty and white on the ground; so
she made her way into the great hall; and then, going to
the window, she saw it bright and soft upon the drive; but
while she stood there, she saw a little girl, not so old as
she was, "but so pretty," said my darling, "and this little
girl beckoned to me to come out; and oh, she was so pretty
and so sweet, I could not choose but go." And then this
other little girl had taken her by the hand, and side by side
the two had gone round the east corner.

"Now you are a naughty little girl, and telling stories,"
said I. "What would your good mamma, that is in heaven,
and never told a story in her life, say to her little Rosamond, if she heard her—and I dare say she does—telling
stories!"

"Indeed, Hester," sobbed out my child, "I'm telling you
true. Indeed I am."

"Don't tell me!" said I, very stern. "I tracked you by
your footmarks through the snow; there were only yours to
be seen: and if you had had a little girl to go hand-in-hand
with you up the hill, don't you think the footprints would
have gone along with yours?"

"I can't help it, dear, dear Hester," said she, crying, "if
they did not; I never looked at her feet, but she held my
hand fast and tight in her little one, and it was very, very
cold. She took me up the Fell-path, up to the holly-trees;

and there I saw a lady weeping and crying; but when she saw me, she hushed her weeping, and smiled very proud and grand, and took me on her knee, and began to lull me to sleep; and I that's all, Hester—but that is true; and my dear mamma knows it is," said she, crying. So I thought the child was in a fever, and pretended to believe her, as she went over her story—over and over again, and always the same. At last Dorothy knocked at the door with Miss Rosamond's breakfast; and she told me the old ladies were down in the eating parlour, and that they wanted to speak to me. They had both been into the night-nursery the evening before, but it was after Miss Rosamond was asleep; so they had only looked at her—not asked me any questions.

"I shall catch it," thought I to myself, as I went along the north gallery. "And yet," I thought, taking courage, "it was in their charge I left her; and it's they that's to blame for letting her steal away unknown and unwatched." So I went in boldly, and told my story. I told it all to Miss Furnivall, shouting it close to her ear; but when I came to the mention of the other little girl out in the snow, coaxing and tempting her out, and wiling her up to the grand and beautiful lady by the holly-tree, she threw her arms up her old and withered arms—and cried aloud, "Oh! Heaven, forgive! Have mercy!"

Mrs. Stark took hold of her; roughly enough, I thought; but she was past Mrs. Stark's management, and spoke to me, in a kind of wild warning and authority.

"Hester! keep her from that child! It will lure her to her death! That evil child! Tell her it is a wicked, naughty child." Then Mrs. Stark hurried me out of the room; where, indeed, I was glad enough to go; but Miss Furnivall kept shrieking out, "Oh! have mercy! Wilt Thou never forgive! It is many a long year ago"—

I was very uneasy in my mind after that. I durst never leave Miss Rosamond, night or day, for fear lest she might slip off again, after some fancy or other; and all the more because I thought I could make out that Miss Furnivall

was crazy, from their odd ways about her; and I was afraid
lest something of the same kind (which might be in the
family, you know) hung over my darling. And the great
frost never ceased all this time; and whenever it was a more
stormy night than usual, between the gusts, and through
the wind, we heard the old lord playing on the great organ.
But, old lord, or not, wherever Miss Rosamond went,
there I followed; for my love for her, pretty helpless orphan, was stronger than my fear for the grand and terrible
sound. Besides, it rested with me to keep her cheerful and
merry, as beseemed her age. So we played together, and
wandered together, here and there, and everywhere; for
I never dared to lose sight of her again in that large and
rambling house. And so it happened, that one afternoon,
not long before Christmas Day, we were playing together
on the billiard-table in the great hall (not that we knew
the way of playing, but she liked to roll the smooth ivory
balls with her pretty hands, and I liked to do whatever she
did); and, by-and-by, without our noticing it, it grew dusk
indoors, though it was still light in the open air, and I was
thinking of taking her back into the nursery, when, all of
a sudden, she cried out:

"Look, Hester! look! there is my poor little girl out in
the snow!"

I turned towards the long narrow windows, and there,
sure enough, I saw a little girl, less than my Miss Rosamond—dressed all unfit to be out-of-doors such a bitter
night—crying, and beating against the window-panes, as
if she wanted to be let in. She seemed to sob and wail,
till Miss Rosamond could bear it no longer, and was flying to the door to open it, when, all of a sudden, and
close up upon us, the great organ pealed out so loud and
thundering, it fairly made me tremble; and all the more,
when I remembered me that, even in the stillness of that
dead-cold weather, I had heard no sound of little battering hands upon the window-glass, although the Phantom
Child had seemed to put forth all its force; and, although

I had seen it wail and cry, no faintest touch of sound had fallen upon my ears. Whether I remembered all this at the very moment, I do not know; the great organ sound had so stunned me into terror; but this I know, I caught up Miss Rosamond before she got the hall-door opened, and clutched her, and carried her away, kicking and screaming, into the large bright kitchen, where Dorothy and Agnes were busy with their mince-pies.

"What is the matter with my sweet one?" cried Dorothy, as I bore in Miss Rosamond, who was sobbing as if her heart would break.

"She won't let me open the door for my little girl to come in; and she'll die if she is out on the Fells all night. Cruel, naughty Hester," she said, slapping me; but she might have struck harder, for I had seen a look of ghastly terror on Dorothy's face, which made my very blood run cold.

"Shut the back-kitchen door fast, and bolt it well," said she to Agnes. She said no more; she gave me raisins and almonds to quiet Miss Rosamond: but she sobbed about the little girl in the snow, and would not touch any of the good things. I was thankful when she cried herself to sleep in bed. Then I stole down to the kitchen, and told Dorothy I had made up my mind. I would carry my darling back to my father's house in Applethwaite; where, if we lived humbly, we lived at peace. I said I had been frightened enough with the old lord's organ-playing; but now that I had seen for myself this little moaning child, all decked out as no child in the neighbourhood could be, beating and battering to get in, yet always without any sound or noise—with the dark wound on its right shoulder; and that Miss Rosamond had known it again for the phantom that had nearly lured her to her death (which Dorothy knew was true); I would stand it no longer.

I saw Dorothy change colour once or twice. When I had done, she told me she did not think I could take Miss Rosamond with me, for that she was my lord's ward, and I had no right over her; and she asked me, would I leave the child that I was so fond of, just for sounds and sights that could do me no harm; and that they had all had to get used to in their turns? I was all in a hot, trembling passion; and I said it was very well for her to talk, that knew what these sights and noises betokened, and that had, perhaps, had something to do with the Spectre-Child while it was alive. And I taunted her so, that she told me all she knew, at last; and then I wished I had never been told, for it only made me afraid more than ever.

She said she had heard the tale from old neighbours, that were alive when she was first married; when folks used to come to the hall sometimes, before it had got such a bad name on the country side: it might not be true, or it might, what she had been told.

The old lord was Miss Furnivall's father—Miss Grace as Dorothy called her, for Miss Maude was the elder, and Miss Furnivall by rights. The old lord was eaten up with pride. Such a proud man was never seen or heard of; and his daughters were like him. No one was good enough to wed them, although they had choice enough; for they were the great beauties of their day, as I had seen by their portraits, where they hung in the state drawing-room. But, as the old saying is, "Pride will have a fall"; and these two haughty beauties fell in love with the same man, and he no better than a foreign musician, whom their father had down from London to play music with him at the Manor House. For, above all things, next to his pride, the old lord loved music. He could play on nearly every instrument that ever was heard of: and it was a strange thing it did not soften him; but he was a fierce dour old man, and had broken his poor wife's heart with his cruelty, they said. He was mad after music, and would pay any money for it. So he got this foreigner to come; who made such beautiful music, that they said the very birds on the trees stopped their singing to listen. And, by degrees, this foreign gentleman got such a hold over the old lord, that nothing would serve him but that he must come every year; and it was he that had the great organ brought from Holland, and built up in the hall, where it stood now. He taught the old lord to play on it; but many and many a time, when Lord Furnivall was thinking of nothing but his fine organ, and his finer music, the dark foreigner was walking abroad in the woods with one of the young ladies: now Miss Maude, and then Miss Grace.

Miss Maude won the day and carried off the prize, such as it was; and he and she were married, all unknown to any one; and before he made his next yearly visit, she had been confined of a little girl at a farm-house on the Moors, while her father and Miss Grace thought she was away at Doncaster Races. But though she was a wife and a mother, she was not a bit softened, but as haughty and as passionate as ever; and perhaps more so, for she was jealous of Miss Grace, to whom her foreign husband paid a deal of court—by way of blinding her—as he told his wife. But Miss Grace triumphed over Miss Maude, and Miss Maude grew fiercer and fiercer, both with her husband and with her sister; and the former—who could easily shake off what was disagreeable, and hide himself in foreign countries—went away a month before his usual time that summer, and half-threatened that he would never come back again. Meanwhile, the little girl was left at the farm-house, and her mother used to have her horse saddled and gallop wildly over the hills to see her once every week, at the very least—for where she loved, she loved; and where she hated, she hated. And the old lord went on playing—playing on his organ; and the servants thought the sweet music he made had soothed down his awful temper, of which (Dorothy said) some terrible tales could be told. He grew infirm too, and had to walk with a crutch; and his son that was the present Lord Furnivall's father was with the army in America, and the other son at sea; so Miss Maude had it pretty much her own way, and she and Miss Grace grew colder and bitterer to each other every day; till at last they hardly ever spoke, except when the old lord was by. The foreign musician came again the next summer, but it was for the last time; for they led him such a life with their jealousy and their passions, that he grew weary, and went away, and never was heard of again. And Miss Maude, who had always meant to have her marriage acknowledged when her father should be dead, was left now a deserted wife whom nobody knew to have been married—with a child that she dared not own, although she loved it to distraction; living with a father whom she feared, and a sister whom she hated. When the next summer passed over and the dark foreigner never came, both Miss Maude and Miss Grace grew gloomy and sad; they had a haggard look about them, though they looked handsome as ever. But by-and-by Miss Maude brightened; for her father grew more and more infirm, and more than ever carried away by his music; and she and Miss Grace lived almost entirely apart, having separate rooms, the one on the west side, Miss Maude on the east those very rooms which were now shut up. So she thought she might have her little girl with her, and no one need ever know except those who dared not speak about it, and were bound to believe that it was, as she said, a cottager's child she had taken a fancy too. All this, Dorothy said, was pretty well known; but what came afterwards no one knew, except Miss Grace, and Mrs. Stark, who was even then her maid, and much more of a friend to her than ever her sister had been. But the servants supposed, from words that were dropped, that Miss Maude had triumphed over Miss Grace, and told her that all the time the dark foreigner had been mocking her with pretended love—he was her own husband; the colour left Miss Grace's cheek and lips that very day for ever, and she was heard to say many a time that sooner or later she would have her revenge; and Mrs. Stark was for ever spying about the east rooms.

One fearful night, just after the New Year had come in, when the snow was lying thick and deep, and the flakes

were still falling—fast enough to blind any one who might
be out and abroad—there was a great and violent noise
heard, and the old lord's voice above all, cursing and swear-
ing awfully—and the cries of a little child—and the proud
defiance of a fierce woman—and the sound of a blow—and
a dead stillness—and moans and wailings dying away on
the hill-side! Then the old lord summoned all his servants,
and told them, with terrible oaths, and words more terrible, that his daughter had disgraced herself, and that he
had turned her out of doors—her, and her child—and that
if ever they gave her help—or food—or shelter—he prayed
that they might never enter Heaven. And, all the while,
Miss Grace stood by him, white and still as any stone; and
when he had ended she heaved a great sigh, as much as
to say her work was done, and her end was accomplished.
But the old lord never touched his organ again, and died
within the year; and no wonder! for, on the morrow of that
wild and fearful night, the shepherds, coming down the
Fell side, found Miss Maude sitting, all crazy and smiling,
under the holly-trees, nursing a dead child—with a terrible mark on its right shoulder. "But that was not what
killed it," said Dorothy; "it was the frost and the cold;
every wild creature was in its hole, and every beast in its
fold—while the child and its mother were turned out to
wander on the Fells! And now you know all! and I wonder
if you are less frightened now?"

I was more frightened than ever; but I said I was not. I
wished Miss Rosamond and myself well out of that dreadful house for ever; but I would not leave her, and I dared
not take her away. But oh! how I watched her, and guarded
her! We bolted the doors and shut the window-shutters
fast, an hour or more before dark, rather than leave them
open five minutes too late. But my little lady still heard
the weird child crying and mourning; and not all we could
do or say could keep her from wanting to go to her, and let
her in from the cruel wind and the snow. All this time, I
kept away from Miss Furnivall and Mrs. Stark, as much as

ever I could; for I feared them—I knew no good could be about them, with their grey hard faces, and their dreamy eyes, looking back into the ghastly years that were gone. But, even in my fear, I had a kind of pity—for Miss Furnivall, at least. Those gone down to the pit can hardly have a more hopeless look than that which was ever on her face. At last I even got so sorry for her—who never said a word but what was quite forced from her—that I prayed for her; and I taught Miss Rosamond to pray for one who had done a deadly sin; but often when she came to those words, she would listen, and start up from her knees, and say, "I hear my little girl plaining and crying very sad—oh! let her in, or she will die!"

One night—just after New Year's Day had come at last, and the long winter had taken a turn, as I hoped—I heard the west drawing-room bell ring three times, which was a signal for me. I would not leave Miss Rosamond alone, for all she was asleep—for the old lord had been playing wilder than ever—and I feared lest my darling should waken to hear the spectre child; see her I knew she could not. I had fastened the windows too well for that. So I took her out of her bed and wrapped her up in such outer clothes as were most handy, and carried her down to the drawing-room, where the old ladies sat at their tapestry work as usual. They looked up when I came in, and Mrs. Stark asked, quite astounded, "Why did I bring Miss Rosamond there, out of her warm bed?" I had begun to whisper, "Because I was afraid of her being tempted out while I was away, by the wild child in the snow," when she stopped me short (with a glance at Miss Furnivall), and said Miss Furnivall wanted me to undo some work she had done wrong, and which neither of them could see to unpick. So I laid my pretty dear on the sofa, and sat down on a stool by them, and hardened my heart against them, as I heard the wind rising and howling.

Miss Rosamond slept on sound, for all the wind blew so; and Miss Furnivall said never a word, nor looked round

when the gusts shook the windows. All at once she started
up to her full height, and put up one hand, as if to bid us
listen.

"I hear voices!" said she, "I hear terrible screams—I
hear my father's voice!"

Just at that moment my darling wakened with a sudden
start: "My little girl is crying, oh, how she is crying!"
and she tried to get up and go to her, but she got her feet
entangled in the blanket, and I caught her up; for my flesh
had begun to creep at these noises, which they heard while
we could catch no sound. In a minute or two the noises
came, and gathered fast, and filled our ears; we, too, heard
voices and screams, and no longer heard the winter's wind
that raged abroad. Mrs. Stark looked at me, and I at her,
but we dared not speak. Suddenly Miss Furnivall went towards the door, out into the ante-room, through the west
lobby, and opened the door into the great hall. Mrs. Stark
followed, and I durst not be left, though my heart almost
stopped beating for fear. I wrapped my darling tight in
my arms, and went out with them. In the hall the screams
were louder than ever; they sounded to come from the
east wing—nearer and nearer—close on the other side of
the locked-up doors—close behind them. Then I noticed
that the great bronze chandelier seemed all alight, though
the hall was dim, and that a fire was blazing in the vast
hearth-place, though it gave no heat; and I shuddered up
with terror, and folded my darling closer to me. But as I
did so, the east door shook, and she, suddenly struggling
to get free from me, cried, "Hester! I must go! My little
girl is there; I hear her; she is coming! Hester, I must go!"

I held her tight with all my strength; with a set will, I
held her. If I had died, my hands would have grasped her
still, I was so resolved in my mind. Miss Furnivall stood
listening, and paid no regard to my darling, who had got
down to the ground, and whom I, upon my knees now, was
holding with both my arms clasped round her neck; she
still striving and crying to get free. All at once the east

door gave way with a thundering crash, as if torn open in a violent passion, and there came into that broad and mysterious light, the figure of a tall old man, with grey hair and gleaming eyes. He drove before him, with many a relentless gesture of abhorrence, a stern and beautiful woman, with a little child clinging to her dress.

"O Hester! Hester!" cried Miss Rosamond. "It's the lady! the lady below the holly-trees; and my little girl is with her. Hester! Hester! let me go to her; they are drawing me to them. I feel them I feel them. I must go!"

Again she was almost convulsed by her efforts to get away; but I held her tighter and tighter, till I feared I should do her a hurt; but rather that than let her go towards those terrible phantoms. They passed along towards the great hall-door, where the winds howled and ravened for their prey; but before they reached that, the lady turned; and I could see that she defied the old man with a fierce and proud defiance; but then she quailed—and then she threw up her arms wildly and piteously to save her child—her little child—from a blow from his uplifted crutch.

And Miss Rosamond was torn as by a power stronger than mine, and writhed in my arms, and sobbed (for by this time the poor darling was growing faint).

"They want me to go with them on to the Fells—they are drawing me to them. Oh, my little girl! I would come, but cruel, wicked Hester holds me very tight." But when she saw the uplifted crutch she swooned away, and I thanked God for it. Just at this moment—when the tall old man, his hair streaming as in the blast of a furnace, was going to strike the little shrinking child Miss Furnivall, the old woman by my side, cried out, "Oh, father! father! spare the little innocent child!" But just then I saw—we all saw—another phantom shape itself, and grow clear out of the blue and misty light that filled the hall; we had not seen her till now, for it was another lady who stood by the old man, with a look of relentless hate and triumphant scorn. That figure was very beautiful to look upon, with a soft white hat drawn down over the proud brows and a red and curling lip. It was dressed in an open robe of blue satin. I had seen that figure before. It was the likeness of Miss Furnivall in her youth; and the terrible phantoms moved on, regardless of old Miss Furnivall's wild entreaty—and the uplifted crutch fell on the right shoulder of the little child, and the younger sister looked on, stony and deadly serene. But at that moment the dim lights, and the fire that gave no heat, went out of themselves, and Miss Furnivall lay at our feet stricken down by the palsy death-stricken.

Yes! she was carried to her bed that night never to rise again. She lay with her face to the wall muttering low but muttering always: "Alas! alas! what is done in youth can never be undone in age! What is done in youth can never be undone in age!"

The Murderer's Violin

Émile Erckmann and Alexandre Chatrian

(1860)

Karl Hâfitz had spent six years in mastering counterpoint. He had studied Haydn, Glick, Mozart, Beethoven, and Rossini; he enjoyed capital health, and was possessed of ample means which permitted him to indulge his artistic tastes—in a word, he possessed all that goes to make up the grand and beautiful in music, except that insignificant but very necessary thing—inspiration!

Every day, fired with a noble ardour, he carried to his worthy instructor, Albertus Kilian, long pieces harmonious enough, but of which every phrase was "cribbed." His master, Albertus, seated in his arm-chair, his feet on the fender, his elbow on a corner of the table, smoking his pipe all the time, set himself to erase, one after the other, the singular discoveries of his pupil. Karl cried with rage, he got very angry, and disputed the point; but the old master quietly opened one of his numerous music-books, and putting his finger on the passage, said—

"Look there, my boy."

Then Karl bowed his head and despaired of the future.

But one fine morning, when he had presented to his master as his own composition a fantasia of Baccherini, varied with Viotti, the good man could no longer remain silent.

"Karl," he exclaimed, "do you take me for a fool? Do you think that I cannot detect your larcenies? This is really too bad!"

And then perceiving the consternation of his pupil, he added—"Listen. I am willing to believe that your memory is to blame, and that you mistake recollection for originality, but you are growing too fat decidedly; you drink too generous a wine, and, above all, too much beer. That is what is shutting up the avenues of your intellect. You must get thinner!"

"Get thinner!"

"Yes, or give up music. You do not lack science, but ideas, and it is very simple; if you pass your whole life covering the strings of your violin with a coat of grease how can they vibrate?"

These words penetrated the depths of Hâfitz's soul.

"If it is necessary for me to get thin," exclaimed he, "I will not shrink from any sacrifice. Since matter oppresses the mind I will starve myself."

His countenance wore such an expression of heroism at that moment that Albertus was touched; he embraced his pupil and wished him every success.

The very next day Karl Hâfitz, knapsack on his back and baton in hand, left the hotel of the Three Pigeons and the brewery sacred to King Gambrinus, and set out upon his travels.

He proceeded towards Switzerland.

Unfortunately at the end of six weeks he was much thinner, but inspiration did not come any the more readily for that.

"Can any one be more unhappy than I am?" he said. "Neither fasting nor good cheer, nor water, wine, or beer can bring me up to the necessary pitch; what have I done to deserve this? While a crowd of ignorant people produce remarkable works, I, with all my science, all my application, all my courage, cannot accomplish anything. Ah! Heaven is not good to me; it is unjust."

Communing thus with himself, he took the road from Brück to Freibourg; night was coming on; he felt weary and footsore. Just then he perceived by the light of the

moon an old ruined hut half-hidden in trees on the opposite side of the way; the door was off its hinges, the small
window-panes were broken, the chimney was in ruins.
Nettles and briars grew around it in wild luxuriance, and
the garret window scarcely topped the heather, in which
the wind blew hard enough to take the horns off a cow.

Karl could also perceive through the mist that a branch
of a fir-tree waved above the door.

"Well," he muttered, "the inn is not prepossessing, it
is rather ill-looking indeed, but we must not judge by
appearances."

So, without hesitation, he knocked at the door with his
stick.

"Who is there? what do you want?" called out rough
voice within.

"Shelter and food," replied the traveller.

"Ah ha! very good."

The door opened suddenly, and Karl found himself con-
fronted by a stout personage with square visage, grey eyes,
his shoulders covered with a great-coat loosely thrown
over them, and carrying an axe in his hand.

Behind this individual a fire was burning on the hearth,
which lighted up the entrance to a small room and the
wooden staircase, and close to the flame was crouched a
pale young girl clad in a miserable brown dress with little
white spots on it. She looked towards the door with an
affrighted air; her black eyes had something sad and an
indescribably wandering expression in them.

Karl took all this in at a glance, and instinctively
grasped his stick tighter.

"Well, come in," said the man; "this is no time to keep
people out of doors."

Then Karl, thinking it bad form to appear alarmed,
came into the room and sat down by the hearth.

"Give me your knapsack and stick," said the man.

For the moment the pupil of Albertus trembled to his
very marrow; but the knapsack was unbuckled and the

stick placed in the corner, and the host was seated quietly before the fire ere he had recovered himself.

This circumstance gave him confidence.

"Landlord," said he, smiling, "I am greatly in want of my supper."

"What would you like for supper, sir?" asked the landlord.

"An omelette, some wine and cheese."

"Ha, ha! you have got an excellent appetite, but our provisions are exhausted."

"You have no cheese, then?"

"No."

"No butter, nor bread, nor milk?"

"No."

"Well, good heavens! what *have* you got?"

"We can roast some potatoes in the embers."

Just then Karl caught sight of a whole regiment of hens perched on the staircase in the gloom, of all sorts, in all attitudes, some pluming themselves in the most nonchalant manner.

"But," said Hâfitz, pointing at this troop of fowls, "you must have some eggs surely?"

"We took them all to market this morning."

"Well, if the worst comes to the worst you can roast a fowl for me."

Scarcely had he spoken when the pale girl, with dishevelled hair, darted to the staircase, crying—

"No one shall touch the fowls! no one shall touch my fowls! Ho, ho, ho! God's creatures must be respected."

Her appearance was so terrible that Hâfitz hastened to say—

"No, no, the fowls shall not be touched. Let us have the potatoes. I devote myself to eating potatoes henceforth. From this moment my object in life is determined. I shall remain here three months—six months—any time that may be necessary to make me as thin as a fakir."

He expressed himself with such animation that the host cried out to the girl—

"Genovéva, Genovéva, look! The Spirit has taken possession of him; just as the other was—"

The north wind blew more fiercely outside; the fire blazed up on the hearth, and puffed great masses of grey smoke up to the ceiling. The hens appeared to dance in the reflection of the flame while the demented girl sang in a shrill voice a wild air, and the log of green wood, hissing in the midst of the fire, accompanied her with its plaintive sibilations.

Hâfitz began to fancy that he had fallen upon the den of the sorcerer Hecker; he devoured a dozen potatoes, and drank a great draught of cold water. Then he felt somewhat calmer; he noticed that the girl had left the chamber, and that only the man sat opposite to him by the hearth.

"Landlord," he said, "show me where I am to sleep."

The host lit a lamp and slowly ascended the worm-eaten staircase; he opened a heavy trap-door with his grey head, and led Karl to a loft beneath the thatch.

"There is your bed," he said, as he deposited the lamp on the floor; "sleep well, and above all things beware of fire."

He then descended, and Hâfitz was left alone stooping beneath the low roof in front of a great mattress covered with a sack of feathers.

He considered for a few seconds whether it would be prudent to sleep in such a place, for the man's countenance did not appear very prepossessing, particularly as, recalling his cold grey eyes, his blue lips, his wide bony forehead, his yellow hue, he suddenly recalled to mind that on the Golzenberg he had encountered three men hanging in chains, and that one of them bore a striking resemblance to the landlord; that he had also those grave eyes, the bony elbows, and that the great toe of his left foot protruded from his shoe cracked by the rain.

He also recollected that that unhappy man named Melchior had been a musician formerly, and that he had been hanged for having murdered the landlord of the

Golden Sheep with his pitcher, because he had asked him
to pay his scanty reckoning.

This poor fellow's music had affected him powerfully
in former days. It was fantastic, and the pupil of Albertus
had envied the Bohemian; but just now when he recalled
the figure on the gibbet, his tatters agitated by the night
wind, and the ravens wheeling around him with discordant
screams, he trembled violently, and his fears augmented
when he discovered, at the farther end of the loft against
the wall, a violin decorated with two faded palm-leaves.

Then indeed he was anxious to escape, but at that moment he heard the rough voice of the landlord.

"Put out that light, will you?" he cried; "go to bed.
I told you particularly to be cautious about fire."

These words froze Karl; he threw himself upon the
mattress and extinguished the light. Silence fell on all the
house.

Now, notwithstanding his determination not to close
his eyes, Hâfitz, in consequence of hearing the sighing
of the wind, the cries of the night-birds, the sound of
the mice pattering over the floor, towards one o'clock fell
asleep; but he was awakened by a bitter, deep, and most
distressing sob. He started up, a cold perspiration standing on his forehead.

He looked up, and saw crouched up beneath the angle
of the roof a man. It was Melchior, the executed crim-
inal. His hair fell down to his emaciated ribs; his chest
and neck were naked. One might compare him to a skeleton of an immense grasshopper, so thin was he; a ray of
moonlight entering through the narrow window gave him
a ghastly blue tint, and all around him hung the long webs
of spiders.

Hâfitz, speechless, with staring eyes and gaping mouth,
kept gazing at this weird object, as one might be expected
to gaze at Death standing at one's bedside when the last
hour has come!

Suddenly the skeleton extended its long bony hand and took the violin from the wall, placed it in position against its shoulder, and began to play.

There was in this ghostly music something of the cadence with which the earth falls upon the coffin of a dearly-loved friend—something solemn as the thunder of the waterfall echoed afar by the surrounding rocks, majestic as the wild blasts of the autumn tempest in the midst of the sonorous forest trees; sometimes it was sad—sad as never-ending despair. Then, in the midst of all this, he would strike into a lively measure, persuasive, silvery as the notes of a flock of goldfinches fluttering from twig, to twig. These pleasing trills soared up with an ineffable tremolo of careless happiness, only to take flight all at once, frightened away by the waltz, foolish, palpitating, bewildering—love, joy, despair—all together singing, weeping, hurrying pell-mell over the quivering strings!

And Karl, notwithstanding his extreme terror, extended his arms and exclaimed—

"Oh, great, great artist! oh, sublime genius! oh, how I lament your sad fate, to be hanged for having murdered that brute of an innkeeper who did not know a note of music!—to wander through the forest by moonlight!—never to live in the world again—and with such talents! O Heaven!"

But as he thus cried out he was interrupted by the rough tones of his host.

"Hullo up there! will you be quiet? Are you ill, or is the house on fire?"

Heavy steps ascended the staircase, a bright light shone through the chinks of the door, which was opened by a thrust of the shoulder, and the landlord appeared.

"Oh!" exclaimed Hâfitz, "what things happen here! First I am awakened by celestial music and entranced by heavenly strains; and then it all vanishes as if it were but a dream."

The innkeeper's face assumed a thoughtful expression.

"Yes, yes," he muttered, "I might have thought as much. Melchior has come to disturb your rest. He will always come. Now we have lost our night's sleep; it is no use to think of rest any more. Come along, friend; get up and smoke a pipe with me."

Karl waited no second bidding; he hastily left the room. But when he got downstairs, seeing that it was still dark night, he buried his head in his hands and remained for a long time plunged in melancholy meditation. The host re-lighted the fire, and taking up his position in the opposite corner of the hearth, smoked in silence.

At length the grey dawn appeared through the little diamond-shaped panes; then the cock crew, and the hens began to hop down from step to step of the staircase.

"How much do I owe you?" asked Karl, as he buckled on his knapsack and resumed his walking-staff.

"You owe us a prayer at the chapel of St. Blaise," said the man, with a curious emphasis—"one prayer for the soul of Melchior, who was hanged, and another for his *fiancée*, Genovéva, the poor idiot."

"Is that all?"

"That is all."

"Well, then, good-bye—I shall not forget."

And, indeed, the first thing that Karl did on his arrival at Freibourg was to offer up a prayer for the poor man and for the girl he had loved, and then he went to the Grape Hotel, spread his sheet of paper upon the table, and, fortified by a bottle of "rikevir," he wrote at the top of the page *The Murderer's Violin,* and then on the spot he traced the score of his first original composition.

A Legend of the North
Anonymous
(1866)

Far away in the wild northern country of long days and short summers, where the weary winter lasts for full nine mouths of twilight, with no sunrise or sunset to mark its monotonous course,—in the wildest part of this wild land wandered a traveller on foot and alone. He carried a long staff in his hand, a rough knapsack strapped upon his back, and his weary step, and the toil-worn expression of hie features, denoted the length and difficulty of his journey, though the bright sparkle of his dark-blue eye seemed almost to repudiate the idea of fatigue. The cold light of the north shone upon him as he toiled along, climbing the steep ascent of a rocky hill, from the summit of which he would enjoy, as well as he knew, the spectacle of a strangely majestic scene. Towering northward were grand lines of snow-capped cliffs, taking those exaggerated pointed forms peculiar to the Norwegian coast; while on his left hand, and far below, stretched the ocean, with its fringe of irregular fiords. Inland lay more hills—mysterious, fanciful hills, with dark chasms and abrupt precipices; conical outlines, almost ghastly in their clear distinctness, standing like giants against the sky, which illumined them faintly with the reflection of the pale yellow flickering light which glowed in the north-west.

We have not time to trace our traveller's previous career in detail. An overwhelming grief had clouded his early life, and the cold hand of sorrow still lay heavy and dead against his heart. He fought against it manfully for a time, but was at last driven to be a voluntary exile from England, and had sought a temporary home amongst the rough but kindly natives of this unfrequented country, who, if they showed no great sympathy for him, at least asked no questions, tortured him with no curiosity, and left him free to wander at his will. And silence and liberty were the greatest alleviation to his troubled mind. His nerves were finely strung, and the misplaced sympathy of his ordinary acquaintance drove him almost to madness. Here, the calmness of nature harmonized with and soothed him, while the fine clear magnetic air of the north gave strength and elasticity to his frame, and excited and kindled his imagination till it almost overpowered the depressing influences of the sad episode of his early life.

Twice or more before he had walked far and fast on purpose to reach this particular mountain rock, to enjoy, in undisturbed solitude, the wonderful mysterious beauty of the aurora borealis in its fullest dignity. It filled his heart with poetry, and awoke fresh and higher thoughts in his soul; and now, as for the third he stood on the top, panting with his struggle up the almost perpendicular steepness of the last twenty yards, he felt that he would be again rewarded, for the aurora promised to be of unusual grandeur, and was already shooting its fiery light along the cloudless sky. Long and earnestly he watched it; the utter stillness; save for the occasional wild cry of some bird, and the almost whispered murmur of the waves amongst the beetling crags far, far below, added to the awe of the scene.

Soon a new sound fell upon his ears—but so faint, so distant, that at first he doubted whether his fancy had not created it by giving a voice to that soft murmur of the sea. Nearer it came, and nearer—sweet, soft, and gentle; but so beautiful, so enchantingly beautiful, that it might have been the voice of angels. Nearer still, as though borne on a breath of air; music, but unlike all earthly music:

such pathos, such harmony, such exquisite tones never fell
on mortal ears before. Scarcely daring to breathe lest he
should lose a note of the melody our traveller listened as
the lovely sounds became clearer and clearer. Intently he
strained his eyes over the wide expanse of ocean as the
divine sound gathered more and more force, now swelling
on his ear, and now dying away to faintness, but never ceas-
ing; and as he gazed on the spot whence the music seemed
to emanate, his eye caught a gleam of light. He could
scarcely tell whether it had been there the moment before
or whether it had that instant appeared, it was so pale, so
uncertain—like a glimmering star. But as he watched it, it
grew brighter, larger and more distinct, spreading softly
over the surface of the water. What could it be? There was
no land in that direction, nothing but the boundless sea,
stretching away to the region of eternal ice. It was not the
sun, rising to begin its unbroken but short-lived course
of summer. It was no reflection from the aurora. It was
entirely inexplicable, as it floated there, not quite on the
horizon, for a dark blue line of sea lay between it and the
sky: but from it the music certainly came.

But what a change in the notes of the music! From the
softest harmony it turned into a wailing dirge of inexpressible agony and despair. For several seconds that sound of
unutterable sorrow wrung our traveller's heart, and made
his blood run cold. Then suddenly it ceased entirely, the
light vanished, there was total silence, and once more the
accustomed murmur of the waves on the crags was the only
sound that broke the stillness of the air.

Our traveller was transfixed—so deeply had the melody, and particularly the heart-rending sadness of the
dirge-like notes, impressed itself on his susceptible spirit!
Long he sat and pondered on this strange vision of the
north; earnestly he desired to hear again the wildly beautiful tones which had stirred his soul to its depths; but
in vain he waited. All nature was wrapped in silence, and
nothing but the heavy flap of a passing eagle's wings gave

token that other life than his own existed in that lonely
spot.

At length he roused himself, and bent his steps in the
direction of the rough shed, which he now called his home.
After some miles of weary walking, he met two or three
carioles, and hailing their occupants, one of them stopped;
and instantly our traveller commenced telling him of what
he had heard and seen. No sooner, however, had he come to
the point of his having actually seen that gleaming light,
than the man put his hands on his ears, and, screaming
with a look of horror—"Do not tell me—do not tell me;
you are lost!"—he tore madly after his companions, and was
out of sight and hearing before another word could be said.

Still more impressed by the man's evident alarm, the
Englishman sought on all sides an explanation of the cause
of his terror. But none of the peasants would talk to him
on the subject; all avoided it; some declared at once they
knew nothing of it, others endeavored to laugh it off: and,
at any rate, though for two months more he continued to
live on in the same place, and often and often re-visited
the rock whence he had heard the supernatural music,
never once during that time did he hear or see anything in
any way whatever that had reference to what had occurred
to him there before.

Some months afterwards, as he was visiting a learned
friend in Bergen, and one who was deeply read in tradi-
tionary lore, he mentioned the circumstance to him. In an
instant the Professor's face glowed with delight.

"Have you then, in real truth, seen the golden light,
my friend?" he exclaimed, with the warmest interest. "You
are, indeed, fortunate. Many a time have I, when at Trond-
heim, explored the coast, passing whole nights on the
rocks in the hope of realising this most beautiful legend.
And you, by mere chance, have seen it!"

"Then you, perhaps, can tell me the history of the legend," said the Englishman, delighted at having at length
found the clue of the mystery.

"That I both can and will," said the Professor; "and I do not wonder that you were unable to learn what you seek to know; for it is so long—hundreds of years, I believe—since the music was last heard, that the tradition has been almost forgotten, and indeed is probably known to very few besides those who live on these shores, and they have reasons, which you shall hear, for avoiding the subject."

"Pray tell me the whole history," said the traveller.

"Most willingly, my friend," answered the Professor. "Know, then, that soon after the misty days of Odin there lived a monarch, young, beautiful, and good, elected to the throne for his virtues by subjects who appreciated them. But it was in a dark day for him, for his great merits, tried and tempered by adversity, were not proof against the temptations of prosperity. At first his people were captivated by the modesty with which he bore his greatness, by the hearty friendliness of his bearing, by his courteous condescension, and the gay and gallant festivity of his court. But pleasure ate into his soul and enervated his iron constitution; feasting was ever the order of the day; luxury and reveling, outdoing the Halls of Walhalla, ruled the royal dwelling. Duties were abandoned, arms were laid aside, that beauty, music, and merriment might take their place. In vain the wise old warriors remonstrated, in vain they detailed before the laughing monarch the evils that would ensue. He bade the music play, and bid the courtiers—young and reckless as himself—listen to those soft sounds, and not to the raven croak of those who sought to make him waste his days in toil and trouble, instead of drinking mead and metheglin from the beaker and the bowl.

"But the evil day came! The foe was in the land. Swiftly the word rang forth—the cry to arms resounded;—but resounded in whose ears? Those enervated arms were too weak to wield the saber and the battle axe as their fathers had done of yore; those alone who would stand up like true men for their country's rights and freedom were

those whom the infirmities of age rendered dependent on
the younger men—their sons, whose sole skill lay in singing, dancing, drinking, and feasting, and who vowed, with
their king, that the secret of life was enjoyment, that toil
was a sin, and pleasure alone was worth the trouble of pur-
suing. And what was their strength as defenders of their
country? Again the cry rang out that the foe was coming
nearer, and then indeed the king took steps for his pres-
ervation. He commanded a golden galley to be built, that
should hold himself and his boon companions, and all the
maidens with the sweetest voices, that with them he might
sail away, and seek a peaceful island, whereon they might
rest in luxury, and wear out life in dreamy happiness. One
wild night of his frantic revelry and mirth was the king's
adieu to his subjects. Next morning saw the foe on the
hills around, and far away on the horizon the gleam of
the never-setting sun caught the topmost points of the
masts—golden like the rest—of the royal galley.

"No mortal eye saw the end of that galley. Never more
were the pleasure-seeking monarch and his crew heard of
by mortal ear. But more than once that light has been seen
to float on the surface of the sea, and each time, in the
middle of the very sweetest song of all, that wild dirge has
rung through the air, and that, they say, is the wail of the
gallant and gay, now weary and worn, seeking the land
they can never reach, and compelled to wander ceaselessly
about those shores in their ill-fated galley. Its appearance
is considered the precursor of some fearful storm or great
national calamity."

"That, then," said the Englishman, who had listened
breathlessly to the narrative, "accounts for the terror of
the Norwegian peasant when I told him to what I had been
listening."

"Yes," said the Professor; "and tradition further says
that to him who actually sees the glowing light, and also
to him to whom he first tells of what he has seen, some
fearful evil is impending."

"Sadness and sorrow are past to me," said the wanderer, with a sigh. "They have done their worst. The brightness of my life is gone—gone with the golden galley beneath the silent sea!"

The Lost Song
M. B. O.
(1872)

It was my grandmother's story, and this is how she came
to tell it to me:

I, Annie Rae, had come down to spend Christmas at "Rae-
burn," the old family homestead. My grandmother and
grandfather had been abroad for years, and this being the
first Christmas for so long that the old house was opened,
they wanted to fill it with bright young faces and merry laughter, to crowd out the voiceless memories which
lurked in every corner, and so a whole party of us had
come—cousins, first, second and third, in fact of all degrees. Speaking of cousins, isn't it strange that very often
the further removed the nearer they seem? At least George
Stewart was only my third cousin by blood, and yet he
always assumed more on the strength of our relationship
than any of my first cousins, and, somehow, in my own
heart I did not mind it at all, though I did tease him so.

But I must go on with my story. It was Christmas Eve,
and the old house was quiet at last. We girls had all gone
to our rooms after a merry evening together. Fannie and
Rose had the room near grandma's, while Kate and Lillie
were just opposite. Some one had to sleep alone at the
other end of the hall, and, after long consultation, it was
decided that I should go, for I had rashly boasted of never
being afraid. I will confess to feeling a little lonely when

all was quiet, and the deep shadows in the corners of the room seemed very dark, for the light of my candle did not reach far. There were three doors in my room, and after fastening securely the one into the entry, I merely turned the handles of the others, and finding them locked inside, did not care to explore any further just then. I must have been a long time undressing, for the clock struck the hour of midnight as I put out my light. Even then I could not go to sleep, but found myself wondering what was behind those doors that I had not opened, and I determined to have a regular exploring expedition the next day. There were so many romantic stories attached to this old house. I had even heard hints of private staircases, shut up rooms, &c., and had always delighted in mysteries.

I think I must have been asleep for a short time when I suddenly found myself awake with a start, and a curious impression that I was listening for something. There certainly was a sound overhead, but what was it? It came again more clearly, and I distinguished a faint, broken melody, and yet imperfect, like some one playing a long-forgotten air on a piano where some of the strings were broken. Three times it came, like the verses of a song, and though there were no words, thought of George, and how sorrowfully he had looked at me that evening as I had passed him without saying "good night." It was only to tease him, and I had pretended not to see his proffered hand, but had taken Willie Thorne's arm instead, and we had walked up the broad staircase together.

Again, all was still, only a long-drawn sigh seemed to echo my own through the room, and came from the direction of the furthest door. Without a sensation of fear, only an ill-defined feeling of pain and regret, I sank to sleep, and when I woke the morning sun was shining brightly enough to dispel all illusions. I resolved to say nothing to the girls, but quietly to explore and see what was to be found, for I knew perfectly well that what I had heard was no dream. So I got up long before breakfast, and after completing my toilet, threw wide the shutters and opened the first door nearest the entry. Only an empty closet! Disappointed but slightly relieved, I closed it and went over to the other.

The key turned hard in the lock as if it had not been opened for a long time. Then the door stood wide, and I saw a flight of stairs, but only prosaic wooden steps, like those leading to any garret. I started bravely up, and soon found myself in a large loft or attic, filled with odds and ends.

First, an old spinning-wheel caught my eye, relic of our most industrious great grandmothers. Then a stack of old firearms. with which our ancestors, the bold Raes, may have shed the blood of daring foes, or, perhaps, and I am afraid more likely, have only done damage among the crows that came to steal from their spacious cornfields. Lastly, beyond these, and behind a pile of mattings and boxes, I came upon an old piano. It quite startled me, at first, but then the broad daylight was very reassuring, and I am not nervous. It was very old and of a most curious shape, and evidently had been very elegant in its day. I tried to lift the lid, and found it locked, but as I touched it a shiver ran through me, for I was convinced now that this was what my ghostly music had come from last night, and I determined to find out before another day had passed who it had belonged to, and what restless spirit still haunted its worn strings.

So, after breakfast, when all the others had gone to church, I went into my grandmother's room to sit with her, for she was not very strong, dear old lady, and rarely went out of the house in Winter.

After we were nicely settled, and had got through our morning's reading, I told her of my last night's adventure, and my subsequent researches, and begged her to tell me all about the old piano that I had found in the attic. She smiled at my eagerness, but did not seem at all surprised or incredulous, for, though she herself had never heard the music I spoke of, there had been others long ago, she said, who, sleeping in that room on Christmas Eve, had been known to hear faint sounds, coming as if from the old piano above, though it was always locked, and the key had been lost. The coincidence, at least, was very strange, taken in connection with the history attached to it, and which my grandmother then proceeded to relate to me.

"Many years ago," said my grandmother, "when your great-great-great-grandfather was alive, this house was full of life and merriment; for your Aunt Annie—your great-great-aunt, for whom you are named, child—lived here with her father and brothers. She was as bright and sunny as the day was long, but so full of mischief and coquetry that she gave the heart-ache to all the young men, far and near, and yet had suffered never a pang herself. I am afraid that a spice of her coquetry has descended to this generation too, my dear," said the old lady, gazing fondly, but reproachfully at me. "I felt sorry to see the look in poor George's eyes, last night, as you turned away from him on the stairs—"

"Oh, do please go on, grandmother dear," said I. "I am so much interested in the story." But in my own wicked little heart I was sorry too, and inwardly resolved to make up for it to him on the first opportunity.

"Well, your Aunt Annie always had the house full, and some of her cousins and young friends were always staying there. Among the gentlemen who were their frequent visitors was a young naval officer, Robert Carrol, whom they suspected Annie of preferring. Of course, as girls will, they all teased her most unmercifully about him, and consequently she would hardly speak to him sometimes, and just because in her own heart she knew that to talk with him one hour was better to her than a whole day with all the others.

"The poor fellow evidently had no eyes for any one else, but he was very reserved and sensitive, and did not go in boldly and make love to her, as any other man would have done, but stood and worshiped afar off. They say he was a very fine musician, and sang beautifully, and not only that but he composed songs for Annie to sing; for she had a lovely voice, and would sing sweet old ballads to us in the long Summer evenings with wonderful pathos and feeling.

"As the days went by the time drew near for Robert to join his ship. Early in December his orders came, and he was to leave the day after Christmas.

"He loved Annie so dearly that he felt he could not go away from her so long without asking for some assurance that his love was returned, and yet he could not bear to think of hearing her say she could never love him. Sometimes she treated him so coldly, almost rudely, and yet again, when they were alone, he could have sworn her eyes spoke a different language.

"The day before Christmas came, and still no word had been spoken. On the morning of that day Robert wrote a note to her, and enclosed in it a little song he had written, and in the note he said"—"But stay," said my grandmother, "I think I can show you the very note itself," and going to her desk she took from it an old yellow piece of manuscript music, so faded as to be almost illegible, and a little sheet of paper. "These," she said, "were found up in the attic among other old letters and private family papers when we came back, and though I destroyed the rest I kept these," and taking up the note she read it aloud. It was very short, and ran thus:

Annie, darling, will you be my wife? and may I go away with the hope warm at my heart that when I come back I may claim you as my own? Little one, if it is to be, and you can love me, will you sing my song for me tonight when I come. If there is no hope for me you will sing something else, and I will know my fate at once, and it will better to learn it so than to give you the pain of telling me. But somehow I feel hopeful in spite of the fact that your sweet voice is to sing me into life or death.

Forever yours, in this world and the next.

Robert.

"He sealed the note enclosing the song, and sent it over by his servant. As the man was going into the gate he met Annie's youngest brother, Harry, a little fellow of ten years old, who snatched the note from him, and said, 'Oh! I'll take it to sister Annie, Tom,' and ran off. So Thomas walked away with an easy conscience, thinking he had delivered the note safely, at least to a 'member of the family.'

"Harry trotted off toward the house with the best intentions in the world, but was diverted on the way by some important business with a small boy of his own age, who suddenly turned up, so by the time he did go home all memory of the note had vanished from his youthful mind.

"Evening came, and the younger children were all in bed, and Harry lay sound asleep, while on a chair hung his little jacket, and in the pocket still, poor Robert's note undelivered. Annie, with cheeks 'like twin roses,' and eyes bright with love and hope, was waiting for the company.

"All the young people were coming from the neighborhood to have a frolic, but she only thought of Robert. 'He must speak to me to-night,' she said to herself. 'I am sure he loves me, and in spite of my bad behavior to him sometimes, he must know my heart.'

"Early in the evening Annie's father, according to his custom, asked her for a song, and as she rose and went to the piano she caught sight of Robert's pale, handsome face. He was near the door, where he had just entered, standing with his arms folded and his eyes fixed upon her with a look that to her dying day she never forgot. As she sat down to the instrument an unaccountable feeling of depression came over her, some unseen influence seemed to hold her hands so that she could scarcely strike the notes, but with an impulse she threw it off, and dashed into some gay, nonsensical song that was popular at the time, and sang it through to the very end.

When she looked up Robert was gone, and she never saw him again in this world. He left home that night and never returned, for his ship, with all on board, was lost on the way out; and went to his grave thinking her cold and heartless. And she—; all the next day she waited for him, wondering that he did not come. That night as she was wearily going to her room a little voice from the nursery called her, and, going in, she found Harry wide awake.

"'Oh! sister Annie,' said he; 'don't scold me, but I forgot your note yesterday, and there it is still in my pocket.' And he pointed to the jacket which hung on a chair. Mechanically, she reached and took it, but when she saw the address in *his* hand she grew as pale as death. She only stooped and kissed the little fellow, who was sobbing bitterly, and no word of reproach passed her lips.

"From that day she was a different being. Her whole life seemed to be but a period of waiting; waiting for news of him.

"You must remember, my dear," added my grandmother, "that in those times there were no such conveniences for communication as we have nowadays, when lovers can change their minds three or four times a day by mail, and can telegraph 'yes' and 'no' sixty times a minute (more or less) if they please.

"And when at last the news of Robert's death came, it was as if some blight had fallen on her, for she seemed to fade away, and grew weaker and weaker, until it got to be so that she never left her room. Then her piano was moved up there, the very room you were in last night—for her music seemed the only thing left in which she took any interest, and often at night when all was still they would

hear her playing, for she had never been known to sing
since that time when, with her own sweet voice, she had
smilingly sounded the death knell of two hearts.

"On Christmas morning, just one year after, when they
came to her room they found her seated at her piano, with
his song before her, and her white hands cold and stiff
resting on the keys. She had gone to meet him, and her
weary waiting was over at last."

This was my grandmother's story of the old piano—and
that evening, as George and I were sitting together on
the broad staircase, while the others were dancing in the
parlor, I told it all over to him, and would you believe it?
when I came to the part about poor Robert's last letter,
George actually said it served him right for not being man
enough to ask for what he wanted when he had the chance,
"as I intend to ask you right here, little Annie," said he,
and then—well, somehow I did not finish the rest of the
story that evening.

Since then, however, we have often talked it over, but
George always smiles when I tell of the ghostly music I
heard on Christmas eve in the old house, and suggests that
though the piano was locked, yet the back had fallen out
from old age, and that there was room from a whole regiment of mice to creep in and run over the rusty strings,
and he further says that I was sleepy and troubled in my
mind for treating him so badly, and thought it was my
aunt's ghost come to warn me. But that is nonsense, of
course, and I shall always believe that it was poor Robert's
lost song that I heard.

The Ensouled Violin

HILARION SMERDIS

(1880)

The almost supernatural or magic art of Nicolo Paganini
—the greatest violin player that the world has ever produced—was often speculated upon, never understood. The
sensation he produced upon his audience was marvellous,
overpowering. The Great Rossini wept like a sentimental
German maiden, upon hearing him play for the first time.
The princess Eliza of Lucca, sister of the great Napolean,
though he was in her service as the director of her private
orchestra, was for a long time unable to hear him play
without fainting. In women he produced nervous fits
and hysterics at his will; stout hearted men he drove to
frenzy. He changed cowards into heroes, and made the
bravest soldiers become as nervous girls. Thousands of
dreary tales circulated about this mysterious Genoese,
the modern Orpheus of Italy. For besides his remarkable
appearance—termed by his friends eccentric, and by his
victims diabolical—he had experienced great difficulties
in refuting certain rumours of his having murdered his
wife, and after her, his mistress, both of whom loved him
passionately. Their unquiet souls, it was whispered, had
been made through his magic art to pass into his violin—
the famous "Cremona:" superstition not utterly unground
in view of his extraordinary facility in drawing out of
his instrument the most unearthly sounds, and positively
human voices. These effects well-nigh startled his audiences

into terror, and, if we add to it the impenetrable mystery connected with a certain period of his youth, we will find the wild tales told of him in a measure excusable; especially among a people whose ancestors knew the Borgias and the Medici of black-art fame.

We will now give a fact—a page from his biography— connected with, and based upon, such a tale. The press got hold of it at the time of its occurrence, and the annals of the literature of Italy preserve the record of it until now, though in many and various other forms.

It was in 1831. The great, the "diabolical" Paganini was creating at the house of the Paris Opera an enthusiasm unsurpassed by any triumph he had previously gleaned. After hearing him, several of the leading musicians of the noblest orchestra in the Western world, broke their instruments . . .

At that time, there lived at Paris another violinist gift- ed with an extraordinary talent, but poor and unknown a German, whose name was Franz Stenio. He was young and a philosopher, imbued with all the mysticism of Hoff- man's *"Chant d' Antonia,"* and nursed in the atmosphere of the old haunted castles on the Rhine. He had studied the occult arts and dabbled in alchemy, but otherwise was in- terested but little in the matters of this world. The whole of his aspirations mounted, incense-like, together with the wave of heavenly harmony which he drew forth from his four-stringed instrument, to a higher and a nobler sphere.

His mother, his only love on earth and whom he had never left, died when he was thirty. It was then that he found he had been left poor indeed; poor in purse, still poorer in earthly affections. His old violin teacher, Samuel Klaus, one of those grotesque figures which look as if they had just stepped out of some old mediaeval panel, with the speaking and piercing voice of a "show Punch," and the fantastic allures of a night-goblin, then took him by the hand, and, leading him to his violin, simply said:—"make yourself famous. I am old and childless, I will be your father, and we will live together." And they went to Paris.

Franz had never heard Paganini. He swore he would either eclipse all the violinists of those days, or, break his instrument and at the same time, put an end to his own life. Old Klaus rejoiced, and jumping on one leg like an old satyr, flattered and incensed him, believing himself all the while to be performing a sacred duty for the holy cause of art.

Franz was making himself ready for his first appearance before the public, when Paganini's arrival in the great capital of fashion was loudly heralded by his fame. The German violinist resolved to postpone his *debut,* and at first smiled at the enthusiastic mentions of the Italian's name. But soon this name became a fiery thorn in the heart of Franz, a threatening phantom in the mind of old Samuel. Both shuddered at the very mention of Paganini's successes.

At last the Italian's first concert was announced, and the prices of admission made enormous. The master and the pupil both pawned their watches and got two modest seats. Who can describe the enthusiasm, the triumphs of this famous, and at the same time, fatal night? At the first touch of Paganini's magic bow, both Franz and Samuel felt is if the icy hand of death had touched them. Carried away by an irresistible enthusiasm which turned into a violent, unearthly mental torture, they dared neither look into each other's faces, nor exchange one word during the whole performance.

At midnight, while the chosen delegates of the Musical Society of Paris unhitching the horses, were dragging in triumph Paganini home in his carriage, the two Germans having returned to their obscure apartment, were sitting mournful and desperate, in their usual places at the fire-corner. "Samuel!" exclaimed Franz, pale as death itself,—"Samuel—it remains for us now but to die! . . . Do you hear me? . . . We are worthless . . . worthless! We were

two mad men to have hoped that any one in this world
would ever rival . . . *him!*—" The name of Paganini stuck
in his throat as in utter despair he fell into his arm-chair.

The old professor's wrinkles suddenly became purple;
and his little greenish eyes gleamed phosphorescently as,
bending toward his pupil, he whispered to him in a hoarse
and broken voice—"Thou art wrong, my Franz! I have
taught thee, and thou hast learned all of the great art that
one simple mortal and a good Christian can learn from
another and as simple a mortal as himself. Am I to be
blamed because these accursed Italians, in order to reign
unequalled in the domain of art, have recourse to Satan
and the diabolical effects of black magic?"

Franz turned his eyes upon his old master. There was
a sinister light burning in those glittering orbs; a light
telling plainly, that to secure such a power, he too, would
not scruple to sell himself, body and soul, to the Evil One.

Samuel understood the cruel thought, but yet went on
with a feigned calmness—"You have heard the unfortunate
tale rumoured about the famous Tartini? He died on one
Sabbath night, strangled by his familiar demon, who had
taught him the way, by means of incantations, to animate
his violin, with a human soul, by shutting up in it, the
soul of a young Virgin . . . Paganini did more; in order to
endow his instrument with the faculty of emitting human
sobs, despairing cries, in short the most heart-rending
notes of the human voice, Paganini became the murderer
of a friend, who was more tenderly attached to him than
any other on this earth. He then made out of the intestines
of his victim the four cords of his magic violin. This is
the secret of his enchanting talent, of that overpowering
melody, and that combination of sounds, which you will
never be able to master, unless . . ."

The old man could not finish the sentence. He staggered before the fiendish look of his pupil, and covered
his face with his hands.—"And . . . you really believe . . .
that had I the means of obtaining human intestines for

strings, I could rival Paganini?" asked Franz, after a moment's pause, and casting down his eyes.

The old German, unveiled his face, and, with a strange look of determination upon it, softly answered—"Human intestines only are not sufficient for our purpose: these must have belonged to one that has loved us well, and with an unselfish, holy, love. Tartini endowed his violin with the life of a virgin; but that virgin had died of unrequited love for him . . . The fiendish artist had prepared beforehand a tube in which he managed to catch her last breath as she expired in pronouncing his beloved name, and, then transferred this breath into his violin. As to Paganini—I have just told you his tale. It was with the consent of his victim though, that he murdered him to get possession of his intestines . . . Oh for the power of the human voice!" Samuel went on, after a brief pause. "What can equal the eloquence, the magic spell, of the human voice! Do you think, my poor boy, I would not have taught you this great, this final secret, were it not, that it throws one right into the clutches of *him* . . . who must remain unnamed at night?"

Franz did not answer. With a calm, awful to behold, he left his place, took down his violin from the wall where it was hanging, and with one powerful grasp of the cords tore them out and flung them into the fire.

The old Samuel suppressed a cry of horror. The cords were hissing upon the coals, where, among the blazing logs, they wriggled and curled like so many living snakes.

Weeks and months passed away. This conversation was never resumed between the master and the pupil. But a profound melancholy had taken possession of Franz, and the two hardly exchanged a word together. The violin hung mute, cordless, and full of dust, upon its habitual place. It was like the presence of a soulless corpse between them.

One night, as Franz sat, looking particularly pale and gloomy, old Samuel, suddenly jumped from his seat, and after hopping about the room in a magpie fashion approached his pupil, imprinted a fond kiss upon the young man's brow, and then squeaked at the top of his voice. "It is time to put an end to all this!" . . . Whereupon starting from his usual lethargy, Franz echoed, as in a dream;—"Yes, it is time to put an end to this." Upon which the two separated and went to bed.

On the following morning, when Franz awoke, he was astonished at not seeing his old teacher at his usual place to give him his first greeting. "Samuel! My good, my dear . . . Samuel!" exclaimed Franz, as he hurriedly jumped from his bed to go into his master's chamber. He staggered back frightened at the sound of his own voice, so changed and hoarse it seemed to him at this moment. No answer came in response to his call. Naught followed but a dead silence . . . There exists in the domain of sounds, a silence which usually denotes death. In the presence of a corpse, as in the lugubrious stillness of a tomb, silence acquires a mysterious power, which strikes the sensitive soul with a nameless terror . . .

Samuel was lying on his bed, cold, stiff and lifeless . . . At the sight of him, who had loved him so well, and had been more than a father, Franz experienced a dreadful shock. But the passion of the fanatical artist got the better of the despair of the man, and smothered the feelings of the latter.

A note addressed with his own name was conspicuously placed upon a table near the corpse. With a trembling hand, the violinist tore open the envelope, and read the following:—

"My beloved Franz,
"When you read this, I will have made the greatest sacrifice, your best and only friend and professor could have accomplished, for your fame. He, who loved you most, is now but an inanimate body; of your old teacher there now remains but a clod of cold organic

matter. I need not prompt you as to what you have to do with it. Fear not stupid prejudices. It is for your future fame that I have made an offering of my body, and you would become guilty of the blackest ingratitude, were you now to render this sacrifice useless. When you shall have replaced the cords upon your violin, and these cords—a portion of my own self,—will acquire under your touch my voice, my groans, my song of welcome, and the sobs of my infinite love for you, my boy,—then, Oh, Franz, fear nobody! Take your instrument along with you, and follow the steps of him who filled our lives with bitterness and despair . . . Appear on the arena, where, hitherto, he has reigned without a rival, and bravely throw the gauntlet of defiance into his face. Oh, Franz! then only wilt thou hear with what a magic power the full note of love will issue forth from thy violin; as with a last caressing touch of its cords, thou wilt, perhaps, remember that they have once formed a portion of thine old teacher, who now embraces and blesses thee for the last time—Samuel."

Two burning tears sparkled in the eyes of Franz, but they dried up instantly under the fiery rush of passionate hope and pride. The eyes of the future magician-artist, rivetted to the ghastly face of the corpse, shone like the eyes of the church-owl.

Our pen refuses to describe what took place later on that day, in the death room, after the legal autopsy was over. Suffice to say, that, after a fortnight had passed, the violin was dusted and four new, stout, cords had been stretched upon it. Franz dared not look at them. He tried to play, but the bow trembled in his hand like a dagger in the grasp of a novice-brigand. He made a vow not to try

again until the portentous night when he should have a
chance to rival—nay, surpass Paganini.

But the famous violinist had left Paris and was now
giving a series of triumphant concerts at an old Flemish
town in Belgium.

One night, as Paganini sat in the bar room of the hotel
at which he stopped, surrounded by a crowd of admirers,
a visiting card was handed to him which had a few words
written in pencil upon its back, by a young man with wild
and staring eyes. Fixing upon the intruder a look which
few persons could bear, but receiving back a glance as determined and calm as his own, Paganini slightly bowed
and then dryly said:—"Sir, it will be as you desire . . .
name the night . . . I am at your service . . ."

On the following morning the whole town was startled
at the sight of numerous bills posted at the corner of every
street. The strange notice ran thus:—

> "To-night at the Grand Theatre of —, and
> for the first time, will appear before the pub-
> lic, Frans Stenio, a German Violinist, arrived
> purposely to throw the gauntlet at, and chal-
> lenge the world-famous Paganini to a duel—
> upon their violins. He purposes to compete
> with the great 'virtuoso' in the execution of
> the most difficult of his compositions. The
> famous Paganini has accepted the challenge.
> Frans Stenio will have to play in competition
> with the unrivalled violinist the celebrat-
> ed 'Fantaisie caprice' of the latter, known as
> 'The Witches.'"

The effect of the notice proved magical. Paganini, who,
amid his greatest triumphs, never lost sight of a profitable
speculation, doubled the usual price of admission. But
still the theatre could not hold the crowds that flocked to
it on that memorable night.

At the terrible hour of the forthcoming struggle, Franz was at his post, calm, resolute, almost smiling. It was arranged that Paganini should begin. When he appeared upon the stage, the thick walls of the theatre shook to their foundation with the applause that greeted him. He began and ended his famous composition "The Witches" amid uninterrupted bravos. The cries of public enthusiasm lasted so long that Franz began to think his turn would never come. When, at last, Paganini, amid the roaring applauses of a frantic public, was allowed to retire behind the scenes, and his eye fell upon Stenio, who was tuning his violin, he felt amazed at the serene calmness, and the air of assurance of the unknown German artist.

When Franz approached the foot-lights, he was received with an icy coldness. But for all that he did not feel in the least disconcerted: he only scornfully smiled, for he was sure of his triumph.

At the first notes of the *Prelude* of "The Witches" the audience became dumb struck with astonishment. It was Paganini's touch, and—it was something else besides. Some—and that some the majority—thought that never, in his best moments of inspiration had the Italian artist himself, while executing this diabolical composition of his, exhibited such an equally diabolical power. Under the pressure of the long muscular fingers, the cords wriggled like the palpitating intestines of a disemboweled victim, the Satanic eye of the artist, fixed upon the sound board, called forth hell itself out of the mysterious depths of his instrument. Sounds transformed themselves into shapes, and gathering thickly, at the evocation of the mighty magician, whirled around him, like a host of fantastic, infernal figures, dancing the witches' "goat dance." In the emptiness of the stage background behind him, a nameless phantasmagoria produced by the concussion of unearthly vibrations, seemed to draw pictures of shameless orgies, and the voluptuous hymens, of the witches' Sabbath. . . . A collective hallucination got hold of the public. Panting

for breath, ghastly, and trickling with the icy perspiration
of an inexpressible terror, they sat spellbound, and unable to break the charm of the music by the slightest motion. They experienced all the illicit enervating delights
of the paradise of Mohammed that come into the disor-
dered fancy of an opium-eating Mussalman, and felt at the
same time the abject terror, the agony of one who struggles against an attack of *delirium tremens* . . . Many ladies
fainted, and strong men gnashed their teeth in a state of
utter helplessness! . . .

Then came the *finale*— The magic bow was just drawing forth its last quivering sounds—imitating the precipi-
tate flight of the witches saturated with the fumes of their
night's saturnalia, when the notes suddenly changed in their
melodious ascension into the squeaking, disagreeable tones
of a street *punchinello*, screaming at the top of his senile
voice: "Art thou satisfied, Franz, my boy? . . . Have I well
kept my promise, eh" . . . And then, the slender graceful
figure of the violinist suddenly appeared to the public as
entirely enveloped in a semitransparent form, which clearly
defined the outlines of a grotesque and grinning but terri-
bly awful-looking old man, whose bowels were protruding
and ended where they were stretched on the violin!

Within this hazy, quivering veil, the violinist was then
seen driving furiously his bow upon the human cords with
the contortions of a demoniac, as represented on a mediaeval Cathedral painting!

An indescribable panic swept over the audience, and,
breaking through the spell which had bound them for so
long motionless in their seats, every living creature in the
theatre made one mad rush to the door. It was like the
sudden outburst of a dam; a human torrent, roaring amid
a shower of discordant notes, idiotic squeaking, prolonged
and whining moans, and cacophonous cries of frenzy, above
which, like the detonations of pistol shots, was heard the
consecutive bursting of the four cords upon the bewitched
violin . . .

When the theatre was emptied of its last occupant, the terrified manager rushed on the stage in search of the unfortunate performer. They found him dead and stiff, behind the foot-lights, twisted up in the most unnatural of postures, and his violin shattered into a thousand fragments.

The Bandsman's Story
HUGH CONWAY
(1882)

At twenty I believed I was sent into the world to become a second Beethoven; at twenty-five I was playing the flu-gel-horn in a German band, and thought myself lucky in getting that appointment.

It seems a great drop—a fall from the stars to the mire; but as my own particular fortunes or misfortunes have little bearing upon the events I am going to relate, I need not dwell upon them at any length. Left an orphan at an early age, bred up in a small village under the care of an old aunt, what wonder that the astonishment caused in the little world around, by the musical talent I gave early evidence of, quite turned my head? The boy who could play upon all and every instrument by ear alone, and, moreover, play melodies which he really thought at the time were original, was looked upon by the simple people about as a heaven-born genius, and naturally felt averse to earning a prosaic living by commerce. So exalted was he, in fact, that having acquired a smattering of harmony, and, through the kindness of some old friends, a hundred pounds to give him a start, he felt little fear of failure when he resolved to wring fortune, if not fame, from Music, heavenly maid.

How soon a man finds his level in London! How soon I found mine! and found, moreover, that within the boundaries of the United Kingdom there must be at least five thousand young fellows whose talents were equal to, if not greater than, mine.

Having learnt my lesson, hard as it was, thoroughly, the next thing was to find out how to live. My money was at last spent, and I think my dreams of success fled entirely as I changed the last sovereign; and then, almost cap in hand, I was fain to wait upon those great publishers whom in my dreams I had patronised, and beg for work, however humble. So then I became a helot, a drawer of water and carrier of wood to the divine mistress, Art. I copied scores, I tuned pianos when I could get that task entrusted to me; I gave elementary lessons when I could find pupils. It was dreary work, but somehow for the next few years I managed to live; and then, tired of the ceaseless and unremunerative drudgery, I sank all pride and donned the gay blue-and-white uniform of the Upper Rhine Band, engaged to perform from May to October at the rising watering-place, Shinglemouth.

It was a hard life, but I believe not an unhealthy one, if a man had a good constitution, sound limbs and lungs. Being on one's feet the whole day was the most fatiguing part of it. It was unpleasant, also, playing in half a gale of wind, or with cold drizzling rain falling but worse than all to me were the burning days in July and August, when the sun glared down upon us,—vicious, it seemed to me, at finding his dazzling rays reflected from our bright brass instruments. Then I confess I looked with envy upon the holiday folks for whom we made sweet music, as they sat placidly under the shade of the trees or their own umbrellas; and I longed to tear off my close-fitting tunic, and revel in the green sea at my feet. Yet in spite of all these drawbacks, after my sedentary life in London, I was contented and comfortable enough.

The Upper Rhine Band was none of those harrowing little atrocities who go about with five or six ignorant performers, braying on battered brass instruments—releasing one of their number every ten minutes to go on a begging expedition. We were a properly organised and fairly musical company, engaged and paid by a committee of the townspeople, to enhance the natural attractions of Shinglemouth. Far too dignified were we to pass the hat round. If our listeners chose to give, there was a box placed for that purpose; but as all such vicarious contributions went to the committee's fund, it mattered nothing to us.

Probably the inner life of a German band would be without general interest, so I will only say that our quarters were in a dingy little street at the back of the fine row of new buildings on the Esplanade. We lodged in twos and threes at various small houses. We met together at a certain hour in the morning to commence our rounds, and at nine o'clock at night our duties were over, our instruments put into their cases, and each man his own master—free to smoke, drink, or go to bed, as he pleased.

Although the name we gave ourselves—"The Upper Rhine Band"—was intended to stamp our origin as Teutonic, there were several in the company who, like myself, only spoke English; but as these were quite as good musicians as their German comrades, the fraud was a very little one. My tale concerns no more than two men, so I need only mention the names of these—Caspar Hoffman, a German, and Stephen Slade, an Englishman. The former played the clarinet—an instrument which, in the constitution of a German band, takes the place of the first violin in an orchestra. The latter played that enormous mass of metal called a serpent.

Hoffman was a tall, light-haired man: his age was about thirty. His face was handsome, and bore an expression of great amiability. His manner invited friendship at once; and my strange new life seemed easier and pleasanter to me when this frank young German chose to discover a kindred spirit in mine, and insisted upon our lodging and chumming together. It took me little time to find out

that he was a man of education and reading, and that his
acquirements were far more than might have been expected
from one in his position. He had lived in England a long
time, and spoke our language easily, and he told me he was
almost as well acquainted with French. It seemed strange
to me that so well educated, I might almost say so accomplished a man, should fill so lowly a post in the world.
Indeed I began to weave a little romance about him, fancy-
ing he must be an exiled nobleman or political offender.
When I knew him well enough to venture to express my
wonder, and ask for an explanation, he laughed a bitter
laugh, saying—

"There is nothing to explain, my friend. My little history is the history of thousands of my countrymen. The
eldest son of a small farmer; given an education that strait-
ened the means of my people; sent out as certain to find
employment and fortune for myself and all belonging to
me in your great London.

"*Ach!* what find I there? Tens of thousands of young
Germans like myself, all striving to get into merchants'
offices and make the promised fortunes. Everywhere I
offered myself—not even a pound a-week could I get. Then
I began to starve, and the consul offered to send me back.
How could I return? Then I found I could make a living
by that gift natural to most of my countrymen. And now
I play the clarinet till Fortune finds me something better
to do."

Any way, if not a prince in disguise, my light-haired
German was a fine fellow: a true friend to me when I
most wanted a friend, and a great favorite with all. Even
the surly toll-taker at the pier gates was civil to him. The
nurserymaids, heedless of their charges, looked upon him
with that openmouthed admiration usually reserved for
the military; and, although with trembling I say it, I have
seen ladies whose rank in life should have forbidden such
condescension, glance with approval at his fine face and
manly figure. Yet when I said above that he was a favorite

with all, I should have made an exception—Stephen Slade, the Englishman.

I knew little of this man, and that little was not pleasing enough to make me wish for a closer acquaintance. I may say, in passing, that I am not a bandsman now. Fortune at last gave the wheel a half-turn, which placed me at least above such struggles for a living. At the time of which I write, I had little enough to be proud of; but, fallen as I was in the world, there were a few men in the band with whom I could scarcely bring myself to associate on intimate terms. This man Slade was one of them.

The son of the poorest parents, his present position was as much a rise in the world to him as it was a fall to Hoffman and myself. Yet he appeared to be a sullen, discontented man. Those who knew him better than I did said he was clever and crafty, but could be pleasant enough company when he chose. I never tried to ascertain the truth of the latter assertion, although I fully believed the former. I disliked the man, his appearance, and his ways. He was broad-shouldered and powerful, although clumsily and coarsely made. That our dislike was mutual, I knew: indeed we had quarreled about some trivial matter the first day we met; and ever since, I had studiously avoided him. I felt that the man was of a vindictive nature, and would do me an evil turn if he found the opportunity; but unless I was foolish enough to be provoked to a personal encounter, in which his great strength would be of service to him, I could scarcely see how he could harm me.

It often pleased him to throw out sneering remarks about gentlemen and their ways—intended, of course, for the benefit of Hoffman and myself. Caspar would parry these attacks with jesting good-humour and ready wit, oftentimes raising a hearty laugh from his listeners at the expense of Stephen Slade. Yet I knew that even if these merry sarcasms struck well home, it was for another cause that Slade hated my friend—that cause which has ever been answerable for so much bad blood between man and man.

One night, when Caspar and I were sitting in our poor
little room, talking, and finishing our pipes before going
to bed, Slade's name was mentioned.

"How that wretch hates you!" I said.

"*So!* hates me!"

"Yes; I can see him glaring sideways at you, even whilst
blowing his heart out over his awful instrument."

"Ah, he is not a pleasant man. Yet I thought it was you
he honored with his dislike, not me."

"He dislikes me, and would no doubt injure me if he
could; but you he hates. I saw it in his look."

"And for what cause?"

"Need we go very far to seek the cause? Certainly not a
quarter of a mile."

Caspar laughed, but made no reply.

The cause of Slade's animosity lay very near at hand.
Where the corner of our dingy little street went round towards the Esplanade, was a second- or third-rate inn: not
an establishment that for a moment dared to enter into
competition with the great hotels on the Esplanade, but
which nevertheless did a fair and lucrative business with
the rank and file of excursionists to Shinglemouth. This
inn we had to pass and repass morning, noon, and evening, going to and coming from the pier. After our work
was over, many of us, when able to afford it, were glad to
pause and drink a glass of beer or spirits. The inn was kept
by a widow named Beane—a woman reported well-to-do in
the world, owning, as she did, the house, and doing good
business there. Now Mrs. Deane had one daughter, an only
child, and reputed heiress to all her mother's wealth,—
wealth that, to the German members of our fraternity,
must have seemed fabulous,—a dower almost large enough
for one of the numerous princesses of Fatherland. This
girl, Mary Deane, was really handsome—dark-eyed, dark-
haired, and rich in color. She was, I must say, a well-con-
ducted, virtuous girl, perhaps showing at times a little of
that coquetry which appears to be inseparable from good

looks, when owned by a girl of her rank in life. As it seems necessary for their comfort that every body of men should raise up a goddess to adore, Mary Deane, by common consent of our unmarried members at least, was exalted to that proud position; and the amount of broken but devoted English wafted to her across the shining counter was enough to give the girl ear-ache, if not heart-ache. Of course I ought to have followed my fellows' example, and fallen in love with her; but somehow—and somehow—in spite of all failures, my dreams had not quite left me, and genius in a white apron drawing beer seemed rather out of the fitness of things. Again, it was not long before I found that my light-haired German, Caspar, was the man on whom the girl had set her heart.

Have I written the above lines in a light vein? If so, it was far from my intention. As I picture him now, smiling at the girl with that frank open smile of his, and calling up on her face that scarcely disguised look of pleasure, my thoughts are only sad ones. Not for a moment did I think that Caspar was wooing the girl either for her undoubted charms or possible possessions; but like other men I have known, without meaning harm, he had a dangerous knack of dropping his voice and softening those clear blue eyes of his when speaking to a pretty woman; and if Mary Deane mistook these symptoms for dawning love, who can blame her? You must always remember that in social standing, and as far as outside appearances went, there was a great gulf between her and a clarinet player in a German band, and she stood on the side nearest heaven. Yet when Hoffman entered the house and gave his modest orders, she invariably came out from the little parlour behind to minister to his wants,—an act of condescension certainly not accorded to many of our comrades.

Let Caspar be grateful or not for the favors shown him, one other man, at least, would have given much for them: this was Stephen Slade.

With all his faults, the man was not a drunkard, yet at
every leisure moment he haunted the corner house, and
in his own unpleasant fashion wooed the girl. First to enter and last to leave, he sat and scowled at all who inter-
changed a word with Mary Deane, till men grew nervous
and uncomfortable under his sullen gaze, and the girl herself could only escape it by taking refuge in the private
sanctum, where no one was allowed, on any pretense, to
enter. Caspar alone heeded not his black looks: he was not
his rival, so troubled nothing about them, but talked as
long as he chose to Mary, letting Slade scowl his blackest
at the broad back hiding his sun from him.

This, I say, was the reason why Caspar Hoffman had
one enemy amongst us.

On that evening when we had the conversation as above,
Caspar, with a sort of mock gallantry, had given the girl a
rose. The act and his manner were harmless enough; but
I felt distressed, having noticed the vivid blush that came
to her cheek as she pinned his gift to her dress, and had
now, in truth, only led up to the subject under discussion
with a view of warning my friend not to make the girl too
fond of him.

So I resumed.

"Slade, you must know, looks upon you as a fortunate
rival. He is madly in love."

"Then I am sorry for it. I am not his rival, although I
fear he will have little chance, for all that."

"But you really ought to be careful. I don't want to
flatter you, but the girl is in love with you."

"Then I am more sorry yet. I am *versprochen*—bespo-
ken. Far away in *Vaterland* dwells a little *Mädchen*, with
eyes of blue, and flaxen hair. True and tender is she; and
years, weary years, has she waited for me. When I can I
will send for her, or else some day I will go back to her,
and till the earth, like my fathers before me, for a living."

I said no more, and Caspar's eyes grew dreamy and
far away as he fell into a deep reverie, thinking doubtless

of the little German maiden waiting and waiting for her lover. Then he sighed, and stretching out his arm, took his clarinet, and played softly, very softly, a plaintive little phrase. It was very simple and very melodious. I was struck with it, but could not remember having heard it before. I listened attentively as he played it over and over again. A sad little tune, and one I should no doubt always have been able to recall, even if events to come had not impressed it for ever upon my memory.

When at last he laid his clarinet down, I asked him what he had been playing.

"A little *Lied*—a setting to one of Heine's songs."

"But who wrote it! It is quite fresh to me."

"A friend of mine, who had dreams once, such as you confess to, *mein Englander,* but who never dreams now."

"You mean you wrote it yourself!"

He laughed and nodded, and at my request played his strange little song several times more; so that, when we went to bed at last, I rocked my brain to repose with its rhythm.

The next day, in spite of the season being summer, was bitterly cold. That evening we played on the pier, with a keen north-east wind cutting our hearts out, and making our scanty audience stamp their feet and clap their hands, more for the promotion of circulation than for applause.

I had not been well all the day. I had only done my part with a great effort; and when at length our hour of freedom came, and we shouldered our music-stands and left the pier, I think I felt worse than ever I did in my life-time. I was thoroughly worn out, and my one desire was for warmth and rest. Hoffman and I walked together, as was our custom; and without tellling him how ill I felt, I said, as we turned out of the Esplanade—

"I am shivering with cold. I think I shall step into Mrs. Deane's and get a glass of brandy."

"Very well; although, after your lecture last night, you cannot expect me to accompany you. I shall go home and write a letter."

I entered the inn, and found the dark-browed Slade there as usual. The spirits I drank seemed to do me little or no good: but as the gas was lit, I found the warmth of the room pleasant; so I sat down in a corner, and, thoroughly ill and tired out, dozed off. I must have slept a long time, for the sound of the shutters being put up for the night aroused me. I opened my eyes, and from the dusk of my corner saw Stephen Slade leaning over the counter, talking to Mary Deane, who kept well out of his reach.

"I tell you I love you," I heard him whisper. "I will slave day and night until I can make a home for you, if you will give me one word of hope."

"Why can't you take your answer, Mr. Slade?" replied the girl. "When you asked me before, I told you I cared nothing for you, and never should. Why can't you leave me alone and go elsewhere?"

I saw the man's back shaking with suppressed passion as he said:

"If that long-legged cur of a German chose to speak to you as I am speaking, you'd give him a very different answer, I'll be bound."

The girl's face flushed. "What do you mean by insult-ing me and a better man than yourself!" she cried, with spirit. "His friend is sitting just behind you, so you had better be careful what you say."

Slade, who had doubtless forgotten my presence, faced round and looked at me. I had the sense to shut my eyes again.

"Damn them both for upstarts," he growled. "The boy is drunk or fast asleep." Then turning again, he said in a hissing whisper, "You mind me, Mary Deane—I'll have you, or no one shall. If I see that fellow making love to you again, I'll shoot him like a dog that he is. I will; I swear it! If it costs me my life I will."

The girl laughed scornfully, and without another word turned her back upon him and vanished through the curtained door.

After waiting a minute on the chance of her reappearing, Slade, with a scowl and a curse at my sleeping form, left the house, from whence, after a proper interval, I followed him and crawled home.

The next morning I should have told Caspar Hoffman all I had overheard, but when I awoke I found myself scarcely able to articulate a word, and suffering from severe pain in my chest. I was seriously ill—there was no doubt about it—and, moreover, rapidly growing worse. That evening I was taken to the hospital, where I lay for a fortnight with inflammation of the lungs. Caspar, like a good fellow, came to see me every morning and evening, until within a day or two before I was pronounced well enough to quit. When that time came and I stepped outside the gates, I felt it would be some time before I could resume my place in the Upper Rhine Band. Slowly, very slowly, I walked home, wondering what had kept Hoffman away from me the last few days, and looking forward to the cheery greeting he would give me when we met. Just before I reached our house I encountered Stephen Slade. To my surprise he stopped, and accosting me with quite a show of friendship, inquired after my health, congratulated me upon my recovery, and even carried his new-born civility far enough to beg me to take some dinner with him, it being now the time allotted for that meat I began to think whether, after all, I had misjudged the man—whether his roughness was but external, and his heart beneath as kind as other people's. However, as I was anxious to get home and see my friend, I declined his well-meant hospitality, saying that Hoffman would be expecting me.

"Hoffman!" he repeated. "Have you not heard the news?"

"What news?"

"Hoffman has left us—suddenly—without a word to any one. He has gone back to Germany, we all believe. Every one thought you were in the secret."

So saying, he bade me good morning, leaving me too much surprised to utter a word.

I entered the room in which Caspar and I had lived together for the last two months, and the first thing I saw was a letter addressed to me lying on the table. I opened it; it ran thus:—

> "Dear Friend,—I am called back to Germa-
> ny at an hour's notice, and deeply regret that
> I cannot find time to see you again. Please
> guard all my belongings, and I will write tell-
> ing you where to send them. My prospects be-
> ing entirely changed, I shall return no more."

Ill, weary, disappointed, and sorely in need of compan-ionship and sympathy as I was, I sank down on one of the rickety chairs, leant my head upon the table, and fairly cried.

The letter was unsigned, but its being written in that peculiar German calligraphy left no doubt as to the writer. After our daily and almost brotherly intercourse, his abrupt departure seemed almost unkind; yet I felt that he was such a true friend to me, that he must have had strong reasons for it, and also for withholding his present address. I could only hope that soon I might hear from him.

In another week I had recovered my health sufficiently to enable me to resume my place among my Teutonic comrades, and found, upon rejoining them, an idea prevailing that Caspar Hoffman had inherited a fortune—hence the reason he had left so suddenly.

I was still weak, and lagged behind the others as we left the pier that evening. Just outside the toll-gate I met Mary Deane. I suppose she must have hidden herself until Slade had passed by. If I looked ill, she looked worse. The rich colour had flown from her cheeks, her lips looked drawn, and dark circles were round her eyes. Glancing hastily around, she said, in a sharp, quick whisper—

"I want to see you—I must speak to you—alone. Be outside our house at twelve o'clock to-night without fail." Then, without waiting for any answer, she turned and hurried away.

Her manner was so emphatic, so earnest, that I never thought of disobeying her command, and twelve o'clock found me waiting outside the corner house. The door opened stealthily, and Mary appearing, beckoned me in. I entered, when, taking my hand, she led me to the parlor. The gas, turned down low, made a dreary twilight in the room, and through it the girl's face looked wan and ghost like. I seated myself, wondering what was the reason of this midnight appointment, when, leaning over me, she whispered in my ear—

"Where is Caspar Hoffman?"

"Caspar Hoffman!" I repeated. "Why, gone home to his friends and to fortune, they say. He left me a letter—read it." And as I spoke I drew the letter from my pocket.

She waved it aside without giving it one look. "He has not," she said; "he is dead—murdered—and that man has murdered him."

"You are dreaming, or you must be mad."

"I am not. I know it. I am sure of it. He threatened to do so the night you were taken ill, and he has done it now. When or how, I know not; but every time I see his black face and wicked eyes I can read the deed there. Oh, my Caspar! my bonny Caspar! I will find out the truth."

"But his letter to me—it is written as a German writes. Look at it."

She turned upon me with something like contempt in her voice.

"And would not a man who murders forge also? Has he never seen a letter written by a German? Ah, Stephen Slade is a cleverer man than either you or Caspar ever suspected. Do you know Caspar's handwriting?"

I was obliged to confess I could not remember having seen it.

"Then I say that letter is only a forgery, written to deceive us. He has killed him. I know it. He comes to me in dreams, in more than dreams, and tells me so. You, who call yourself his friend, aid me in bringing his murderer to justice. Oh, my Caspar! my Caspar!" and she threw her arms across the table, and leaning her head upon them, sobbed convulsively.

The girl's passionate words, excited manner, and, above all, absolute, unswerving belief in her wild statement, greatly impressed me. Her dark suspicions were infectious; and as my former opinion of Slade again reasserted itself, I began almost to think that her horrible fancy might have some foundation. It may have been my ill health, or the mystery of this midnight meeting, that induced me to give any weight to her words; but any way, I promised to leave no stone unturned, but try and ascertain whether Hoffman really wrote the letter, and whether he had gone back to Germany. Calmed, apparently calmed by my promise, she bade me good night.

As she opened the door for me to go out—as her hand lay in mine—as I was looking into her great dark eyes, shining through the dusk; solemn at one moment with the horror they pictured; fierce at another with fire of revenge,—as we stood thus, I say, a sound came on the night wind—a sound that sent a tremor through me and made the blood run cold in every vein with unspeakable fear. And I knew, from the way in which her fingers closed on mine, that as I heard it and trembled, so it was with my companion. It was nearly one o'clock. The street was deserted by all save ourselves. So quiet was all around, that we could catch the dash of the waves on the shingle, audible, even at that distance, through the stillness of the summer night; and then—soft, yet clear and well defined—rose, as it were close to us, a strain of plaintive music. So close it seemed, that I turned instinctively to see the player; but we were alone in the street, which, although dimly lighted, held no recess where one might hide; and I felt, soft as the music sounded, it was not distance that diminished the power of the notes. Whoever or whatever produced it, was almost within arm's-length. And bar after bar of the strange music came sighing to us until I had recovered sense enough to understand the language of the notes, and then my fear was linked with horror, for this was the melody that fell upon my ear:—

Over and over again I heard the pathetic little phrase floating, it seemed, in the air around me; at times so low that I could scarcely say I heard it—at times so clear and distinct that I turned again and again to detect the player, but each attempt was futile.

Many minutes did Mary Deane and I stand, hand in hand, listening with all our power, neither speaking nor trying to speak, until the notes grew fainter and fainter, and finally died into the silence of the night, and the distant murmur of the waves was the only sound left. I looked into the girl's face, but said nothing.

"You heard it?" she whispered.

I nodded assent—my agitation was too great for speech.

"I did not tell you before," she said; "but I have heard it three times. But never so clearly or for so long as to-night. What does it mean? Tell me."

"I do not know," I replied; and then with an effort said, "Let us meet here again to-morrow night at the same hour, and try and find its meaning."

She assented, and closed the door as I turned away towards my home. Agitation is no word to express the state of my mind; for although I dared not tell Mary Deane so, the unearthly melody that came sighing so softly to us that night, was that same plaintive little air that Caspar Hoffman had played to me the last time we had sat together in the room which now seemed so desolate without his cheery presence.

I knew not what to think—what to do. My sleep that night was restless, broken, and dreamful. All sorts of horrors came to me, but running through and in some way entwined with every dream was that haunting melody. The figures in my visions moved to its notes; their voices, when they spoke, kept time to them. I seemed to breathe to their rhythm and glad I was when I awoke altogether and found it was broad daylight.

Somehow I dragged through the next day, studiously avoiding Stephen Slade's eyes, lest he should read in my look the growing but as yet undefined suspicions I felt my eyes must utter. At half-past nine I threw myself on my bed and slept with my clothes on for three hours. At one o'clock I was waiting outside the inn. There was no moon, but the stars were bright above. I had not long to wait; the girl soon appeared, and closed the door behind her. Her head was covered with a thick hood that almost prevented recognition. We shook hands, and, without a word, waited with nerves intent on catching the first strains of the mysterious music, if indeed it should be again audible to us. For some time we listened in vain, and I was just on the point of saying, "It must have been our fancy," when close at my right hand arose the plaintive and familiar strain. Mary's cold fingers stole trembling into mine as, in spite of last night's experience, I turned sharply round, feeling convinced that some bodily player must be close by. Up and down the street I looked, but we were alone, and yet the notes lay on the air. Now they seemed at the right, now at the left, now behind, now in front—departing, returning, circling around, yet ever with us. I am not ashamed to say dread—mortal dread—came over me, as with a mournful monotony I heard, over and over again, Caspar Hollman's sad little melody sighing through the night, whilst with the girl's hand ever in my own we stood still, neither knowing what to do nor how to account for the phenomenon. At last, in an awestruck whisper, Mary Deane said—

"It is Caspar playing. I know it is—I feel it. What are we to do?"

The sound of her voice recalled my reasoning faculties, and, unbeliever as I had ever been in the supernatural, I felt now that it might be for some weighty reason we were permitted to hear this strange music on these two occasions. I was brave now; fear had left me. I was only eager to learn what message the music bore.

I drew my companion's arm through mine. "Let us move up the street a few paces, and see if the music follows us," I said.

We did so, but after walking some twenty yards could hear it no longer. Then we returned to the spot where at first we stood, and the notes sounded as before. We then walked a little way in the other direction, and yet we heard the melody: farther yet we went, and it was with us; farther and farther yet, right to the end of the street, and yet it kept near us. We turned to the left, and heard it not. We retraced our steps, and took the road to the right, and clearly we heard each note once more.

We neither were frightened now: my companion, like myself, had caught the meaning of the music. It was not accompanying us, nor following us, but, as a bird might, hovering before us—guiding us for some purpose, to some end, although we knew not to what or whither it might lead us. The girl seemed transformed. Her step grew firm and sure; her arm trembled on mine no longer. She turned her wild eyes to mine, and said, almost in exultation—

"I knew it—I knew that music meant something. Listen! it calls us to follow, and it will lead us on and on until we learn the truth. Yes, my Caspar, my love," she continued, speaking in a softer voice, as if addressing one near at hand,—"yes, follow it we will, even to the ends of the earth."

She said no more; and silently, for what seemed hours, we followed as the music led us. All fatigue had left me, and every nerve was strung with excitement and curiosity. Far along the main road we went, turning neither to the right nor the left, with the music ever circling and floating around us, but ever advancing, as the mother bird that seeks to draw the stranger from her nest and its treasure. On and on for perhaps three miles it led us by the road, till, glancing back, I could only see the lights of Shinglemouth dim in the distance. Then the notes stayed, and near us was a gate. We passed through it, and the music passed before us. We entered a grove of pine-trees, with which the country round about is thickly studded. Spectral and weird the trunks looked as they threw their straight shadows on the light brown ground beneath, carpeted many inches deep with cast needles. The pungent aromatic odour of the pines perfumed the air, and to this day that odour sets my heart beating with the memories it bears. Then out again to the open, with nothing between us and the clear stars shining overhead. We were now on the sward that stretched away towards the sea-cliff. There was no road, not even a footpath, over the springy turf; but on and on our feet were led, straight as the crow flies—the girl's step ever falling in unison with mine, and as firm and resolute. Gradually we seemed to be bearing across the downs towards the sea; and I was wondering whether our destination was the sea-coast, when I found we were descending the side of a deepish hollow. We reached the bottom, which was thickly covered with large-sized stones, and then with one accord we stopped short, for we heard the music no longer. Suddenly as it came, so it went: one moment we heard it, as we had heard it for so long, close at hand; the next, and not a sound broke the stillness of the night. I raised my eyes and peered around. Just in front of us was a small, square, grey building; old and venerable it looked, like a ruin of some sort. The sides of the hollow in which we stood sloped upwards towards its roof, which seemed almost on a level with the higher ground. As I knew but little of the neighbourhood round about, I turned to the girl.

"Where are we?" I asked.

"At the old limekiln, about five miles from home."

"Is it worked now?"

"No; it hasn't been worked for years. No one ever comes near it."

"What shall we do now?"

"I shall wait," she answered, decisively.

"Wait!" I echoed; "for what? The music has left us. It has led us here, but perhaps can do no more. Its mission is accomplished. Let us return by daylight and try if we can find out anything."

"No matter—I shall wait. You can leave me if you like; I am not afraid."

This was entirely out of the question; so finding persuasion useless, I determined to make the best of it. After all, some inner voice I could not hear might be telling the girl what course to take. I pressed her no more, but begged her to sit down and rest herself, and upon her complying, seated myself beside her and longed for the morning to break.

And thus we sat and waited—neither speaking—both listening for the weird music to come again for our guidance,—sat until I feared we should be numbed with cold, for we were not far from the sea, and the night was chilly.

Being summer time, the nights were very short, and with joy I saw at last the welcome greyness tempering the eastern sky. With the coming dawn a mist seemed to be gathering, and a cold wind began to blow in from the sea. I was shivering, and suggested to my companion, who sat motionless as a statue beside me, that it would be well if we took shelter under the side of the limekiln. She made no remark, but rising, followed where I led her. I placed her as comfortably as I could; and then, pressing her hands on her eyes, she sat silent, ever thinking, I well knew, of the man she loved. The morning was now fairly breaking; and I was resolved, as soon as there was sufficient light, to thoroughly examine the place, and ascertain if what I dreaded to think of might be hidden there. I had even risen to commence my investigations—quietly, without disturbing my silent companion, thinking that whatever fearful discovery was to be made had better be made by me alone—when the noise of a stone rolling down the declivity and falling with a slight crash upon its fellows at the bottom, drove all the blood back to my heart, and grasping Mary's arm, I forcibly pushed her back into the darkness cast by the side of the limekiln, as through the grey mist of the morning a man strode down into the hollow and stood within a few paces of us; and as he stood there, for a moment we heard once more the melancholy notes that had led us so far.

The girl clutched my arm with an energy almost painful.

"See," she whispered —"see, there is Caspar's murderer, led here, as we were led, for us to know and accuse."

And the man standing there with pallid face and distorted features, with great drops of sweat rolling from his forehead, was Stephen Slade. Had he looked our way he must have seen us, so close we were to each other; but all his attention seemed to be riveted on one spot, the entrance to the disused kiln, now almost hidden by a pile of stones. He was breathing hard and quick, and stood gesticulating, shaking his fists and glaring in that one direction.

"Devil! devil!" we heard him mutter, "why will you not rest in peace and leave me alone? Three times has that cursed music drawn me here against my will. I hate you dead worse than living."

Then, as if with an effort, he turned away and began to retrace his steps. As he moved, the girl broke from my hold and sprang after him. Her hood had fallen back, her long dark hair streamed loose about her shoulders, and her eyes from under her black and knitted brows gleamed like fire—an avenging fury she looked, claiming blood for blood. Heedless of the consequences, she grasped his arm and cried with a shrill voice, "Murder! murder!" I had followed her, both to protect and assist her; but as I did so, the danger of bearding this desperate man flashed through my brain like lightning. As he felt her touch, I think he screamed with horror, and with a livid face staggered back, seeming about to fall. So helpless he appeared, that I believe had we then and there thrown ourselves upon him we might have bound him as easily as a child. We let the opportunity slip, and the delay was fatal. In a few moments he had recognised us; then, knowing he had to deal with mortals like himself, not with avenging spirits, the man's horrible courage and ferocity came to his aid. His cruel eyes met mine in the early twilight; and well, from their expression, I knew what was coming, and framed an inward prayer for deliverance.

"So you have spied and tracked me," he said. "You two, at any rate, will never tell the tale. I can make room for both of you beside your friend."

Then, with fell murder written on his face, he came towards me, and I braced myself for the struggle, which I felt was hopeless.

Slade, as I said before, was a broad-shouldered man of great strength. What chance could I have with him, broken as I was with sickness, and worn-out with the night-watching? I had no weapon, not even a pocket-knife. Fly, and leave the girl to his mercies, I could not. Truly, death seemed very near to me at the moment when I felt those muscular arms thrown round me, and my ribs bending beneath their strong grip. I was an infant in his hands. Yet I was not altogether unaided. Bravely the girl stood by me, tore at his arms, at his face, to make him release me. It was but for a moment, however. He loosened his left arm, and, with one backward sweep of it, hurled her, stunned and senseless, upon a heap of stones. "You and I will have another kind of reckoning by-and-by, my pretty maid," I heard him mutter as he closed with me once more. Death was very, very near me now. Backwards and forwards we swayed, then we fell together—Slade uppermost. I was utterly exhausted, and could struggle no more. The ruffian tore himself from my feeble grip, and kneeling on my arms, pressed his thumbs upon my throat. As I lay helpless, I could look straight into his wicked eyes, but saw no gleam of mercy or relenting there. In three seconds my head felt bursting, sense was failing me; I seemed trying to articulate these words, "How hor—ri—ble—to—die—like—this!" when—waking, dreaming, or dying—I heard close, close to me, the wail of Caspar Hoffman's *Lied*,—the same ghostly music that had led us to this spot, and brought the murderer face to face with us. And as I heard it, I knew I was saved. Slade's villainous grip on my throat relaxed; I breathed once more; and although too far gone to move hand or foot to save my life, I could see the ruffian rise, stare around him in a bewildered manner, then, muttering like one in a dream, and with a face as set as a somnambulist's, ascend the side of the hollow, and vanish over the level ground. Then I fainted.

When my senses returned I found Mary Deane kneeling beside me and chafing my hands. She had not been much injured, and upon coming to herself found me lying dead, as she thought, and Slade gone.

We were too much exhausted, indeed terrified, to make any investigation that might solve the mystery of the night. Painfully we dragged ourselves over the downs until we reached the main road; then having removed, as far as we could, all traces of the recent deadly struggle, managed by the aid of a passing waggon to reach Shinglemouth before its inhabitants were astir.

What could I do now? My only course seemed to be that of going to the police and accusing Slade of the murder of Hoffman. I could give no common-sense reasons for the accusation, but I might beg that the limekiln be searched, and the man kept in sight at least during the operation. It should be no fault of mine if Slade escaped justice. And so I went.

The inspector I saw was rather a friend of mine, and gave me an attentive hearing. Upon learning the gist of my errand, he said—

"You are an hour too late. The man is in custody now, upon his own confession. Says he murdered him and stuck the body in the entrance of the limekiln, making a heap of stones in front of it. We thought him drunk or raving— kept on talking about music that was driving him mad. Any way, he's here safe enough, and some of our men have gone off down coast to find out whether his tale is true or false."

And true enough they found it. Three hours afterwards I saw all that remained of my light-hearted German friend; and two months afterwards Stephen Slade was hanged at Dorchester jail.

He simply confessed to the murder, but would enter into no particulars. Plenty of circumstantial evidence was forthcoming to establish his guilt, but it was never ascertained how he decoyed his victim to that lonely and distant spot. A pistol-bullet through the breast told the way the deed was done, and that was all.

Slade died sullen and impenitent. The prison doctor thought there were grounds for a reprieve, as the man was for ever talking wildly about music he, but no one else, could hear. This was, however, attributed to the profession he had followed, not to higher causes; so as he had no friends to take up his case, and as his character was not such as to enlist strangers in his favour, no steps were taken to mitigate his sentence, and he met the fate he fully merited.

Since that night I have never heard that ghostly music. Its mission was no doubt accomplished when the mysterious power it wielded caused the murderer's hand to drop nerveless from my throat, and drove him, cruel, remorseless, and impenitent as he was, to make confession of a crime that might else have remained undiscovered, and to reveal the tragic end of Caspar Hoffman.

The Haunted Organist of Hurly Burly

Rosa Mulholland

(1886)

There had been a thunderstorm in the village of Hurly Burly. Every door was shut, every dog in his kennel, every rut and gutter a flowing river after the deluge of rain that had fallen. Up at the great house, a mile from the town, the rooks were calling to one another about the fright they had been in, the fawns in the deer-park were venturing their timid heads from behind the trunks of trees, and the old woman at the gate-lodge had risen from her knees, and was putting back her prayer-book on the shelf In the garden, July roses, unwieldy with their full-blown richness, and saturated with rain, hung their heads heavily to the earth; others, already fallen, lay flat upon their blooming faces on the path, where Bess, Mistress Hurly's maid, would find them, when going on her morning quest of rose-leaves for her lady's pot-pourri. Ranks of white lilies, just brought to perfection by today's sun, lay dabbled in the mire of flooded mould. Tears ran down the amber cheeks of the plums on the south wall, and not a bee had ventured out of the hives, though the scent of the air was sweet enough to tempt the laziest drone. The sky was still lurid behind the boles of the upland oaks, but the birds had begun to dive in and out of the ivy that wrapped up the home of the Hurlys of Hurly Burly.

This thunderstorm took place more than half a century ago, and we must remember that Mistress Hurly was

dressed in the fashion of that time as she crept out from
behind the squire's chair, now that the lightning was over,
and, with many nervous glances towards the window, sat
down before her husband, the tea-urn, and the muffins.
We can picture her fine lace cap, with its peachy ribbons,
the frill on the hem of her cambric gown just touching
her ankles, the embroidered clocks on her stockings, the
rosettes on her shoes, but not so easily the lilac shade of
her mild eyes, the satin skin, which still kept its delicate
bloom, though wrinkled with advancing age, and the pale,
sweet, puckered mouth, that time and sorrow had made
angelic while trying vainly to deface its beauty.

The squire was as rugged as his wife was gentle, his skin
as brown as hers was white, his grey hair as bristling as
hers was glossed; the years had ploughed his face into ruts
and channels; a bluff, choleric, noisy man he had been;
but of late a dimness had come on his eyes, a hush on his
loud voice, and a check on the spring of his hale step. He
looked at his wife often, and very often she looked at him.
She was not a tall woman, and he was only a head higher.
They were a quaintly well-matched couple, despite their
differences. She turned to you with nervous sharpness and
revealed her tender voice and eye; he spoke and glanced
roughly, but the turn of his head was courteous. Of late
they fitted one another better than they had ever done
in the heyday of their youthful love. A common sorrow
had developed a singular likeness between them. In former
years the cry from the wife had been, 'Don't curb my son
too much!' and from the husband, 'You ruin the lad with
softness.' But now the idol that had stood between them
was removed, and they saw each other better.

The room in which they sat was a pleasant old-fashioned drawing-room, with a general spider-legged character about the fittings; spinnet and guitar in their places,
with a great deal of copied music beside them; carpet,
tawny wreaths on the pale blue; blue flutings on the walls,
and faint gilding on the furniture. A huge urn, crammed

with roses, in the open bay-window, through which came delicious airs from the garden, the twittering of birds settling to sleep in the ivy close by, and occasionally the pattering of a flight of rain-drops, swept to the ground as a bough bent in the breeze. The urn on the table was ancient silver, and the china rare. There was nothing in the room for luxurious ease of the body, but everything of delicate refinement for the eye.

There was a great hush all over Hurly Burly, except in the neighbourhood of the rooks. Every living thing had suffered from heat for the past month, and now, in common with all Nature, was receiving the boon of refreshed air in silent peace. The mistress and master of Hurly Burly shared the general spirit that was abroad, and were not talkative over their tea.

"Do you know," said Mistress Hurly, at last, "when I heard the first of the thunder beginning I thought it was— it was—"

The lady broke down, her lips trembling, and the peachy ribbons of her cap stirring with great agitation.

"Pshaw!" cried the old squire, making his cup suddenly ring upon the saucer, "we ought to have forgotten that. Nothing has been heard for three months."

At this moment a rolling sound struck upon the ears of both. The lady rose from her seat trembling, and folded her hands together, while the tea-urn flooded the tray.

"Nonsense, my love," said the squire; "that is the noise of wheels. Who can be arriving?"

"Who, indeed?" murmured the lady, reseating herself in agitation.

Presently pretty Bess of the rose-leaves appeared at the door in a flutter of blue ribbons.

"Please, madam, a lady has arrived, and says she is expected. She asked for her apartment, and I put her into the room that was got ready for Miss Calderwood. And she sends her respects to you, madam, and she'll be down with you presently."

The squire looked at his wife, and his wife looked at the squire.

"It is some mistake," murmured madam. "Some visitor for Calderwood or the Grange. It is very singular."

Hardly had she spoken when the door again opened, and the stranger appeared—a small creature, whether girl or woman it would be hard to say—dressed in a scanty black silk dress, her narrow shoulders covered with a white muslin pelerine. Her hair was swept up to the crown of her head, all but a little fringe hanging over her low forehead within an inch of her brows. Her face was brown and thin, eyes black and long, with blacker settings, mouth large, sweet, and melancholy. She was all head, mouth, and eyes; her nose and chin were nothing.

This visitor crossed the floor hastily, dropped a courtesy in the middle of the room, and approached the table, saying abruptly, with a soft Italian accent:

"Sir and madam, I am here. I am come to play your organ."

"The organ!" gasped Mistress Hurly.

"The organ!" stammered the squire.

"Yes, the organ," said the little stranger lady, playing on the back of a chair with her fingers, as if she felt notes under them. "It was but last week that the handsome signor, your son, came to my little house, where I have lived teaching music since my English father and my Italian mother and brothers and sisters died and left me so lonely."

Here the fingers left off drumming, and two great tears were brushed off, one from each eye with each hand, child's fashion. But the next moment the fingers were at work again, as if only whilst they were moving the tongue could speak.

"The noble signor, your son," said the little woman, looking trustfully from one to the other of the old couple, while a bright blush shone through her brown skin, "he often came to see me before that, always in the evening, when the sun was warm and yellow all through my little studio, and the music was swelling my heart, and I could play out grand with all my soul; then he used to come and say, 'Hurry, little Lisa, and play better, better still. I have work for you to do.by-and-by.' Sometimes he said, 'Brava!' and sometimes he said 'Eccellentissima!' but one night last week he came to me and said, 'It is enough. Will you swear to do my bidding, whatever it may be?' Here the black eyes fell. And I said, 'Yes.' And he said, 'Now you are my betrothed.' And I said, 'Yes.' And he said, 'Pack up your music, little Lisa, and go off to England to my English father and mother, who have an organ in their house which must be played upon. If they refuse to let you play, tell them I sent you, and they will give you leave. You must play all day, and you must get up in the night and play. You must never tire. You are my betrothed, and you have sworn to do my work.' I said, 'Shall I see you there, signor?' And he said, 'Yes, you shall see me there.' I said, 'I will keep my vow, Signor.' And so, sir and madam, I am come."

The soft foreign voice left off talking, the fingers left off thrumming on the chair, and the little stranger gazed in dismay at her auditors, both pale with agitation.

"You are deceived. You make a mistake," said they in one breath.

"Our son—" began Mistress Hurly, but her mouth twitched, her voice broke, and she looked piteously towards her husband.

"Our son," said the squire, making an effort to conquer the quavering in his voice, "our son is long dead."

"Nay, nay," said the little foreigner. "If you have thought him dead have good cheer, dear sir and madam. He is alive; he is well, and strong, and handsome. But one, two, three, four, five" (on the fingers) "days ago he stood by my side."

"It is some strange mistake, some wonderful coincidence!" said the mistress and master of Hurly Burly.

"Let us take her to the gallery," murmured the mother of this son who was thus dead and alive.

"There is yet light to see the pictures. She will not know his portrait."

The bewildered wife and husband led their strange visitor away to a long gloomy room at the west side of the house, where the faint gleams from the darkening sky still lingered on the portraits of the Hurly family.

"Doubtless he is like this," said the squire, pointing to a fair-haired young man with a mild face, a brother of his own who had been lost at sea.

But Lisa shook her head, and went softly on tiptoe from one picture to another, peering into the canvas, and still turning away troubled. But at last a shriek of delight startled the shadowy chamber.

"Ah, here he is! See, here he is, the noble signor, the beautiful signor, not half so handsome as he looked five days ago, when talking to poor little Lisa! Dear sir and madam, you are now content. Now take me to the organ, that I may commence to do his bidding at once."

The mistress of Hurly Burly clung fast by her husband's arm. "How old are you, girl?" she said faintly.

"Eighteen," said the visitor impatiently, moving towards the door.

"And my son has been dead for twenty years!" said his mother, and swooned on her husband's breast.

"Order the carriage at once," said Mistress Hurly, recovering from her swoon; "I will take her to Margaret Calderwood. Margaret will tell her the story. Margaret will bring her to reason. No, not tomorrow; I cannot bear tomorrow, it is so far away. We must go tonight."

The little signora thought the old lady mad, but she put on her cloak again obediently, and took her seat beside Mistress Hurly in the Hurly family coach. The moon that looked in at them through the pane as they lumbered along was not whiter than the aged face of the squire's wife, whose dim faded eyes were fixed upon it in doubt and awe too great for tears or words. Lisa, too, from her corner gloated upon the moon, her black eyes shining with passionate dreams.

A carriage rolled away from the Calderwood door as the Hurly coach drew up at the steps.

Margaret Calderwood had just returned from a dinner-party, and at the open door a splendid figure was standing, a tall woman dressed in brown velvet, the diamonds on her bosom glistening in the moonlight that revealed her, pouring, as it did, over the house from eaves to basement. Mistress Hurly fell into her outstretched arms with a groan, and the strong woman carried her aged friend, like a baby, into the house. Little Lisa was overlooked, and sat down contentedly on the threshold to gloat awhile longer on the moon, and to thrum imaginary sonatas on the doorstep.

There were tears and sobs in the dusk, moonlit room into which Margaret Calderwood carried her friend. There was a long consultation, and then Margaret, having hushed away the grieving woman into some quiet corner, came forth to look for the little dark-faced stranger, who had arrived, so unwelcome, from beyond the seas, with such wild communication from the dead.

Up the grand staircase of handsome Calderwood the little woman followed the tall one into a large chamber where a lamp burned, showing Lisa, if she cared to see it, that this mansion of Calderwood was fitted with much greater luxury and richness than was that of Hurly Burly. The appointments of this room announced it the sanctum of a woman who depended for the interest of her life upon resources of intellect and taste. Lisa noticed nothing but a morsel of biscuit that was lying on a plate.

"May I have it?" said she eagerly. "It is so long since I have eaten. I am hungry."

Margaret Calderwood gazed at her with a sorrowful, motherly look, and, parting the fringing hair on her forehead, kissed her. Lisa, staring at her in wonder, returned the caress with ardour.

Margaret's large fair shoulders, Madonna face, and yellow braided hair, excited a rapture within her. But when food was brought her, she flew to it and ate.

"It is better than I have ever eaten at home!" she said gratefully. And Margaret Calderwood murmured, "She is physically healthy, at least."

"And now, Lisa," said Margaret Calderwood, "come and tell me the whole history of the grand signor who sent you to England to play the organ."

Then Lisa crept in behind a chair, and her eyes began to bum and her fingers to thrum, and she repeated word for word her story as she had told it at Hurly Burly.

When she had finished, Margaret Calderwood began to pace up and down the floor with a very troubled face. Lisa watched her, fascinated, and, when she bade her listen to a story which she would relate to her, folded her restless hands together meekly, and listened.

"Twenty years ago, Lisa, Mr. and Mrs. Hurly had a son. He was handsome, like that portrait you saw in the gallery, and he had brilliant talents. He was idolized by his father and mother, and all who knew him felt obliged to love him. I was then a happy girl of twenty. I was an orphan, and Mrs. Hurly, who had been my mother's friend, was like a mother to me. I, too, was petted and caressed by all my friends, and I was very wealthy; but I only valued admiration, riches—every good gift that fell to my share—just in proportion as they seemed of worth in the eyes of Lewis Hurly. I was his affianced wife, and I loved him well.

"All the fondness and pride that were lavished on him could not keep him from falling into evil ways, nor from becoming rapidly more and more abandoned to wickedness, till even those who loved him best despaired of seeing his reformation. I prayed him with tears, for my sake, if not for that of his grieving mother, to save himself before it was too late. But to my horror I found that my power was gone, my words did not even move him; he loved me no more. I tried to think that this was some fit of madness that would pass, and still clung to hope. At last his own mother forbade me to see him."

Here Margaret Calderwood paused, seemingly in bitter thought, but resumed:

"He and a party of his boon companions, named by themselves the 'Devil's Club,' were in the habit of practising all kinds of unholy pranks in the country. They had midnight carousings on the tomb-stones in the village graveyard; they carried away helpless old men and children, whom they tortured by making believe to bury them alive; they raised the dead and placed them sitting round the tombstones at a mock feast. On one occasion there was a very sad funeral from the village. The corpse was carried into the church, and prayers were read over the coffin, the chief mourner, the aged father of the dead man, standing weeping by. In the midst of this solemn scene the organ suddenly pealed forth a profane tune, and a number of voices shouted a drinking chorus. A groan of execration burst from the crowd, the clergyman turned pale and closed his book, and the old man, the father of the dead, climbed the altar steps, and, raising his arms above his head, uttered a terrible curse. He cursed Lewis Hurly to all eternity, he cursed the organ he played, that it might be dumb henceforth, except under the fingers that had now profaned it, which, he prayed, might be forced to labour upon it till they stiffened in death. And the curse seemed to work, for the organ stood dumb in the church from that day, except when touched by Lewis Hurly.

"For a bravado he had the organ taken down and conveyed to his father's house, where he had it put up in the chamber where it now stands. It was also for a bravado that he played on it every day. But, by-and-by, the amount of time which he spent at it daily began to increase rapidly. We wondered long at this whim, as we called it, and his poor mother thanked God that he had set his heart upon an occupation which would keep him out of harm's way. I was the first to suspect that it was not his own will that kept him hammering at the organ so many laborious hours, while his boon companions tried vainly to draw him away. He used to lock himself up in the room with the organ, but one day I hid myself among the curtains, and saw him writhing on his seat, and heard him groaning as he strove to wrench his hands from the keys, to which they flew back like a needle to a magnet. It was soon plainly to be seen that he was an involuntary slave to the organ; but whether through a madness that had grown within himself, or by some supernatural doom, having its cause in the old man's curse, we did not dare to say. By-and-by there came a time when we were wakened out of our sleep at nights by the rolling of the organ. He wrought now night and day. Food and rest were denied him. His face got haggard, his beard grew long, his eyes started from their sockets. His body became wasted, and his cramped fingers like the claws of a bird. He groaned piteously as he stooped over his cruel toil. All save his mother and I were afraid to go near him. She, poor, tender woman, tried to put wine and food between his lips, while the tortured fingers crawled over the keys; but he only gnashed his teeth at her with curses, and she retreated from him in terror, to pray. At last, one dreadful hour, we found him a ghastly corpse on the ground before the organ.

"From that hour the organ was dumb to the touch of all human fingers. Many, unwilling to believe the story, made persevering endeavours to draw sound from it, in vain. But when the darkened empty room was locked up and left, we heard as loud as ever the well-known sounds humming and rolling through the walls. Night and day the tones of the organ boomed on as before. It seemed that the doom of the wretched man was not yet fulfilled, although his tortured body had been worn out in the terrible struggle to accomplish it. Even his own mother was afraid to go near the room then. So the time went on, and the curse of this perpetual music was not removed from the house.

Servants refused to stay about the place. Visitors shunned it. The squire and his wife left their home for years, and returned; left it, and returned again, to find their ears still tortured and their hearts wrung by the unceasing persecution of terrible sounds. At last, but a few months ago, a holy man was found, who locked himself up in the cursed chamber for many days, praying and wrestling with the demon. After he came forth and went away the sounds ceased, and the organ was heard no more. Since then there has been peace in the house. And now, Lisa, your strange appearance and your strange story convince us that you are a victim of a ruse of the Evil One. Be warned in time, and place yourself under the protection of God, that you may be saved from the fearful influences that are at work upon you. Come—"

Margaret Calderwood turned to the corner where the stranger sat, as she had supposed, listening intently. Little Lisa was fast asleep, her hands spread before her as if she played an organ in her dreams.

Margaret took the soft brown face to her motherly breast, and kissed the swelling temples, too big with wonder and fancy.

"We will save you from a horrible fate!" she murmured, and carried the girl to bed.

In the morning Lisa was gone. Margaret Calderwood, coming early from her own chamber, went into the girl's room and found the bed empty.

"She is just such a wild thing," thought Margaret, "as would rush out at sunrise to hear the larks!" and she went forth to look for her in the meadows, behind the beech hedges and in the home park. Mistress Hurly, from the breakfast-room window, saw Margaret Calderwood, large and fair in her white morning gown, coming down the garden-path between the rose bushes, with her fresh draperies dabbled by the dew, and a look of trouble on her calm face. Her quest had been unsuccessful. The little foreigner had vanished.

A second search after breakfast proved also fruitless, and towards evening the two women drove back to Hurly Burly together. There all was panic and distress. The squire sat in his study with the doors shut, and his hands over his ears. The servants, with pale faces, were huddled together in whispering groups. The haunted organ was pealing through the house as of old.

Margaret Calderwood hastened to the fatal chamber, and there, sure enough, was Lisa, perched upon the high seat before the organ, beating the keys with her small hands, her slight figure swaying, and the evening sunshine playing about her weird head. Sweet unearthly music she wrung from the groaning heart of the organ—wild melodies, mounting to rapturous heights and falling to mournful depths. She wandered from Mendelssohn to Mozart, and from Mozart to Beethoven. Margaret stood fascinated awhile by the ravishing beauty of the sounds she heard, but, rousing herself quickly, put her arms round the musician and forced her away from the chamber. Lisa returned next day, however, and was not so easily coaxed from her post again.

Day after day she laboured at the organ, growing paler and thinner and more weird-looking as time went on.

"I work so hard," she said to Mrs. Hurly. "The signor, your son, is he pleased? Ask him to come and tell me himself if he is pleased."

Mistress Hurly got ill and took to her bed. The squire swore at the young foreign baggage, and roamed abroad. Margaret Calderwood was the only one who stood by to watch the fate of the little organist. The curse of the organ was upon Lisa; it spoke under her hand, and her hand was its slave.

At last she announced rapturously that she had had a visit from the brave signor, who had commended her industry, and urged her to work yet harder. After that she ceased to hold any communication with the living. Time after time Margaret Calderwood wrapped her arms about the frail thing, and carried her away by force, locking the door of the fatal chamber. But locking the chamber and burying the key were of no avail. The door stood open again, and Lisa was labouring on her perch.

One night, wakened from her sleep by the well-known humming and moaning of the organ, Margaret dressed hurriedly and hastened to the unholy room. Moonlight was pouring down the staircase and passages of Hurly Burly. It shone on the marble bust of the dead Lewis Hurly, that stood in the niche above his mother's sitting-room door. The organ room was full of it when Margaret pushed open the door and entered—full of the pale green moonlight from the window, mingled with another light, a dull lurid glare which seemed to centre round a dark shadow, like the figure of a man standing by the organ, and throwing out in fantastic relief the slight form of Lisa writhing, rather than swaying, back and forward, as if in agony. The sounds that came from the organ were broken and meaningless, as if the hands of the player lagged and stumbled on the keys. Between the intermittent chords low moaning cries broke from Lisa, and the dark figure bent towards her with menacing gestures. Trembling with the sickness of supernatural fear, yet strong of will, Margaret Calderwood crept forward within the lurid light, and was drawn into its influence. It grew and intensified upon her, it dazzled and blinded her at first; but presently, by a daring effort of will, she raised her eyes, and beheld Lisa's face convulsed with torture in the burning glare, and bending over her the figure and the features of Lewis Hurly! Smitten with horror, Margaret did not even then lose her presence of mind. She wound her strong arms around the wretched girl and dragged her from her seat and out of the influence of the lurid light, which immediately paled away and vanished. She carried her to her own bed, where Lisa lay, a wasted wreck, raving about the cruelty of the pitiless signor who would not see that she was labouring her best. Her poor cramped hands kept

beating the coverlet, as though she were still at her ago-
nizing task.

Margaret Calderwood bathed her burning temples, and
placed fresh flowers upon her pillow.

She opened the blinds and windows, and let in the
sweet morning air and sunshine, and then, looking up
at the newly awakened sky with its fair promise of hope
for the day, and down at the dewy fields, and afar off at
the dark green woods with the purple mists still hovering
about them, she prayed that a way might be shown her by
which to put an end to this curse. She prayed for Lisa,
and then, thinking that the girl rested somewhat, stole
from the room. She thought that she had locked the door
behind her.

She went downstairs with a pale, resolved face, and,
without consulting anyone, sent to the village for a bricklayer. Afterwards she sat by Mistress Hurly's bedside, and
explained to her what was to be done. Presently she went
to the door of Lisa's room, and hearing no sound, thought
the girl slept, and stole away. By-and-by she went downstairs, and found that the bricklayer had arrived and already begun his task of building up the organ-room door.
He was a swift workman, and the chamber was soon sealed
safely with stone and mortar.

Having seen this work finished, Margaret Calderwood
went and listened again at Lisa's door; and still hearing
no sound, she returned, and took her seat at Mrs. Hurly's
bedside once more. It was towards evening that she at last
entered her room to assure herself of the comfort of Lisa's
sleep. But the bed and room were empty. Lisa had disappeared.

Then the search began, upstairs and downstairs, in the
garden, in the grounds, in the fields and meadows. No
Lisa. Margaret Calderwood ordered the carriage and drove
to Calderwood to see if the strange little Will-o'-the-wisp
might have made her way there; then to the village, and
to many other places in the neighbourhood which it was

not possible she could have reached. She made enquiries everywhere; she pondered and puzzled over the matter. In the weak, suffering state that the girl was in, how far could she have crawled?

After two days' search, Margaret returned to Hurly Burly. She was sad and tired, and the evening was chill. She sat over the fire wrapped in her shawl when little Bess came to her, weeping behind her muslin apron.

"If you'd speak to Mistress Hurly about it, please, ma'am," she said. "I love her dearly, and it breaks my heart to go away, but the organ haven't done yet, ma'am, and I'm frightened out of my life, so I can't stay."

"Who has heard the organ, and when?" asked Margaret Calderwood, rising to her feet.

"Please, ma'am, I heard it the night you went away—the night after the door was built up!"

"And not since?"

"No, ma'am," hesitatingly, "not since. Hist! hark, ma'am! Is not that like the sound of it now?"

"No," said Margaret Calderwood; "it is only the wind." But pale as death she flew down the stairs and laid her ear to the yet damp mortar of the newly built wall. All was silent. There was no sound but the monotonous sough of the wind in the trees outside. Then Margaret began to dash her soft shoulder against the strong wall, and to pick the mortar away with her white fingers, and to cry out for the bricklayer who had built up the door.

It was midnight, but the bricklayer left his bed in the village, and obeyed the summons to Hurly Burly. The pale woman stood by and watched him undo all his work of three days ago, and the servants gathered about in trembling groups, wondering what was to happen next.

What happened next was this: When an opening was made the man entered the room with a light, Margaret Calderwood and others following. A heap of something dark was lying on the ground at the foot of the organ. Many groans arose in the fatal chamber. Here was little Lisa dead!

When Mistress Hurly was able to move, the squire and his wife went to live in France, where they remained till their death. Hurly Burly was shut up and deserted for many years. Lately it has passed into new hands. The organ has been taken down and banished, and the room is a bed-chamber, more luxuriously furnished than any in the house. But no one sleeps in it twice.

Margaret Calderwood was carried to her grave the other day a very aged woman.

A Far-Away Melody

MARY E. WILKINS

(1890)

The clothes-line was wound securely around the trunks of four gnarled, crooked old apple-trees, which stood promiscuously about the yard back of the cottage. It was tree-blossoming time, but these were too aged and sapless to blossom freely, and there was only a white bough here and there shaking itself triumphantly from among the rest, which had only their new green leaves. There was a branch occasionally which had not even these, but pierced the tender green and the flossy white in hard, grey nakedness. All over the yard, the grass was young and green and short, and had not yet gotten any feathery heads. Once in a while there was a dandelion set closely down among it.

The cottage was low, of a dark-red color, with white facings around the windows, which had no blinds, only green paper curtains.

The back door was in the center of the house, and opened directly into the green yard, with hardly a pretense of a step, only a flat oval stone before it.

Through this door, stepping cautiously on the stone, came presently two tall, lank women in chocolate-colored calico gowns, with a basket of clothes between them. They set the basket underneath the line on the grass, with a little clothes-pin bag beside it, and then proceeded methodically to hang out the clothes. Everything of a kind went together, and the best things on the outside line, which could be seen from the street in front of the cottage.

The two women were curiously alike. They were about the same height, and moved in the same way. Even their faces were so similar in feature and expression that it might have been a difficult matter to distinguish between them. All the difference, and that would have been scarcely apparent to an ordinary observer, was a difference of degree, if it might be so expressed. In one face the features were both bolder and sharper in outline, the eyes were a trifle larger and brighter, and the whole expression more animated and decided than in the other.

One woman's scanty drab hair was a shade darker than the other's, and the negative fairness of complexion, which generally accompanies drab hair, was in one relieved by a slight tinge of warm red on the cheeks.

This slightly intensified woman had been commonly considered the more attractive of the two, although in reality there was very little to choose between the personal appearance of these twin sisters, Priscilla and Mary Brown. They moved about the clothes-line, pinning the sweet white linen on securely, their thick, white-stockinged ankles showing beneath their limp calicoes as they stepped, and their large feet in cloth slippers flattening down the short, green grass. Their sleeves were rolled up, displaying their long, thin, muscular arms, which were sharply pointed at the elbows.

They were homely women; they were fifty and over now, but they never could have been pretty in their 'teens, their features were too irredeemably irregular for that. No youthful freshness of complexion or expression could have possibly done away with the impression that they gave. Their plainness had probably only been enhanced by the contrast, and these women, to people generally, seemed better-looking than when they were young. There was an honesty and patience in both faces that showed all the plainer for their homeliness.

One, the sister with the darker hair, moved a little quicker than the other, and lifted the wet clothes from the basket to the line more frequently. She was the first to speak, too, after they had been hanging out the clothes for some little time in silence. She stopped as she did so, with a wet pillow-case in her hand, and looked up reflectively at the flowering apple-boughs overhead, and the blue sky showing between, while the sweet spring wind ruffled her scanty hair a little.

"I wonder, Mary," said she, "if it would seem so very queer to die a mornin' like this, say. Don't you believe there's apple branches a-hangin' over them walls made out of precious stones, like these, only there ain't any dead limbs among 'em, an' they're all covered thick with flowers? An' I wonder if it would seem such an awful change to go from this air into the air of the New Jerusalem." Just then a robin hidden somewhere in the trees began to sing. "I s'pose," she went on, "that there's angels instead of robins, though, and they don't roost up in trees to sing, but stand on the ground, with lilies growin' round their feet, may be, up to their knees, or on the gold stones in the street, an' play on their harps to go with the singin'."

The other sister gave a scared, awed look at her. "Lor, don't talk that way, sister," said she. "What has got into you lately? You make me crawl all over, talkin' so much about dyin'. You feel well, don't you?"

"Lor, yes," replied the other, laughing, and picking up a clothes-pin for her pillow-case; "I feel well enough, an' I don't know what has got me to talkin' so much about dyin' lately, or thinkin' about it. I guess it's the spring weather. P'r'aps flowers growin' make anybody think of wings sproutin' kinder naterally. I won't talk so much about it if it bothers you, an' I don't know but it's sorter nateral it should. Did you get the potatoes before we came out, sister?"—with an awkward and kindly effort to change the subject.

"No," replied the other, stooping over the clothes-basket. There was such a film of tears in her dull blue eyes that she could not distinguish one article from another.

"Well, I guess you had better go in an' get 'em, then; they ain't worth anything, this time of year, unless they soak a while, an I'll finish hangin' out the clothes while you do it."

"Well, p'r'aps I'd better," the other woman replied, straightening herself up from the clothes-basket. Then she went into the house without another word; but down in the damp cellar, a minute later, she sobbed over the potato barrel as if her heart would break. Her sister's remarks had filled her with a vague apprehension and grief which she could not throw off. And there was something a little singular about it. Both these women had always been of a deeply religious cast of mind. They had studied the Bible faithfully, if not understandingly, and their religion had strongly tinctured their daily life. They knew almost as much about the Old Testament prophets as they did about their neighbors; and that was saying a good deal of two single women in a New England country town. Still this religious element in their natures could hardly have been termed spirituality. It deviated from that as much as anything of religion—which is in one way spirituality itself—could.

Both sisters were eminently practical in all affairs of life, down to their very dreams, and Priscilla especially so. She had dealt in religion with the bare facts of sin and repentance, future punishment and reward. She had dwelt very little, probably, upon the poetic splendors of the Eternal City, and talked about them still less. Indeed, she had always been reticent about her religious convictions, and had said very little about them even to her sister.

The two women, with God in their thoughts every moment, seldom had spoken his name to each other. For Priscilla to talk in the strain that she had to-day, and for a week or two previous, off and on, was, from its extreme deviation from her usual custom, certainly startling.

Poor Mary, sobbing over the potato barrel, thought it was a sign of approaching death. She had a few superstitious-like grafts upon her practical, commonplace character.

She wiped her eyes finally, and went up-stairs with her tin basin of potatoes, which were carefully washed and put to soak by the time her sister came in with the empty basket.

At twelve exactly the two sat down to dinner in the clean kitchen, which was one of the two rooms the cottage boasted. The narrow entry ran from the front door to the back. On one side was the kitchen and living-room; on the other, the room where the sisters slept. There were two small unfinished lofts overhead, reached by a step-ladder through a little scuttle in the entry ceiling: and that was all. The sisters had earned the cottage and paid for it years before, by working as tailoresses. They had, besides, quite a snug little sum in the bank, which they had saved out of their hard earnings. There was no need for Priscilla and Mary to work so hard, people said; but work hard they did, and work hard they would as long as they lived. The mere habit of work had become as necessary to them as breathing.

Just as soon as they had finished their meal and cleared away the dishes, they put on some clean starched purple prints, which were their afternoon dresses, and seated themselves with their work at the two front windows; the house faced south-west, so the sunlight streamed through both. It was a very warm day for the season, and the windows were open. Close to them in the yard outside stood great clumps of lilac bushes. They grew on the other side of the front door too; a little later the low cottage would look half-buried in them. The shadows of their leaves made a dancing network over the freshly washed yellow floor.

The two sisters sat there and sewed on some coarse vests all the afternoon. Neither made a remark often. The room, with its glossy little cooking-stove, its eight-day clock on the mantel, its chintz-cushioned rocking-chairs, and the dancing shadows of the lilac leaves on its yellow floor, looked pleasant and peaceful.

Just before six o'clock a neighbor dropped in with her cream pitcher to borrow some milk for tea, and she sat

down for a minute's chat after she had got it filled. They
had been talking a few moments on neighborhood topics,
when all of a sudden Priscilla let her work fall and raised
her hand. "Hush!" whispered she.

The other two stopped talking, and listened, staring at
her wonderingly, but they could hear nothing.

"What is it, Miss Priscilla?" asked the neighbor, with
round blue eyes. She was a pretty young thing, who had
not been married long.

"Hush! Don't speak. Don't you hear that beautiful music?" Her ear was inclined towards the open window, her
hand still raised warningly, and her eyes fixed on the opposite wall beyond them.

Mary turned visibly paler than her usual dull paleness,
and shuddered. "I don't hear any music," she said. "Do
you, Miss Moore?"

"No-o," replied the caller, her simple little face beginning to put on a scared look, from a vague sense of a
mystery she could not fathom. Mary Brown rose and went
to the door, and looked eagerly up and down the street.
"There ain't no organ-man in sight anywhere," said she,
returning, "an' I can't hear any music, an' Miss Moore
can't, an' we're both sharp enough o' hearin'. You're jest
imaginin' it, sister."

"I never imagined anything in my life," returned the
other, "an' it ain't likely I'm goin' to begin now. It's the
beautifulest music. It comes from over the orchard there.
Can't you hear it? But it seems to me it's growin' a little
fainter like now. I guess it's movin' off, perhaps."

Mary Brown set her lips hard. The grief and anxiety
she had felt lately turned suddenly to unreasoning anger
against the cause of it; through her very love she fired with
quick wrath at the beloved object. Still she did not say
much, only, "I guess it must be movin' off," with a laugh,
which had an unpleasant ring in it.

After the neighbor had gone, however, she said more,
standing before her sister with her arms folded squarely

across her bosom. "Now, Priscilla Brown," she exclaimed, "I think it's about time to put a stop to this. I've heard about enough of it. What do you s'pose Miss Moore thought of you? Next thing it'll be all over town that you're gettin' spiritual notions. To-day it's music that nobody else can hear, an' yesterday you smelled roses, and there ain't one in blossom this time o' year, and all the time you're talkin' about dyin'. For my part, I don't see why you ain't as likely to live as I am. You're uncommon hearty on vittles. You ate a pretty good dinner to-day for a dyin' person."

"I didn't say I was goin' to die," replied Priscilla meekly: the two sisters seemed suddenly to have changed natures. "An' I'll try not to talk so, if it plagues you. I told you I wouldn't this mornin', but the music kinder took me by surprise like, an' I thought may be you an' Miss Moore could hear it. I can jest hear it a little bit now, like the dyin' away of a bell."

"There you go agin!" cried the other sharply. "Do, for mercy's sake, stop, Priscilla. There ain't no music."

"Well, I won't talk any more about it," she answered patiently; and she rose and began setting the table for tea, while Mary sat down and resumed her sewing, drawing the thread through the cloth with quick, uneven jerks.

That night the pretty girl neighbor was aroused from her first sleep by a distressed voice at her bedroom window, crying, "Miss Moore! Miss Moore!"

She spoke to her husband, who opened the window. "What's wanted?" he asked, peering out into the darkness.

"Priscilla's sick," moaned the distressed voice; "awful sick. She's fainted, an' I can't bring her to. Go for the doctor—quick! quick! *quick!*" The voice ended in a shriek on the last word, and the speaker turned and ran back to the cottage, where, on the bed, lay a pale, gaunt woman, who had not stirred since she left it. Immovable through all her sister's agony, she lay there, her features shaping themselves out more and more from the shadows, the bed-clothes that covered her limbs taking on an awful rigidity.

"She must have died in her sleep," the doctor said, when he came, "without a struggle."

When Mary Brown really understood that her sister was dead, she left her to the kindly ministrations of the good women who are always ready at such times in a country place, and went and sat by the kitchen window in the chair which her sister had occupied that afternoon.

There the women found her when the last offices had been done for the dead.

"Come home with me to-night," one said; "Miss Green will stay with *her*," with a turn of her head towards the opposite room, and an emphasis on the pronoun which distinguished it at once from one applied to a living person.

"No," said Mary Brown; "I'm a goin' to set here an' listen." She had the window wide open, leaning her head out into the chilly night air.

The women looked at each other; one tapped her head, another nodded hers. "Poor thing!" said a third.

"You see," went on Mary Brown, still speaking with her head leaned out of the window, "I was cross with her this afternoon because she talked about hearin' music. I was cross, an' spoke up sharp to her, because I loved her, but I don't think she knew. I didn't want to think she was goin' to die, but she was. An' she heard the music. It was true. An' now I'm a-goin' to set here an' listen till I hear it too, an' then I'll know she ain't laid up what I said agin me, an' that I'm a-goin' to die too."

They found it impossible to reason with her; there she sat till morning, with a pitying woman beside her, listening all in vain for unearthly melody.

Next day they sent for a widowed niece of the sisters, who came at once, bringing her little boy with her. She was a kindly young woman, and took up her abode in the little cottage, and did the best she could for her poor aunt, who, it soon became evident, would never be quite herself again. There she would sit at the kitchen window and listen day after day. She took a great fancy to her niece's little boy, and used often to hold him in her lap as she sat there. Once in a while she would ask him if he heard any music. "An innocent little thing like him might hear quicker than a hard, unbelievin' old woman like me," she told his mother once.

She lived so for nearly a year after her sister died. It was evident that she failed gradually and surely, though there was no apparent disease. It seemed to trouble her exceedingly that she never heard the music she listened for. She had an idea that she could not die unless she did, and her whole soul seemed filled with longing to join her beloved twin sister, and be assured of her forgiveness. This sister-love was all she had ever felt, besides her love of God, in any strong degree; all the passion of devotion of which this homely, commonplace woman was capable was centered in that, and the unsatisfied strength of it was killing her. The weaker she grew, the more earnestly she listened. She was too feeble to sit up, but she would not consent to lie in bed, and made them bolster her up with pillows in a rocking-chair by the window. At last she died, in the spring, a week or two before her sister had the preceding year. The season was a little more advanced this year, and the apple-trees were blossomed out further than they were then. She died about ten o'clock in the morning. The day before her niece had been called into the room by a shrill cry of rapture from her: "I've heard it! I've heard it!" she cried. "A faint sound o' music, like the dyin' away of a bell."

A Wicked Voice
Vernon Lee
(1890)

To M.W.,
In remembrance of the last song at Palazzo Barbaro,
Chi ha inteso, intenda.

They have been congratulating me again today upon being the only composer of our days—of these days of deafening orchestral effects and poetical quackery—who has despised the new-fangled nonsense of Wagner, and returned boldly to the traditions of Handel and Gluck and the divine Mozart, to the supremacy of melody and the respect of the human voice.

O cursed human voice, violin of flesh and blood, fashioned with the subtle tools, the cunning hands, of Satan! O execrable art of singing, have you not wrought mischief enough in the past, degrading so much noble genius, corrupting the purity of Mozart, reducing Handel to a writer of high-class singing-exercises, and defrauding the world of the only inspiration worthy of Sophocles and Euripides, the poetry of the great poet Gluck? Is it not enough to have dishonored a whole century in idolatry of that wicked and contemptible wretch the singer, without persecuting an obscure young composer of our days, whose only wealth is his love of nobility in art, and perhaps some few grains of genius?

And then they compliment me upon the perfection with which I imitate the style of the great dead masters; or ask

119

me very seriously whether, even if I could gain over the modern public to this bygone style of music, I could hope to find singers to perform it. Sometimes, when people talk as they have been talking today, and laugh when I declare myself a follower of Wagner, I burst into a paroxysm of unintelligible, childish rage, and exclaim, "We shall see that some day!"

Yes; some day we shall see! For, after all, may I not recover from this strangest of maladies? It is still possible that the day may come when all these things shall seem but an incredible nightmare; the day when *Ogier the Dane* shall be completed, and men shall know whether I am a follower of the great master of the Future or the miserable singing-masters of the Past. I am but half-bewitched, since I am conscious of the spell that binds me. My old nurse, far off in Norway, used to tell me that were-wolves are ordinary men and women half their days, and that if, during that period, they become aware of their horrid transformation they may find the means to forestall it. May this not be the case with me? My reason, after all, is free, although my artistic inspiration be enslaved; and I can despise and loathe the music I am forced to compose, and the execrable power that forces me.

Nay, is it not because I have studied with the doggedness of hatred this corrupt and corrupting music of the Past, seeking for every little peculiarity of style and every biographical trifle merely to display its vileness, is it not for this presumptuous courage that I have been overtaken by such mysterious, incredible vengeance?

And meanwhile, my only relief consists in going over and over again in my mind the tale of my miseries. This time I will write it, writing only to tear up, to throw the manuscript unread into the fire. And yet, who knows? As the last charred pages shall crackle and slowly sink into the red embers, perhaps the spell may be broken, and I may possess once more my long-lost liberty, my vanished genius.

It was a breathless evening under the full moon, that implacable full moon beneath which, even more than beneath the dreamy splendor of noon-tide, Venice seemed to swelter in the midst of the waters, exhaling, like some great lily, mysterious influences, which make the brain swim and the heart faint—a moral malaria, distilled, as I thought, from those languishing melodies, those cooing vocalizations which I had found in the musty music-books of a century ago. I see that moonlight evening as if it were present. I see my fellow-lodgers of that little artists' boarding-house. The table on which they lean after supper is strewn with bits of bread, with napkins rolled in tapestry rollers, spots of wine here and there, and at regular intervals chipped pepper-pots, stands of toothpicks, and heaps of those huge hard peaches which nature imitates from the marble-shops of Pisa. The whole pension-full is assembled, and examining stupidly the engraving which the American etcher has just brought for me, knowing me to be mad about eighteenth century music and musicians, and having noticed, as he turned over the heaps of penny prints in the square of San Polo, that the portrait is that of a singer of those days.

Singer, thing of evil, stupid and wicked slave of the voice, of that instrument which was not invented by the human intellect, but begotten of the body, and which, instead of moving the soul, merely stirs up the dregs of our nature! For what is the voice but the Beast calling, awakening that other Beast sleeping in the depths of mankind, the Beast which all great art has ever sought to chain up, as the archangel chains up, in old pictures, the demon with his woman's face? How could the creature attached to this voice, its owner and its victim, the singer, the great, the real singer who once ruled over every heart, be otherwise than wicked and contemptible? But let me try and get on with my story.

I can see all my fellow-boarders, leaning on the table, contemplating the print, this effeminate beau, his hair curled into *ailes de pigeon,* his sword passed through his embroidered pocket, seated under a triumphal arch somewhere among the clouds, surrounded by puffy Cupids and crowned with laurels by a bouncing goddess of fame. I hear again all the insipid exclamations, the insipid questions about this singer:—"When did he live? Was he very famous? Are you sure, Magnus, that this is really a portrait," &c. &c. And I hear my own voice, as if in the far distance, giving them all sorts of information, biographical and critical, out of a battered little volume called *The Theatre of Musical Glory; or, Opinions upon the most Famous Chapel-masters and Virtuosi of this Century,* by Father Prosdocimo Sabatelli, Barnalite, Professor of Eloquence at the College of Modena, and Member of the Arcadian Academy, under the pastoral name of Evander Lilybaean, Venice, 1785, with the approbation of the Superiors. I tell them all how this singer, this Balthasar Cesari, was nicknamed Zaffirino because of a sapphire engraved with cabalistic signs presented to him one evening by a masked stranger, in whom wise folk recognized that great cultivator of the human voice, the devil; how much more wonderful had been this Zaffirino's vocal gifts than those of any singer of ancient or modern times; how his brief life had been but a series of triumphs, petted by the greatest kings, sung by the most famous poets, and finally, adds Father Prosdocimo, "courted (if the grave Muse of history may incline her ear to the gossip of gallantry) by the most charming nymphs, even of the very highest quality."

My friends glance once more at the engraving; more insipid remarks are made; I am requested—especially by the American young ladies—to play or sing one of this Zaffirino's favorite songs—"For of course you know them, dear Maestro Magnus, you who have such a passion for all old music. Do be good, and sit down to the piano." I refuse, rudely enough, rolling the print in my fingers. How fearfully this cursed heat, these cursed moonlight nights, must have unstrung me! This Venice would certainly kill me in the long-run! Why, the sight of this idiotic engraving, the mere name of that coxcomb of a singer, have made my heart beat and my limbs turn to water like a love-sick hobbledehoy.

After my gruff refusal, the company begins to disperse; they prepare to go out, some to have a row on the lagoon, others to saunter before the *cafés* at St. Mark's; family discussions arise, gruntings of fathers, murmurs of mothers, peals of laughing from young girls and young men. And the moon, pouring in by the wide-open windows, turns this old palace ballroom, nowadays an inn dining-room, into a lagoon, scintillating, undulating like the other lagoon, the real one, which stretches out yonder furrowed by invisible gondolas betrayed by the red prow-lights. At last the whole lot of them are on the move. I shall be able to get some quiet in my room, and to work a little at my opera of *Ogier the Dane*. But no! Conversation revives, and, of all things, about that singer, that Zaffirino, whose absurd portrait I am crunching in my fingers.

The principal speaker is Count Alvise, an old Venetian with dyed whiskers, a great check tie fastened with two pins and a chain; a threadbare patrician who is dying to secure for his lanky son that pretty American girl, whose mother is intoxicated by all his mooning anecdotes about the past glories of Venice in general, and of his illustrious family in particular. Why, in Heaven's name, must he pitch upon Zaffirino for his mooning, this old duffer of a patrician?

"Zaffirino,—ah yes, to be sure! Balthasar Cesari, called Zaffirino," snuffles the voice of Count Alvise, who always repeats the last word of every sentence at least three times. "Yes, Zaffirino, to be sure! A famous singer of the days of my forefathers; yes, of my forefathers, dear lady!" Then a lot of rubbish about the former greatness of Venice, the glories of old music, the former Conservatoires, all mixed up with anecdotes of Rossini and Donizetti, whom he

pretends to have known intimately. Finally, a story, of
course containing plenty about his illustrious family:—
"My great grand-aunt, the Procuratessa Vendramin, from
whom we have inherited our estate of Mistrà, on the
Brenta"—a hopelessly muddled story, apparently, fully of
digressions, but of which that singer Zaffirino is the hero.
The narrative, little by little, becomes more intelligible,
or perhaps it is I who am giving it more attention.

"It seems," says the Count, "that there was one of his
songs in particular which was called the 'Husbands' Air'—
L'Aria dei Mariti—because they didn't enjoy it quite as
much as their better-halves. . . . My grand-aunt, Pisana
Renier, married to the Procuratore Vendramin, was a
patrician of the old school, of the style that was getting
rare a hundred years ago. Her virtue and her pride rendered her unapproachable. Zaffirino, on his part, was in
the habit of boasting that no woman had ever been able
to resist his singing, which, it appears, had its foundation
in fact—the ideal changes, my dear lady, the ideal changes
a good deal from one century to another!—and that his
first song could make any woman turn pale and lower her
eyes, the second make her madly in love, while the third
song could kill her off on the spot, kill her for love, there
under his very eyes, if he only felt inclined. My grandaunt
Vendramin laughed when this story was told her, refused
to go to hear this insolent dog, and added that it might
be quite possible by the aid of spells and infernal pacts to
kill a *gentildonna,* but as to making her fall in love with a
lackey—never! This answer was naturally reported to Zaffirino, who piqued himself upon always getting the better
of any one who was wanting in deference to his voice. Like
the ancient Romans, *parcere subjectis et debellare superbos.*
You American ladies, who are so learned, will appreciate
this little quotation from the divine Virgil. While seeming
to avoid the Procuratessa Vendramin, Zaffirino took the
opportunity, one evening at a large assembly, to sing in
her presence. He sang and sang and sang until the poor

grand-aunt Pisana fell ill for love. The most skilful physicians were kept unable to explain the mysterious malady
which was visibly killing the poor young lady; and the
Procuratore Vendramin applied in vain to the most ven-
erated Madonnas, and vainly promised an altar of silver,
with massive gold candlesticks, to Saints Cosmas and Da-
mian, patrons of the art of healing. At last the brother-
in-law of the Procuratessa, Monsignor Almorò Vendramin,
Patriarch of Aquileia, a prelate famous for the sanctity of
his life, obtained in a vision of Saint Justina, for whom
he entertained a particular devotion, the information that
the only thing which could benefit the strange illness of
his sister-in-law was the voice of Zaffirino. Take notice
that my poor grand-aunt had never condescended to such
a revelation.

"The Procuratore was enchanted at this happy solution; and his lordship the Patriarch went to seek Zaffirino
in person, and carried him in his own coach to the Villa of
Mistrà, where the Procuratessa was residing. On being told
what was about to happen, my poor grand-aunt went into
fits of rage, which were succeeded immediately by equally
violent fits of joy. However, she never forgot what was due
to her great position. Although sick almost unto death,
she had herself arrayed with the greatest pomp, caused her
face to be painted, and put on all her diamonds: it would
seem as if she were anxious to affirm her full dignity before this singer. Accordingly she received Zaffirino reclining on a sofa which had been placed in the great ballroom
of the Villa of Mistrà, and beneath the princely canopy;
for the Vendramins, who had intermarried with the house
of Mantua, possessed imperial fiefs and were princes of
the Holy Roman Empire. Zaffirino saluted her with the
most profound respect, but not a word passed between
them. Only, the singer inquired from the Procuratore
whether the illustrious lady had received the Sacraments
of the Church. Being told that the Procuratessa had herself
asked to be given extreme unction from the hands of her

brother-in-law, he declared his readiness to obey the orders of His Excellency, and sat down at once to the harpsichord.

"Never had he sung so divinely. At the end of the first song the Procuratessa Vendramin had already revived most extraordinarily; by the end of the second she appeared entirely cured and beaming with beauty and happiness; but at the third air—the *Aria dei Mariti,* no doubt—she began to change frightfully; she gave a dreadful cry, and fell into the convulsions of death. In a quarter of an hour she was dead! Zaffirino did not wait to see her die. Having finished his song, he withdrew instantly, took post-horses, and traveled day and night as far as Munich. People remarked that he had presented himself at Mistrà dressed in mourning, although he had mentioned no death among his relatives; also that he had prepared everything for his departure, as if fearing the wrath of so powerful a family. Then there was also the extraordinary question he had asked before beginning to sing, about the Procuratessa having confessed and received extreme unction. . . . No, thanks, my dear lady, no cigarettes for me. But if it does not distress you or your charming daughter, may I humbly beg permission to smoke a cigar?"

And Count Alvise, enchanted with his talent for narrative, and sure of having secured for his son the heart and the dollars of his fair audience, proceeds to light a candle, and at the candle one of those long black Italian cigars which require preliminary disinfection before smoking.

. . . If this state of things goes on I shall just have to ask the doctor for a bottle; this ridiculous beating of my heart and disgusting cold perspiration have increased steadily during Count Alvise's narrative. To keep myself in countenance among the various idiotic commentaries on this cock-and-bull story of a vocal coxcomb and a vaporing great lady, I begin to unroll the engraving, and to examine stupidly the portrait of Zaffirino, once so renowned, now so forgotten. A ridiculous ass, this singer, under his triumphal arch, with his stuffed Cupids and the great fat winged kitchenmaid crowning him with laurels. How flat and vapid and vulgar it is, to be sure, all this odious eighteenth century!

But he, personally, is not so utterly vapid as I had thought. That effeminate, fat face of his is almost beautiful, with an odd smile, brazen and cruel. I have seen faces like this, if not in real life, at least in my boyish romantic dreams, when I read Swinburne and Baudelaire, the faces of wicked, vindictive women. Oh yes! he is decidedly a beautiful creature, this Zaffirino, and his voice must have had the same sort of beauty and the same expression of wickedness. . . .

"Come on, Magnus," sound the voices of my fellow-boarders, "be a good fellow and sing us one of the old chap's songs; or at least something or other of that day, and we'll make believe it was the air with which he killed that poor lady."

"Oh yes! the *Aria dei Mariti,* the 'Husbands' Air,'" mumbles old Alvise, between the puffs at his impossible black cigar. "My poor grand-aunt, Pisana Vendramin; he went and killed her with those songs of his, with that *Aria dei Mariti.*"

I feel senseless rage overcoming me. Is it that horrible palpitation (by the way, there is a Norwegian doctor, my fellow-countryman, at Venice just now) which is sending the blood to my brain and making me mad? The people round the piano, the furniture, everything together seems to get mixed and to turn into moving blobs of color. I set to singing; the only thing which remains distinct before my eyes being the portrait of Zaffirino, on the edge of that boarding-house piano; the sensual, effeminate face, with its wicked, cynical smile, keeps appearing and disappearing as the print wavers about in the draught that makes the candles smoke and gutter. And I set to singing madly,

singing I don't know what. Yes; I begin to identify it: 'tis
the *Biondina in Gondoleta,* the only song of the eighteenth
century which is still remembered by the Venetian people.
I sing it, mimicking every old-school grace; shakes, cadences, languishingly swelled and diminished notes, and
adding all manner of buffooneries, until the audience,
recovering from its surprise, begins to shake with laughing;
until I begin to laugh myself, madly, frantically, between
the phrases of the melody, my voice finally smothered in
this dull, brutal laughter. . . . And then, to crown it all, I
shake my fist at this long-dead singer, looking at me with
his wicked woman's face, with his mocking, fatuous smile.

"Ah! you would like to be revenged on me also!" I exclaim. "You would like me to write you nice roulades and
flourishes, another nice *Aria dei Mariti,* my fine Zaffirino!"

That night I dreamed a very strange dream. Even in the big
half-furnished room the heat and closeness were stifling.
The air seemed laden with the scent of all manner of white
flowers, faint and heavy in their intolerable sweetness:
tuberoses, gardenias, and jasmines drooping I know not
where in neglected vases. The moonlight had transformed
the marble floor around me into a shallow, shining, pool.
On account of the heat I had exchanged my bed for a
big old-fashioned sofa of light wood, painted with little
nosegays and sprigs, like an old silk; and I lay there, not
attempting to sleep, and letting my thoughts go vaguely to
my opera of *Ogier the Dane,* of which I had long finished
writing the words, and for whose music I had hoped to
find some inspiration in this strange Venice, floating, as
it were, in the stagnant lagoon of the past. But Venice had
merely put all my ideas into hopeless confusion; it was as
if there arose out of its shallow waters a miasma of long-
dead melodies, which sickened but intoxicated my soul. I
lay on my sofa watching that pool of whitish light, which
rose higher and higher, little trickles of light meeting it

here and there, wherever the moon's rays struck upon some polished surface; while huge shadows waved to and fro in the draught of the open balcony.

I went over and over that old Norse story: how the Paladin, Ogier, one of the knights of Charlemagne, was decoyed during his homeward wanderings from the Holy Land by the arts of an enchantress, the same who had once held in bondage the great Emperor Caesar and given him King Oberon for a son; how Ogier had tarried in that island only one day and one night, and yet, when he came home to his kingdom, he found all changed, his friends dead, his family dethroned, and not a man who knew his face; until at last, driven hither and thither like a beggar, a poor minstrel had taken compassion of his sufferings and given him all he could give—a song, the song of the prowess of a hero dead for hundreds of years, the Paladin Ogier the Dane.

The story of Ogier ran into a dream, as vivid as my waking thoughts had been vague. I was looking no longer at the pool of moonlight spreading round my couch, with its trickles of light and looming, waving shadows, but the frescoed walls of a great saloon. It was not, as I recognized in a second, the dining-room of that Venetian palace now turned into a boarding-house. It was a far larger room, a real ballroom, almost circular in its octagon shape, with eight huge white doors surrounded by stucco moldings, and, high on the vault of the ceiling, eight little galleries or recesses like boxes at a theatre, intended no doubt for musicians and spectators. The place was imperfectly lighted by only one of the eight chandeliers, which revolved slowly, like huge spiders, each on its long cord. But the light struck upon the gilt stuccoes opposite me, and on a large expanse of fresco, the sacrifice of Iphigenia, with Agamemnon and Achilles in Roman helmets, lappets, and knee-breeches. It discovered also one of the oil panels let into the moldings of the roof, a goddess in lemon and lilac draperies, foreshortened over a great green peacock.

Round the room, where the light reached, I could make out big yellow satin sofas and heavy gilded consoles; in the shadow of a corner was what looked like a piano, and farther in the shade one of those big canopies which decorate the anterooms of Roman palaces. I looked about me, wondering where I was: a heavy, sweet smell, reminding me of the flavor of a peach, filled the place.

Little by little I began to perceive sounds; little, sharp, metallic, detached notes, like those of a mandolin; and there was united to them a voice, very low and sweet, almost a whisper, which grew and grew and grew, until the whole place was filled with that exquisite vibrating note, of a strange, exotic, unique quality. The note went on, swelling and swelling. Suddenly there was a horrible piercing shriek, and the thud of a body on the floor, and all manner of smothered exclamations. There, close by the canopy, a light suddenly appeared; and I could see, among the dark figures moving to and fro in the room, a woman lying on the ground, surrounded by other women. Her blond hair, tangled, full of diamond-sparkles which cut through the half-darkness, was hanging disheveled; the laces of her bodice had been cut, and her white breast shone among the sheen of jeweled brocade; her face was bent forwards, and a thin white arm trailed, like a broken limb, across the knees of one of the women who were endeavoring to lift her. There was a sudden splash of water against the floor, more confused exclamations, a hoarse, broken moan, and a gurgling, dreadful sound. . . . I awoke with a start and rushed to the window.

Outside, in the blue haze of the moon, the church and belfry of St. George loomed blue and hazy, with the black hull and rigging, the red lights, of a large steamer moored before them. From the lagoon rose a damp sea-breeze. What was it all? Ah! I began to understand: that story of old Count Alvise's, the death of his grand-aunt, Pisana Vendramin. Yes, it was about that I had been dreaming.

I returned to my room; I struck a light, and sat down to my writing-table. Sleep had become impossible. I tried to work at my opera. Once or twice I thought I had got hold of what I had looked for so long. . . . But as soon as I tried to lay hold of my theme, there arose in my mind the distant echo of that voice, of that long note swelled slowly by insensible degrees, that long note whose tone was so strong and so subtle.

There are in the life of an artist moments when, still unable to seize his own inspiration, or even clearly to discern it, he becomes aware of the approach of that long-invoked idea. A mingled joy and terror warn him that before another day, another hour have passed, the inspiration shall have crossed the threshold of his soul and flooded it with its rapture. All day I had felt the need of isolation and quiet, and at nightfall I went for a row on the most solitary part of the lagoon. All things seemed to tell that I was going to meet my inspiration, and I awaited its coming as a lover awaits his beloved.

I had stopped my gondola for a moment, and as I gently swayed to and fro on the water, all paved with moonbeams, it seemed to me that I was on the confines of an imaginary world. It lay close at hand, enveloped in luminous, pale blue mist, through which the moon had cut a wide and glistening path; out to sea, the little islands, like moored black boats, only accentuated the solitude of this region of moonbeams and wavelets; while the hum of the insects in orchards hard by merely added to the impression of untroubled silence. On some such seas, I thought, must the Paladin Ogier, have sailed when about to discover that during that sleep at the enchantress's knees centuries had elapsed and the heroic world had set, and the kingdom of prose had come.

While my gondola rocked stationary on that sea of moonbeams, I pondered over that twilight of the heroic

world. In the soft rattle of the water on the hull I seemed
to hear the rattle of all that armor, of all those swords
swinging rusty on the walls, neglected by the degenerate
sons of the great champions of old. I had long been in
search of a theme which I called the theme of the "Prowess
of Ogier;" it was to appear from time to time in the course
of my opera, to develop at last into that song of the Minstrel, which reveals to the hero that he is one of a long-
dead world. And at this moment I seemed to feel the presence of that theme. Yet an instant, and my mind would be
overwhelmed by that savage music, heroic, funereal.

Suddenly there came across the lagoon, cleaving, check-
ering, and fretting the silence with a lacework of sound
even as the moon was fretting and cleaving the water, a
ripple of music, a voice breaking itself in a shower of little
scales and cadences and trills.

I sank back upon my cushions. The vision of heroic
days had vanished, and before my closed eyes there seemed
to dance multitudes of little stars of light, chasing and
interlacing like those sudden vocalizations.

"To shore! Quick!" I cried to the gondolier.

But the sounds had ceased; and there came from the
orchards, with their mulberry-trees glistening in the
moonlight, and their black swaying cypress-plumes, nothing save the confused hum, the monotonous chirp, of the
crickets.

I looked around me: on one side empty dunes, orchards,
and meadows, without house or steeple; on the other, the
blue and misty sea, empty to where distant islets were pro-
filed black on the horizon.

A faintness overcame me, and I felt myself dissolve.
For all of a sudden a second ripple of voice swept over the
lagoon, a shower of little notes, which seemed to form a
little mocking laugh.

Then again all was still. This silence lasted so long
that I fell once more to meditating on my opera. I lay in
wait once more for the half-caught theme. But no. It was

not that theme for which I was waiting and watching with baited breath. I realized my delusion when, on rounding the point of the Giudecca, the murmur of a voice arose from the midst of the waters, a thread of sound slender as a moonbeam, scarce audible, but exquisite, which expanded slowly, insensibly, taking volume and body, taking flesh almost and fire, an ineffable quality, full, passionate, but veiled, as it were, in a subtle, downy wrapper. The note grew stronger and stronger, and warmer and more passionate, until it burst through that strange and charming veil, and emerged beaming, to break itself in the luminous facets of a wonderful shake, long, superb, triumphant.

There was a dead silence.

"Row to St. Mark's!" I exclaimed. "Quick!"

The gondola glided through the long, glittering track of moonbeams, and rent the great band of yellow, reflected light, mirroring the cupolas of St. Mark's, the lace-like pinnacles of the palace, and the slender pink belfry, which rose from the lit-up water to the pale and bluish evening sky.

In the larger of the two squares the military band was blaring through the last spirals of a *crescendo* of Rossini. The crowd was dispersing in this great open-air ballroom, and the sounds arose which invariably follow upon out-of-door music. A clatter of spoons and glasses, a rustle and grating of frocks and of chairs, and the click of scabbards on the pavement. I pushed my way among the fashionable youths contemplating the ladies while sucking the knob of their sticks; through the serried ranks of respectable families, marching arm in arm with their white frocked young ladies close in front. I took a seat before Florian's, among the customers stretching themselves before departing, and the waiters hurrying to and fro, clattering their empty cups and trays. Two imitation Neapolitans were slipping their guitar and violin under their arm, ready to leave the place.

"Stop!" I cried to them; "don't go yet. Sing me something—sing *La Camesella* or *Funiculì, funiculà*—no matter what, provided you make a row;" and as they screamed and scraped their utmost, I added, "But can't you sing louder, d—n you!—sing louder, do you understand?"

I felt the need of noise, of yells and false notes, of something vulgar and hideous to drive away that ghost-voice which was haunting me.

Again and again I told myself that it had been some silly prank of a romantic amateur, hidden in the gardens of the shore or gliding unperceived on the lagoon; and that the sorcery of moonlight and sea-mist had transfigured for my excited brain mere humdrum roulades out of exercises of Bordogni or Crescentini.

But all the same I continued to be haunted by that voice. My work was interrupted ever and anon by the attempt to catch its imaginary echo; and the heroic harmonies of my Scandinavian legend were strangely interwoven with voluptuous phrases and florid cadences in which I seemed to hear again that same accursed voice.

To be haunted by singing-exercises! It seemed too ridiculous for a man who professedly despised the art of singing. And still, I preferred to believe in that childish amateur, amusing himself with warbling to the moon.

One day, while making these reflections the hundredth time over, my eyes chanced to light upon the portrait of Zaffirino, which my friend had pinned against the wall. I pulled it down and tore it into half a dozen shreds. Then, already ashamed of my folly, I watched the torn pieces float down from the window, wafted hither and thither by the sea-breeze. One scrap got caught in a yellow blind below me; the others fell into the canal, and were speedily lost to sight in the dark water. I was overcome with shame. My heart beat like bursting. What a miserable, unnerved worm I had become in this cursed Venice, with its languishing moonlights, its atmosphere as of some stuffy boudoir, long unused, full of old stuffs and potpourri!

That night, however, things seemed to be going better. I was able to settle down to my opera, and even to work at it. In the intervals my thoughts returned, not without a certain pleasure, to those scattered fragments of the torn engraving fluttering down to the water. I was disturbed at my piano by the hoarse voices and the scraping of violins which rose from one of those music-boats that station at night under the hotels of the Grand Canal. The moon had set. Under my balcony the water stretched black into the distance, its darkness cut by the still darker outlines of the flotilla of gondolas in attendance on the music-boat, where the faces of the singers, and the guitars and violins, gleamed reddish under the unsteady light of the Chinese-lanterns.

"*Jammo, jammo; jammo, jammo jà,*" sang the loud, hoarse voices; then a tremendous scrape and twang, and the yelled-out burden, "*Funiculì, funiculà; funiculì, funiculà; jammo, jammo, jammo, jammo, jammo jà.*"

Then came a few cries of "*Bis, Bis!*" from a neighboring hotel, a brief clapping of hands, the sound of a handful of coppers rattling into the boat, and the oar-stroke of some gondolier making ready to turn away.

"Sing the *Camesella*," ordered some voice with a foreign accent.

"No, no! *Santa Lucia.*"

"I want the *Camesella.*"

"No! *Santa Lucia.* Hi! sing *Santa Lucia*—d'you hear?"

The musicians, under their green and yellow and red lamps, held a whispered consultation on the manner of conciliating these contradictory demands. Then, after a minute's hesitation, the violins began the prelude of that once famous air, which has remained popular in Venice— the words written, some hundred years ago, by the patrician Gritti, the music by an unknown composer—*La Biondina in Gondoleta.*

That cursed eighteenth century! It seemed a malignant fatality that made these brutes choose just this piece to interrupt me.

At last the long prelude came to an end; and above the cracked guitars and squeaking fiddles there arose, not the expected nasal chorus, but a single voice singing below its breath.

My arteries throbbed. How well I knew that voice! It was singing, as I have said, below its breath, yet none the less it sufficed to fill all that reach of the canal with its strange quality of tone, exquisite, far-fetched.

They were long-drawn-out notes, of intense but peculiar sweetness, a man's voice which had much of a woman's, but more even of a chorister's, but a chorister's voice without its limpidity and innocence; its youthfulness was veiled, muffled, as it were, in a sort of downy vagueness, as if a passion of tears withheld.

There was a burst of applause, and the old palaces re-echoed with the clapping. "Bravo, bravo! Thank you, thank you! Sing again—please, sing again. Who can it be?"

And then a bumping of hulls, a splashing of oars, and the oaths of gondoliers trying to push each other away, as the red prow-lamps of the gondolas pressed round the gaily lit singing-boat.

But no one stirred on board. It was to none of them that this applause was due. And while every one pressed on, and clapped and vociferated, one little red prow-lamp dropped away from the fleet; for a moment a single gondola stood forth black upon the black water, and then was lost in the night.

For several days the mysterious singer was the universal topic. The people of the music-boat swore that no one besides themselves had been on board, and that they knew as little as ourselves about the owner of that voice. The gondoliers, despite their descent from the spies of the old Republic, were equally unable to furnish any clue. No musical celebrity was known or suspected to be at Venice; and every one agreed that such a singer must be a European celebrity. The strangest thing in this strange business was, that even among those learned in music there was no

agreement on the subject of this voice: it was called by all
sorts of names and described by all manner of incongruous adjectives; people went so far as to dispute whether
the voice belonged to a man or to a woman: every one had
some new definition.

In all these musical discussions I, alone, brought forward no opinion. I felt a repugnance, an impossibility almost, of speaking about that voice; and the more or less
commonplace conjectures of my friend had the invariable
effect of sending me out of the room.

Meanwhile my work was becoming daily more difficult, and I soon passed from utter impotence to a state
of inexplicable agitation. Every morning I arose with fine
resolutions and grand projects of work; only to go to bed
that night without having accomplished anything. I spent
hours leaning on my balcony, or wandering through the
network of lanes with their ribbon of blue sky, endeavoring vainly to expel the thought of that voice, or endeavoring in reality to reproduce it in my memory; for the more
I tried to banish it from my thoughts, the more I grew to
thirst for that extraordinary tone, for those mysteriously
downy, veiled notes; and no sooner did I make an effort to
work at my opera than my head was full of scraps of forgotten eighteenth century airs, of frivolous or languishing
little phrases; and I fell to wondering with a bitter-sweet
longing how those songs would have sounded if sung by
that voice.

At length it became necessary to see a doctor, from
whom, however, I carefully hid away all the stranger symptoms of my malady. The air of the lagoons, the great heat,
he answered cheerfully, had pulled me down a little; a
tonic and a month in the country, with plenty of riding
and no work, would make me myself again. That old idler,
Count Alvise, who had insisted on accompanying me to
the physician's, immediately suggested that I should go
and stay with his son, who was boring himself to death
superintending the maize harvest on the mainland: he

could promise me excellent air, plenty of horses, and all the peaceful surroundings and the delightful occupations of a rural life—"Be sensible, my dear Magnus, and just go quietly to Mistrà."

Mistrà—the name sent a shiver all down me. I was about to decline the invitation, when a thought suddenly loomed vaguely in my mind.

"Yes, dear Count," I answered; "I accept your invitation with gratitude and pleasure. I will start tomorrow for Mistrà."

The next day found me at Padua, on my way to the Villa of Mistrà. It seemed as if I had left an intolerable burden behind me. I was, for the first time since how long, quite light of heart. The tortuous, rough-paved streets, with their empty, gloomy porticoes; the ill-plastered palaces, with closed, discolored shutters; the little rambling square, with meager trees and stubborn grass; the Venetian garden-houses reflecting their crumbling graces in the muddy canal; the gardens without gates and the gates without gardens, the avenues leading nowhere; and the population of blind and legless beggars, of whining sacristans, which issued as by magic from between the flag-stones and dust-heaps and weeds under the fierce August sun, all this dreariness merely amused and pleased me. My good spirits were heightened by a musical mass which I had the good fortune to hear at St. Anthony's.

Never in all my days had I heard anything comparable, although Italy affords many strange things in the way of sacred music. Into the deep nasal chanting of the priests there had suddenly burst a chorus of children, singing absolutely independent of all time and tune; grunting of priests answered by squealing of boys, slow Gregorian modulation interrupted by jaunty barrel-organ pipings, an insane, insanely merry jumble of bellowing and barking, mewing and cackling and braying, such as would have enlivened a witches' meeting, or rather some mediaeval

Feast of Fools. And, to make the grotesqueness of such music still more fantastic and Hoffmannlike, there was, besides, the magnificence of the piles of sculptured marbles and gilded bronzes, the tradition of the musical splendor for which St. Anthony's had been famous in days gone by. I had read in old travelers, Lalande and Burney, that the Republic of St. Mark had squandered immense sums not merely on the monuments and decoration, but on the musical establishment of its great cathedral of Terra Firma. In the midst of this ineffable concert of impossible voices and instruments, I tried to imagine the voice of Guadagni, the soprano for whom Gluck had written *Che farò senza Euridice,* and the fiddle of Tartini, that Tartini with whom the devil had once come and made music. And the delight in anything so absolutely, barbarously, grotesquely, fantastically incongruous as such a performance in such a place was heightened by a sense of profanation: such were the successors of those wonderful musicians of that hated eighteenth century!

The whole thing had delighted me so much, so very much more than the most faultless performance could have done, that I determined to enjoy it once more; and towards vesper-time, after a cheerful dinner with two bagmen at the inn of the Golden Star, and a pipe over the rough sketch of a possible cantata upon the music which the devil made for Tartini, I turned my steps once more towards St. Anthony's.

The bells were ringing for sunset, and a muffled sound of organs seemed to issue from the huge, solitary church; I pushed my way under the heavy leathern curtain, expecting to be greeted by the grotesque performance of that morning.

I proved mistaken. Vespers must long have been over. A smell of stale incense, a crypt-like damp filled my mouth; it was already night in that vast cathedral. Out of the darkness glimmered the votive-lamps of the chapels, throwing wavering lights upon the red polished marble, the gilded

railing, and chandeliers, and plaqueing with yellow the
muscles of some sculptured figure. In a corner a burning
taper put a halo about the head of a priest, burnishing his
shining bald skull, his white surplice, and the open book
before him. "Amen" he chanted; the book was closed with
a snap, the light moved up the apse, some dark figures of
women rose from their knees and passed quickly towards
the door; a man saying his prayers before a chapel also got
up, making a great clatter in dropping his stick.

The church was empty, and I expected every minute to
be turned out by the sacristan making his evening round
to close the doors. I was leaning against a pillar, looking
into the greyness of the great arches, when the organ suddenly burst out into a series of chords, rolling through
the echoes of the church: it seemed to be the conclusion
of some service. And above the organ rose the notes of a
voice; high, soft, enveloped in a kind of downiness, like
a cloud of incense, and which ran through the mazes of
a long cadence. The voice dropped into silence; with two
thundering chords the organ closed in. All was silent. For
a moment I stood leaning against one of the pillars of the
nave: my hair was clammy, my knees sank beneath me, an
enervating heat spread through my body; I tried to breathe
more largely, to suck in the sounds with the incense-laden
air. I was supremely happy, and yet as if I were dying; then
suddenly a chill ran through me, and with it a vague panic.
I turned away and hurried out into the open.

The evening sky lay pure and blue along the jagged line
of roofs; the bats and swallows were wheeling about; and
from the belfries all around, half-drowned by the deep bell
of St. Anthony's, jangled the peel of the *Ave Maria*.

"You really don't seem well," young Count Alvise had said
the previous evening, as he welcomed me, in the light of
a lantern held up by a peasant, in the weedy back-garden
of the Villa of Mistrà. Everything had seemed to me like
a dream: the jingle of the horse's bells driving in the dark

from Padua, as the lantern swept the acacia-hedges with their wide yellow light; the grating of the wheels on the gravel; the supper-table, illumined by a single petroleum lamp for fear of attracting mosquitoes, where a broken old lackey, in an old stable jacket, handed round the dishes among the fumes of onion; Alvise's fat mother gabbling dialect in a shrill, benevolent voice behind the bullfights on her fan; the unshaven village priest, perpetually fidgeting with his glass and foot, and sticking one shoulder up above the other. And now, in the afternoon, I felt as if I had been in this long, rambling, tumble-down Villa of Mistrà—a villa three-quarters of which was given up to the storage of grain and garden tools, or to the exercise of rats, mice, scorpions, and centipedes—all my life; as if I had always sat there, in Count Alvise's study, among the pile of undusted books on agriculture, the sheaves of accounts, the samples of grain and silkworm seed, the ink-stains and the cigar-ends; as if I had never heard of anything save the cereal basis of Italian agriculture, the diseases of maize, the peronospora of the vine, the breeds of bullocks, and the iniquities of farm laborers; with the blue cones of the Euganean hills closing in the green shimmer of plain outside the window.

After an early dinner, again with the screaming gabble of the fat old Countess, the fidgeting and shoulder-raising of the unshaven priest, the smell of fried oil and stewed onions, Count Alvise made me get into the cart beside him, and whirled me along among clouds of dust, between the endless glister of poplars, acacias, and maples, to one of his farms.

In the burning sun some twenty or thirty girls, in colored skirts, laced bodices, and big straw-hats, were threshing the maize on the big red brick threshing-floor, while others were winnowing the grain in great sieves. Young Alvise III. (the old one was Alvise II.: every one is Alvise, that is to say, Lewis, in that family; the name is on the house, the carts, the barrows, the very pails) picked up the

maize, touched it, tasted it, said something to the girls
that made them laugh, and something to the head farmer
that made him look very glum; and then led me into a
huge stable, where some twenty or thirty white bullocks
were stamping, switching their tails, hitting their horns
against the mangers in the dark. Alvise III. patted each,
called him by his name, gave him some salt or a turnip,
and explained which was the Mantuan breed, which the
Apulian, which the Romagnolo, and so on. Then he bade
me jump into the trap, and off we went again through the
dust, among the hedges and ditches, till we came to some
more brick farm buildings with pinkish roofs smoking
against the blue sky. Here there were more young women
threshing and winnowing the maize, which made a great
golden Danaë cloud; more bullocks stamping and lowing
in the cool darkness; more joking, fault-finding, explain-
ing; and thus through five farms, until I seemed to see
the rhythmical rising and falling of the flails against the
hot sky, the shower of golden grains, the yellow dust from
the winnowing-sieves on to the bricks, the switching of
innumerable tails and plunging of innumerable horns, the
glistening of huge white flanks and foreheads, whenever I
closed my eyes.

"A good day's work!" cried Count Alvise, stretching out
his long legs with the tight trousers riding up over the
Wellington boots. "Mamma, give us some aniseed-syrup
after dinner; it is an excellent restorative and precaution
against the fevers of this country."

"Oh! you've got fever in this part of the world, have
you? Why, your father said the air was so good!"

"Nothing, nothing," soothed the old Countess. "The
only thing to be dreaded are mosquitoes; take care to fas-
ten your shutters before lighting the candle."

"Well," rejoined young Alvise, with an effort of conscience, "of course there *are* fevers. But they needn't
hurt you. Only, don' go out into the garden at night, if
you don't want to catch them. Papa told me that you have

fancies for moonlight rambles. It won't do in this climate, my dear fellow; it won't do. If you must stalk about at night, being a genius, take a turn inside the house; you can get quite exercise enough."

After dinner the aniseed-syrup was produced, together with brandy and cigars, and they all sat in the long, narrow, half-furnished room on the first floor; the old Countess knitting a garment of uncertain shape and destination, the priest reading out the newspaper; Count Alvise puffing at his long, crooked cigar, and pulling the ears of a long, lean dog with a suspicion of mange and a stiff eye. From the dark garden outside rose the hum and whirr of countless insects, and the smell of the grapes which hung black against the starlit, blue sky, on the trellis. I went to the balcony. The garden lay dark beneath; against the twinkling horizon stood out the tall poplars. There was the sharp cry of an owl; the barking of a dog; a sudden whiff of warm, enervating perfume, a perfume that made me think of the taste of certain peaches, and suggested white, thick, wax-like petals. I seemed to have smelt that flower once before: it made me feel languid, almost faint.

"I am very tired," I said to Count Alvise. "See how feeble we city folk become!"

But, despite my fatigue, I found it quite impossible to sleep. The night seemed perfectly stifling. I had felt nothing like it at Venice. Despite the injunctions of the Countess I opened the solid wooden shutters, hermetically closed against mosquitoes, and looked out.

The moon had risen; and beneath it lay the big lawns, the rounded tree-tops, bathed in a blue, luminous mist, every leaf glistening and trembling in what seemed a heaving sea of light. Beneath the window was the long trellis, with the white shining piece of pavement under it. It was so bright that I could distinguish the green of the vine-leaves, the dull red of the catalpa-flowers. There was in the air a vague scent of cut grass, of ripe American grapes,

of that white flower (it must be white) which made me
think of the taste of peaches all melting into the delicious
freshness of falling dew. From the village church came the
stroke of one: Heaven knows how long I had been vainly
attempting to sleep. A shiver ran through me, and my head
suddenly filled as with the fumes of some subtle wine; I
remembered all those weedy embankments, those canals
full of stagnant water, the yellow faces of the peasants; the
word malaria returned to my mind. No matter! I remained
leaning on the window, with a thirsty longing to plunge
myself into this blue moon-mist, this dew and perfume and
silence, which seemed to vibrate and quiver like the stars
that strewed the depths of heaven. . . . What music, even
Wagner's, or of that great singer of starry nights, the divine Schumann, what music could ever compare with this
great silence, with this great concert of voiceless things
that sing within one's soul?

As I made this reflection, a note, high, vibrating, and
sweet, rent the silence, which immediately closed around
it. I leaned out of the window, my heart beating as though
it must burst. After a brief space the silence was cloven
once more by that note, as the darkness is cloven by a
falling star or a firefly rising slowly like a rocket. But this
time it was plain that the voice did not come, as I had
imagined, from the garden, but from the house itself, from
some corner of this rambling old villa of Mistrà.

Mistrà—Mistrà! The name rang in my ears, and I began
at length to grasp its significance, which seems to have
escaped me till then. "Yes," I said to myself, "it is quite
natural." And with this odd impression of naturalness was
mixed a feverish, impatient pleasure. It was as if I had
come to Mistrà on purpose, and that I was about to meet
the object of my long and weary hopes.

Grasping the lamp with its singed green shade, I gently opened the door and made my way through a series of
long passages and of big, empty rooms, in which my steps
re-echoed as in a church, and my light disturbed whole

swarms of bats. I wandered at random, farther and farther from the inhabited part of the buildings.

This silence made me feel sick; I gasped as under a sudden disappointment.

All of a sudden there came a sound—chords, metallic, sharp, rather like the tone of a mandolin—close to my ear. Yes, quite close: I was separated from the sounds only by a partition. I fumbled for a door; the unsteady light of my lamp was insufficient for my eyes, which were swimming like those of a drunkard. At last I found a latch, and, after a moment's hesitation, I lifted it and gently pushed open the door. At first I could not understand what manner of place I was in. It was dark all round me, but a brilliant light blinded me, a light coming from below and striking the opposite wall. It was as if I had entered a dark box in a half-lighted theatre. I was, in fact, in something of the kind, a sort of dark hole with a high balustrade, half-hidden by an up-drawn curtain. I remembered those little galleries or recesses for the use of musicians or lookers-on—which exist under the ceiling of the ballrooms in certain old Italian palaces. Yes; it must have been one like that. Opposite me was a vaulted ceiling covered with gilt moldings, which framed great time-blackened canvases; and lower down, in the light thrown up from below, stretched a wall covered with faded frescoes. Where had I seen that goddess in lilac and lemon draperies foreshortened over a big, green peacock? For she was familiar to me, and the stucco Tritons also who twisted their tails round her gilded frame. And that fresco, with warriors in Roman cuirasses and green and blue lappets, and knee-breeches—where could I have seen them before? I asked myself these questions without experiencing any surprise. Moreover, I was very calm, as one is calm sometimes in extraordinary dreams—could I be dreaming?

I advanced gently and leaned over the balustrade. My eyes were met at first by the darkness above me, where, like gigantic spiders, the big chandeliers rotated slowly, hanging from the ceiling. Only one of them was lit, and its Murano-glass pendants, its carnations and roses, shone opalescent in the light of the guttering wax. This chandelier lighted up the opposite wall and that piece of ceiling with the goddess and the green peacock; it illumined, but far less well, a corner of the huge room, where, in the shadow of a kind of canopy, a little group of people were crowding round a yellow satin sofa, of the same kind as those that lined the walls. On the sofa, half-screened from me by the surrounding persons, a woman was stretched out: the silver of her embroidered dress and the rays of her diamonds gleamed and shot forth as she moved uneasily. And immediately under the chandelier, in the full light, a man stooped over a harpsichord, his head bent slightly, as if collecting his thoughts before singing.

He struck a few chords and sang. Yes, sure enough, it was the voice, the voice that had so long been persecuting me! I recognized at once that delicate, voluptuous quality, strange, exquisite, sweet beyond words, but lacking all youth and clearness. That passion veiled in tears which had troubled my brain that night on the lagoon, and again on the Grand Canal singing the *Biondina,* and yet again, only two days since, in the deserted cathedral of Padua. But I recognized now what seemed to have been hidden from me till then, that this voice was what I cared most for in all the wide world.

The voice wound and unwound itself in long, languishing phrases, in rich, voluptuous *rifiorituras,* all fretted with tiny scales and exquisite, crisp shakes; it stopped ever and anon, swaying as if panting in languid delight. And I felt my body melt even as wax in the sunshine, and it seemed to me that I too was turning fluid and vaporous, in order to mingle with these sounds as the moonbeams mingle with the dew.

Suddenly, from the dimly lighted corner by the canopy, came a little piteous wail; then another followed, and was lost in the singer's voice. During a long phrase on the harpsichord, sharp and tinkling, the singer turned his head towards the dais, and there came a plaintive little sob. But he, instead of stopping, struck a sharp chord; and with a thread of voice so hushed as to be scarcely audible, slid softly into a long *cadenza*. At the same moment he threw his head backwards, and the light fell full upon the handsome, effeminate face, with its ashy pallor and big, black brows, of the singer Zaffirino. At the sight of that face, sensual and sullen, of that smile which was cruel and mocking like a bad woman's, I understood—I knew not why, by what process—that his singing *must* be cut short, that the accursed phrase *must* never be finished. I understood that I was before an assassin, that he was killing this woman, and killing me also, with his wicked voice.

I rushed down the narrow stair which led down from the box, pursued, as it were, by that exquisite voice, swelling, swelling by insensible degrees. I flung myself on the door which must be that of the big saloon. I could see its light between the panels. I bruised my hands in trying to wrench the latch. The door was fastened tight, and while I was struggling with that locked door I heard the voice swelling, swelling, rending asunder that downy veil which wrapped it, leaping forth clear, resplendent, like the sharp and glittering blade of a knife that seemed to enter deep into my breast. Then, once more, a wail, a death-groan, and that dreadful noise, that hideous gurgle of breath strangled by a rush of blood. And then a long shake, acute, brilliant, triumphant.

The door gave way beneath my weight, one half crashed in. I entered. I was blinded by a flood of blue moonlight. It poured in through four great windows, peaceful and diaphanous, a pale blue mist of moonlight, and turned the huge room into a kind of submarine cave, paved with moonbeams, full of shimmers, of pools of moonlight. It was as bright as at midday, but the brightness was cold, blue, vaporous, supernatural. The room was completely empty, like a great hayloft. Only, there hung from the ceiling the ropes which had once supported a chandelier; and in a corner, among stacks of wood and heaps of Indian-corn, whence spread a sickly smell of damp and mildew, there stood a long, thin harpsichord, with spindle-legs, and its cover cracked from end to end.

I felt, all of a sudden, very calm. The one thing that mattered was the phrase that kept moving in my head, the phrase of that unfinished cadence which I had heard but an instant before. I opened the harpsichord, and my fingers came down boldly upon its keys. A jingle-jangle of broken strings, laughable and dreadful, was the only answer.

Then an extraordinary fear overtook me. I clambered out of one of the windows; I rushed up the garden and wandered through the fields, among the canals and the embankments, until the moon had set and the dawn began to shiver, followed, pursued for ever by that jangle of broken strings.

People expressed much satisfaction at my recovery.

It seems that one dies of those fevers.

Recovery? But have I recovered? I walk, and eat and drink and talk; I can even sleep. I live the life of other living creatures. But I am wasted by a strange and deadly disease. I can never lay hold of my own inspiration. My head is filled with music which is certainly by me, since I have never heard it before, but which still is not my own, which I despise and abhor: little, tripping flourishes and languishing phrases, and long-drawn, echoing cadences.

O wicked, wicked voice, violin of flesh and blood made by the Evil One's hand, may I not even execrate thee in peace; but is it necessary that, at the moment when I curse, the longing to hear thee again should parch my soul like hell-thirst? And since I have satiated thy lust for revenge, since thou hast withered my life and withered my genius, is it not time for pity? May I not hear one note, only one note of thine, O singer, O wicked and contemptible wretch?

The Weird Violin
Anonymous
(1893)

The great Polish violinist, S—, was strolling aimlessly about the town, on a sunny, but cold afternoon, in November of a certain year. He was to play, at night, at one of the great concerts which made the town so musically famous, and, according to his usual custom he was observing passers-by, looking in shop windows, and thinking of anything rather than the approaching ordeal. Not that he was nervous, for none could be less so, but he came to his work all the fresher for an hour or two of idle forgetfulness, and astonished his audiences the more.

Turning out of the busiest street, he ambled into a comparatively quiet thoroughfare, and, throwing away an inch of cigar-end, produced a new Havannah, lighting up with every sign of enjoyment. Now, it was part of his rule, when out on these refreshing excursions, to avoid music shops, and he had already passed half-a-dozen without doing more than barely recognise them. It is therefore very remarkable that, walking by a large music warehouse in this quiet thoroughfare, he should suddenly stop, and, after remaining in doubt for a few moments, go straight to the window and look in.

He had not seen anything when he first passed, and, indeed, he had merely ascertained, out of the corner of his eye, that one of the forbidden shops was near. Why, then, did he feel impelled to return?

The window was stocked, as all such windows are, with instruments, music, and such appurtenances as resin, bows, chin-rests, mutes, strings, bridges and pegs. An old Guanerius, valued at several hundred guineas, lay alongside a shilling set of bones, and a flageolet, all ocarina, and several mouth-organs were gracefully grouped upon a gilt-edged copy of "Elijah."

Amongst the carefully-arranged violins was a curious old instrument the like of which the virtuoso had never seen before, and at this he now stared with all his eyes. It was an ugly, squat violin, of heavy pattern, and ancient appearance. The maker, whoever he had been, had displayed considerable eccentricity throughout its manufacture, but more especially in the scroll, which, owing to some freak, he had carved into the semblance of a hideous, grinning face. There was something horribly repulsive about this strange work of art, and yet it also possessed a subtle fascination. The violinist, keeping his eyes upon the face, which seemed to follow his movements with fiendish persistency, slowly edged to the door, and entered the shop.

The attendant came forward, and recognising the well-known performer, bowed low.

"That is a curious-looking fiddle in the window," began the artist, at once, with a wave of his hand in the direction of the fiend.

"Which one, sir?" inquired the attendant. "Oh, the one with the remarkable scroll, you mean. I'll get it for you." Drawing aside a little curtain, he dived into the window-bay, and produced the instrument, whose face seemed to be grinning more maliciously than ever.

"A fair tone, sir," added the man, "but nothing to suit you, I'm sure."

As soon as Herr S— touched the neck of the violin he gripped it convulsively, and raised the instrument to his chin. Then, for a few moments, he stood, firm as a rock, his eyes fixed upon the awe-stricken attendant, evidently without seeing him.

"A bow," said the musician, at length, in a low voice. He stretched out his disengaged hand and took it, without moving his eyes. Then he stopped four strings with his long fingers, and drew the horse-hair smartly over them with one rapid sweep, producing a rich chord in a minor key.

A slight shiver passed over his frame as the notes were struck, and the look of concentration upon his face, changed to one of horror; but he did not cease. Slowly drooping his gaze, the performer met the gibing glance of the scroll-face, and though his own countenance blanched, and his lips tightened, as if to suppress a cry, the bow was raised again, and the violin spoke.

Did the demon whisper to those moving, nervous fingers? It almost seemed to be doing so; and surely such a melody as came from the instrument was born of no human mind. It was slow and measured, but no solemnity was suggested; it thrilled the frame, but with terror, not delight; it was a chain of sounds, which like a sick man's passing fancy, slipped out of the memory as soon as it was evolved, and was incapable of being recalled.

Slowly, when the last strains were lost, the great violinist dropped both arms to his side, and stood for a few moments, grasping violin and bow, without speaking. There were drops of perspiration on his forehead, and he was pale and weary-looking; when he spoke, it was in a faint voice, and he seemed to address himself to something invisible.

"I cannot endure it now," he said. "I will play again to-night."

"Do you wish to play on the instrument at this evening's concert, sir?" inquired the dealer, not without some astonishment at the choice, much as the performance had affected him.

"Yes—yes, of course!" was the reply, given with some irritability, the speaker having apparently roused himself from his semi-stupor.

As the dealer took back the fiddle, he chanced to turn it back uppermost. It was a curiously marked piece of wood, a black patch spreading over a large portion, and throwing an ugly blur upon the otherwise exquisite purfling.

"See!" gasped the artist, pointing a shaking finger at this blotch, and clutching at the shopkeeper's shoulder. "Blood!"

"Good gracious!" ejaculated the other, shrinking back in alarm. "Are you ill, sir?"

"Blood, blood!" repeated the half-demented musician, and he staggered out of the shop.

It was night, and the concert-room was crowded to excess. The performers upon the platform, accustomed as they were to such sights, could not but gaze with interest at the restless sea of eager, expectant faces which stretched before them.

That indescribable noise, a multitude of subdued murmurs, accompanied by the discordant scraping of strings, and blowing of reeds, was at its height; now and then a loud trombone would momentarily assert itself, or an oboe's plaintive notes would rise above the tumult; and, in short, the moment of intense excitement which immediately precedes the entrance of the conductor was at hand.

Suddenly, the long-continued confusion ceased, and, for an incalculably short space of time, silence reigned. Then a storm of deafening applause burst forth; necks were craned, and eyes strained in vain attempts to catch an early glimpse of the great violinist who was to open the concert by playing a difficult Concerto of Spohr.

It was noticed, that as the virtuoso followed the grey-haired conductor to the center of the platform, he was unusually pale; and those who were seated at no great distance from the orchestra, observed also that he carried a curious violin, instead of the Stradivarius upon which he was wont to perform.

A tap on the conductor's desk, a short, breathless silence, and the sweet strains of the opening bars issued from the instruments of a hundred able musicians.

The soloist, with a sinking at the heart which he could scarcely account for, raised the violin to his shoulder, and saw, for the first time, that it had been re-strung. As he invariably left stringing and tuning to others, this would appear to have been a matter of no moment, and yet it had a strange effect upon him. Again that shudder passed through his body, and again he unwillingly met the glance of those diabolical eyes upon the scroll. Horror of horrors! was the face alive, or was he going mad?

The band, which had swelled out to a loud forte, now dropped to a pianissimo. The moment had arrived. Herr S— raised his bow, and commenced the lovely adagio.

What had come to him? Where were the concert room, the orchestra, the anxious crowd of people? What sounds were these? This was not Spohr, this sweet melody so like, and yet so unlike the weird music which he had played in the dealer's shop. What subtle magic had so acted upon those strains that their horror, their cruel mockery had entirely vanished, and sweet, pure harmony alone remained?

It seemed to the player that he stood within a small, but comfortably furnished room. Two figures were in the room, those of a beautiful young girl, and of a dark, handsome, foreign-looking man.

There was something in the face of the latter which vividly recalled the face upon the scroll, and, strange to say, a counterpart of the violin itself rested under the man's chin.

The girl was seated at a harpsichord, and, as she played, her companion accompanied her upon his strange instrument. From the costume of both, the dreamer concluded that they were phantoms of a hundred years ago.

"Ernestine," the man was saying, in a low voice, as he passed his bow over the strings, "tell me to-night that you have not dismissed me for ever. I can wait for your love."

"It is useless," replied the girl —"oh, it is quite useless! Why importune me further? I could never love you, even if I were not already promised to another."

A savage light gleamed in the man's eye, and more than ever he looked like the face on the violin; but he did not immediately reply and the music went on.

"You tell me it is useless," he said, at length, "and I tell you that it is useless. Useless for you to think of him. Do you hear?" he continued, lowering his violin, and leaning towards her. "You shall never marry him; I swear it by my soul."

The girl shrank from him, and the music ceased. Though he did not know it, the dreaming violinist had reached the conclusion of the adagio movement. He did not hear the deafening plaudits which greeted the fall of his bow; he knew nothing of the enthusiasm of the orchestra, or the praise of the conductor; he heard no more music.

Look! what is this? The girl has seated herself upon a couch, and her lover, his violin still in his left hand, is kneeling at her feet, passionately imploring her to listen. She expostulates for awhile, then repulses him and rises. A malignant fire darts from the furious foreigner's eyes; something bright gleams in his hand; he rushes forward, raises his arm to strike—

The presto movement had commenced, and an extraordinary circumstance soon made itself apparent to the audience. The violinist was running away with the band. Greatly to the horror of the conductor, the tempo had to be increased until a prestissimo was reached. Still the performer was not satisfied, there seemed no limit to his powers to-night; his fingers literally flew up and down the fingerboard; his bow shot to-and-fro with incredible swiftness; and yet the music grew quicker, quicker, until the unhappy conductor, who with difficulty pulled along the toiling band, felt that a fiasco was inevitable.

On, on rushed the fingers and the bow, faster, and faster still: a few of the bandsmen fell off from sheer exhaustion, and stared, horror-stricken, at the mad violinist. Some of the listeners rose in alarm, and many were only detained, by extreme anxiety, from bursting into loud and frantic applause.

Suddenly, with the loud snap of a string, the spell was broken. The orchestra, unable now to proceed, stopped in utter confusion, and a loud sigh of released suspense went up from thousands of throats. Then the whole mass rose in sudden horror, as the violinist dropped his instrument with a crash upon the platform, stared wildly around, clasped a hand to his side, and, with a strange cry, fell to the ground insensible.

For weeks the great violinist lay between life and death; then nature reasserted herself, and he recovered. But it was long, very long, ere he could again appear in public; whilst the weird and mysterious violin never again sent forth its strange and mysterious influence. It had been hopelessly shattered in that last night of its performance, which had well-nigh proved fatal to the world-famed player.

The Piano Next Door
Elia Wilkinson Peattie
(1898)

Babette had gone away for the summer; the furniture was in its summer linens; the curtains were down, and Babette's husband, John Boyce, was alone in the house. It was the first year of his marriage, and he missed Babette. But then, as he often said to himself, he ought never to have married her. He did it from pure selfishness, and because he was determined to possess the most illusive, tantalizing, elegant, and utterly unmoral little creature that the sun shone upon. He wanted her because she reminded him of birds, and flowers, and summer winds, and other exquisite things created for the delectation of mankind. He neither expected nor desired her to think. He had half-frightened her into marrying him, had taken her to a poor man's home, provided her with no society such as she had been accustomed to, and he had no reasonable cause of complaint when she answered the call of summer and flitted away, like a butterfly in the morning sunshine, to the place where the flowers grew.

He wrote to her every evening, sitting in the stifling, ugly house, and poured out his soul as if it were a libation to a goddess. She sometimes answered by telegraph, sometimes by a perfumed note. He schooled himself not to feel hurt. Why should Babette write? Does a goldfinch indict epistles; or a humming-bird study composition; or a glancing, red-scaled fish in summer shallows consider the meaning of words?

He knew at the beginning what Babette was—guessed her limitations—trembled when he buttoned her tiny glove—kissed her dainty slipper when he found it in the closet after she was gone— thrilled at the sound of her laugh, or the memory of it! That was all. A mere case of love. He was in bonds. Babette was not. Therefore he was in the city, working overhours to pay for Babette's pretty follies down at the seaside. It was quite right and proper. He was a grub in the furrow; she a lark in the blue. Those had always been and always must be their relative positions.

Having attained a mood of philosophic calm, in which he was prepared to spend his evenings alone—as became a grub—and to await with dignified patience the return of his wife, it was in the nature of an inconsistency that he should have walked the floor of the dull little drawing-room like a lion in cage. It did not seem in keeping with the position of superior serenity which he had assumed, that, reading Babette's notes, he should have raged with jealousy, or that, in the loneliness of his unkempt chamber, he should have stretched out arms of longing. Even if Babette had been present, she would only have smiled her gay little smile and co- quetted with him. She could not understand. He had known, of course, from the first moment, that she could not understand! And so, why the ache, ache, ache of the heart! Or was it the heart, or the brain, or the soul?

Sometimes, when the evenings were so hot that he could not endure the close air of the house, he sat on the narrow, dusty front porch and looked about him at his neighbors. The street had once been smart and aspiring, but it had fallen into decay and dejection. Pale young men, with flurried-looking wives, seemed to Boyce to occupy most of the houses. Sometimes three or four couples would live in one house. Most of these appeared to be childless. The women made a pretence at fashionable dressing, and wore their hair elaborately in fashions which somehow suggested boarding-houses to Boyce, though he could not have told why. Every house in the block needed fresh paint. Lacking this renovation, the householders tried to make up for it by a display of lace curtains which, at every window, swayed in the smoke-weighted breeze. Strips of carpeting were laid down the front steps of the houses where the communities of young couples lived, and here, evenings, the inmates of the houses gathered, committing mild extravagances such as the treating of each other to ginger ale, or beer, or ice-cream.

Boyce watched these tawdry makeshifts at sociability with bitterness and loathing. He wondered how he could have been such a fool as to bring his exquisite Babette to this neighborhood. How could he expect that she would return to him? It was not reasonable. He ought to go down on his knees with gratitude that she even condescended to write him.

Sitting one night till late,—so late that the fashionable young wives with their husbands had retired from the strips of stair carpeting,—and raging at the loneliness which ate at his heart like a cancer, he heard, softly creeping through the windows of the house adjoin- ing his own, the sound of comfortable melody.

It breathed upon his ear like a spirit of consolation, speaking of peace, of love which needs no reward save its own sweetness, of aspiration which looks forever beyond the thing of the hour to find attainment in that which is eternal. So insidiously did it whisper these things, so delicately did the simple and perfect melodies creep upon the spirit—that Boyce felt no resentment, but from the first listened as one who listens to learn, or as one who, fainting on the hot road, hears, far in the ferny deeps below, the gurgle of a spring.

Then came harmonies more intricate: fair fabrics of woven sound, in the midst of which gleamed golden threads of joy; a tapestry of sound, multi-tinted, gallant with story and achievement, and beautiful things. Boyce, sitting on

his absurd piazza, with his knees jambed against the balustrade, and his chair back against the dun-colored wall
of his house, seemed to be walking in the cathedral of the
redwood forest, with blue above him, a vast hymn in his
ears, pungent perfume in his nostrils, and mighty shafts of
trees lifting themselves to heaven, proud and erect as pure
men before their Judge. He stood on a mountain at sunrise, and saw the marvels of the amethystine clouds below
his feet, heard an eternal and white silence, such as broods
among the everlasting snows, and saw an eagle winging
for the sun. He was in a city, and away from him, diverg-
ing like the spokes of a wheel, ran thronging streets, and
to his sense came the beat, beat, beat of the city's heart.
He saw the golden alchemy of a chosen race; saw greed
transmitted to progress; saw that which had enslaved men,
work at last to their liberation; heard the roar of mighty
mills, and on the streets all the peoples of earth walking
with common purposes, in fealty and understanding. And
then, from the swelling of this concourse of great sounds,
came a diminuendo, calm as philosophy, and from that,
nothingness.

Boyce sat still for a long time, listening to the echoes
which this music had awakened in his soul. He retired,
at length, content, but determined that upon the morrow
he would watch—the day being Sunday—for the musician
who had so moved and taught him.

He arose early, therefore, and having prepared his own
simple breakfast of fruit and coffee, took his station by
the window to watch for the man. For he felt convinced
that the exposition he had heard was that of a masculine
mind. The long, hot hours of the morning went by, but the
front door of the house next to his did not open.

"These artists sleep late," he complained. Still he
watched. He was too much afraid of losing him to go out
for dinner. By three in the afternoon he had grown impatient. He went to the house next door and rang the bell.

There was no response. He thundered another appeal. An old woman with a cloth about her head answered the door. She was very deaf, and Boyce had difficulty in making himself understood.

"The family is in the country," was all she would say. "The family will not be home till September."

"But there is some one living here?" shouted Boyce.

"I live here," she said with dignity, putting back a wisp of dirty gray hair behind her ear. "It is my house. I sublet to the family."

"What family?"

But the old creature was not communicative.

"The family that lives here," she said.

"Then who plays the piano in this house?" roared Boyce. "Do you?"

He thought a shade of pallor showed itself on her ash-colored cheeks. Yet she smiled a little at the idea of her playing.

"There is no piano," she said, and she put an enigmatical emphasis to the words.

"Nonsense," cried Boyce, indignantly. "I heard a piano being played in this very house for hours last night!"

"You may enter," said the old woman, with an accent more vicious than hospitable.

Boyce almost burst into the drawing-room. It was a dusty and forbidding place, with ugly furniture and gaudy walls. No piano nor any other musical instrument stood in it. The intruder turned an angry and baffled face to the old woman, who was smiling with ill-concealed exultation.

"I shall see the other rooms," he announced. The old woman did not appear to be surprised at his impertinence.

"As you please," she said.

So, with the hobbling creature, with her bandaged head, for a guide, he explored every room of the house, which being identical with his own, he could do without fear of leaving any apartment unentered. But no piano did he find!

"Explain," roared Boyce at length, turning upon the leering old hag beside him. "Explain! For surely I heard music more beautiful than I can tell."

"I know nothing," she said. "But it is true I once had a lodger who rented the front room, and that he played upon the piano. I am poor at hearing, but he must have played well, for all the neighbors used to come in front of the house to listen, and sometimes they applauded him, and sometimes they were still. I could tell by watching their hands. Sometimes little children came and danced. Other times young men and women came and listened. But the young man died. The neighbors were angry. They came to look at him and said he had starved to death. It was no fault of mine. I sold his piano to pay his funeral expenses—and it took every cent to pay for them too, I'd have you know. But since then, sometimes—still, it must be nonsense, for I never heard it—folks say that he plays the piano in my room. It has kept me out of the letting of it more than once. But the family doesn't seem to mind—the family that lives here, you know. They will be back in September. Yes."

Boyce left her nodding her thanks at what he had placed in her hand, and went home to write it all to Babette—Babette who would laugh so merrily when she read it!

The Violin
RICHARD MARSH
(1900)

I am unable to say exactly why I bought it. I suspect that the
purchase had a certain connection with the price. Three-
and-sixpence for a "Full-sized violin, splendid instrument;
rich tone; in perfect condition; best bow" did not strike
me as extravagant. In fact, it tickled me. The shop looked
liked a marine-store dealer's. There were old books, old
boots, old bottles and jampots, cheek by jowl with that
"fine violin." Had it—that "splendid instrument"!—been
the last resource of a street musician, I wondered.

The proprietor of the shop appeared to be a lady. She
was very dirty and very fat. I asked to see the fiddle. Taking it from the window, without a word she placed it in
my hands. I am not a judge of violins. I should not know
an Amati if I saw one. As to Straduarius, Ernest told me
the other day that violins—posthumous violins—of his
manufacture are being turned out by the dozen, cheap, at
a little town in Germany. I know very little more about
Straduarius than that. But Ernest does; he is a musician.
And I thought it would amuse him if I made him a present
of a "fine violin" and "best bow," which together cost me
three-and-sixpence.

"How much for the case?"

The fiddle had been reclining on the lid of an ordinary
baize-lined wooden case.

"Shilling," said the lady.

163

It did not occur to me that this was dear. The lady, however, seemed to suppose that my temporary silence conveyed a hint that it was. Because, presently, she observed—

"I won't charge you anything for the case."

"You will let me have the violin, the bow, and the case for three-and-sixpence?"

"Yes," said the lady.

I struck the bargain. As I bore away the prize it crossed my mind that there was something perhaps a little remarkable about that violin. A suspicion, say, of a receiver and a thief. One must purchase violins, bows, and cases at a very low price to be enabled to sell them at a profit for three-and-sixpence. My morality may have been lax, but I told myself that that was the lady's affair, not mine.

Ernest came to dinner that night.

"I have been buying you a present," I remarked as he came in.

He looked at me and laughed. I don't know if he imagined that my words contained a joke.

"A present? What sort of present?"

"A violin."

He glanced at the case upon the table.

"A violin! I say, uncle, I hope you haven't—"

"Been making a fool of yourself," he was on the point of saying, but he wisely stopped in time.

"Just look at that violin, and tell me what you think of it."

He opened the case. He glanced at the violin as it lay within; then he took it out. He handled it reverently. I have noticed that a genuine musician always does handle a fiddle—even a common fiddle—with a sort of reverence. He turned it over and over; he rapped its back softly with his knuckles; he peeped into its belly; he smelt it; he tucked it under his chin; then, putting it down, he fixed his eyes on me, with a light in them as of a smile.

"It's odd, but, do you know, I seem to have seen this violin somewhere before."

"Where have you seen it?"

"I fancy you know better than I. You have a little secret, uncle; come, what is it?"

"Is it a good violin?"

He drew the bow across it, tightening the strings. Then he played a little exercise and a snatch of some quaint melody. Then he lowered it and looked at it with glistening eyes.

"It is a good violin."

"How much is it worth?"

"It depends upon the man who buys it, and upon the length of his purse. I hope you did not give a fancy price."

"Is it dear at three-and-sixpence?"

"Three-and-sixpence? You are joking."

"That is what I gave for it—fiddle, bow, case, and all."

He was turning it over and over.

"Where did you get it?"

"In a dirty shop, in a dirty street, off Lisson Grove."

"I feel sure I have seen it before."

"Do you recognise it by any mark?"

"I recognise it by every mark, and"—he touched it with the bow—"I recognise it by its voice."

The idea struck me as fanciful. In an orchestra of violins, all playing the same music, if one among them could be recognised by its voice, it seems to me that that violin would not be popular. But he *is* fanciful, is Ernest.

We went down to dinner. During the meal he told me about a young man in whom he was much interested. The name of this young man was Philip Coursault, and he, too, was a musician. According to Ernest, he was a strange and wild young man. Poor and proud. Impracticable, too. He relied upon his art for bread. And his art had failed him. Nor was it strange, from all that Ernest said. He had composed oratorios, and grand operas, and elaborate symphonies—all the heavy artillery of music. Ernest declared that genius had inspired them all—that unmistakable genius which rings clear and true. But an unknown young man cannot go into the market with a grand opera in his hand, and have it produced and paid for on the spot, especially when that young man is a crotchety young man, who has ideas of his own as to the way in which he wishes his work produced.

So Mr. Coursault found. Pupils he scorned. Ernest, for instance, had found him one or two. But his treatment of them was so extraordinary, that, as a matter of course, he lost them. He was never punctual. He kept them waiting hours. Sometimes he never came at all. And when he did appear he spent his breath, and exhausted a considerable vocabulary in reviling them for their musical incompetence and crass-headed ignorance. Young lady pupils, too, and in the presence of their mothers! Mrs. Jones told him that he need not call again, which was not strange of Mrs. Jones, who did not pay to have the pleasure of hearing her daughter rated as being lower than the beasts that grovel.

As I have said, my nephew was telling me about that friend of his as we were eating our dinner. My dining-room is under the drawing-room, and in the drawing-room we had left that three-and-sixpenny fiddle. While the fish was being removed we distinctly heard, above our heads, the sound of a violia. It was Ernest who heard it first.

"You have a musician in the house."

"A musician? What do you mean?"

For the change of themes was sudden. He was in the very middle of the story of his friend.

"Someone in the drawing-room is favouring us with a solo on the violin."

I listened It was as he said. The sound was unmistakable. Someone was fiddling while we dined.

"Which of your maids is a mistress of harmony?"

"I was not aware that I had such a paragon. It is the first I have heard of it." Just then Rouse came in with the entrée. "Rouse, who is in the drawing-room?"

The question appeared to surprise him.

"I am not aware, sir, that anyone is."

"There is someone. Go up, and see who it is."

Rouse went. Almost immediately the sound of playing ceased.

"Rouse has stopped the concert."

The man returned.

"Well, who was it?"

"No one, sir, is in the drawing-room."

"No one is, or no one was?"

"No one was, sir."

He smiled. I glanced at Ernest, and Ernest glanced at me. He seemed to be a trifle incredulous.

"Then who was that playing the violin?"

"I fancy, sir, that it must have been someone in the street."

If it was someone in the street then my ears had played me a curious trick. I thought it possible that Rouse was screening one of the maids. I chose to let it pass. I recurred to the subject of our conversation.

"Well, and about your friend?"

"He has disappeared."

"Disappeared?"

"Into thin air, like that performer on the violin." There was a suggestive twitching about the corners of Ernest's lips. I am afraid he thought that Rouse had been guilty of what may be politely termed a subterfuge. "More than a week ago he left his lodgings, with his violin-case in his hand, and he has not been heard of since. Ha! there is the performer back again."

There was. This time it sounded as though someone upstairs was tuning the violin.

"Rouse, who is upstairs?"

The man stood listening.

"I will go and see, sir. There was certainly no one there just now."

As before, the sound ceased almost directly he had left the room.

"Rouse has stopped the concert for the second time. Just as the fair musician was tuning up too!"

Ernest seemed to take it for granted that it was a maid. When Rouse reappeared in the room his bearing was a trifle disturbed.

"There was no one upstairs, sir. It must have been in the street."

I kicked at this.

"Come, Rouse, that won't do. Did it sound to you as though it were in the street?"

"It didn't, sir. But it must have been. There's no one upstairs, and the maids are all below. Besides, sir, there's no one in the house as plays the fiddle."

Ernest interposed. A smile was twinkling in his eyes.

"Where was the violin?"

"There's a violin-case upon the table, sir. I don't know if a violin is in it. The case is closed."

"I *left* it closed."

Ernest's tone was dry. I could see he had his doubts as to the man's veracity. Rouse has been in my service nearly thirty years, and I do not remember having once detected him in a lie. If he was screening anyone, I would have it out with him when my visitor had gone. I did not intend to humiliate a tried and faithful servant in the presence of my young gentleman. I returned to the erratic Mr. Coursault.

"I suppose when your friend disappeared he left a little bill behind."

"You little know Coursault! He had the most astonishing notions about money matters. Some time ago, when I knew he was in a tight place, I ventured to offer him a loan. I never ventured to repeat the offer."

"That sort of thing sounds very well, my boy, among boys! But *did* he leave a little bill?"

"Not a ghost of one. He paid up his week's lodging the very day he left. His landlady says that she believes he expended his last penny in doing so. She says, too, that she believes that he has been starving himself for weeks. I myself have noticed that he has become worn almost to a shadow. But, with such a man as that, what could you do? The more he needed help the farther he would shrink from it. In his uttermost extremity he would owe nothing, even to his dearest friend."

"Do you know his haunts?"

"I ought to—none better! But he has been seen nowhere, and by no one. As is the case with our friend upstairs, he has vanished into air."

I did not like the allusion myself. As for Rouse I saw he winced.

"Did this remarkable friend of yours burden himself with any portion of his baggage?"

"He took nothing but his violin."

"Was that his instrument?"

"All instruments were his. But it was his first love, and his last! He used to say of his violin that to him it was mother, father, wife, and friend."

As I was hesitating whether to smile at the folly of these young men Ernest half rose from his seat. He pointed upwards with his hand.

"Back again!"

As he put it the sound of the violin was back again.

"Listen! Don't trouble yourself, Rouse, to go upstairs and stop the concert, but stand a bit and listen. Let us hear of what metal the performer's made."

We listened the while Ernest held up his hand, as if commanding silence.

"Is that in the street?"

It did not *sound* as though it were. Ernest moved a little from the table.

"Come! let us go upstairs and surprise this fair musician. Possibly this is the case of a light which hitherto has shone unseen."

He went to the door. He opened it softly, so as to make no noise. With the handle in his hand he stood and listened.

"Hark! Let us hear what it is she, or he, is playing."

We all were silent, listening to the music, which came floating through the open door.

"Uncle!" Ernest turned to me. A startled look was on his face. "Surely—surely I know that air!"

It was strange to me. Quaint and sweet and mournful, like the refrain of an old-world song. I would I were a musician. I would write it here.

"It is a thing of Coursault's!"

Suddenly Ernest threw the door wide open. He went into the hall.

I went with him, amused at his eagerness. We stood at the foot of the stairs and listened.

"Do you mean that it is a composition of the friend of whom you have been telling me?"

"I do. I'll swear to it! I've heard him playing it!"

"Then, possibly, he has attained to greater fame than he imagines."

"But it's unpublished. Uncle, Coursault is upstairs!"

He grasped my arm with a degree of force which was a little disconcerting.

"Nonsense! Your friend would scarcely carry his eccentricity so far as to enter, uninvited and unannounced, the house of a perfect stranger—that is, unless he is burglariously inclined."

"I know his touch. Do you think that anyone but a master could play like that?"

It was fine playing. Very soft and delicate, but instinct with a strength, and a force, and a passion, which was perceptible even at our post of disadvantage at the foot of the stairs. A street musician would scarcely play like that—and a parlour-maid!

"It is one of his freaks. He has heard that I was here, and thought he would surprise me. The presence of the violin upon the table was a temptation beyond his strength—it is the man all over! Uncle, let's turn the tables—we'll surprise him!"

He, began gingerly to ascend the stairs. I followed a step or two behind. About half-way up he stopped.

"I call that playing!"

So did I. As we mounted higher the sound was clearer. The voice of the violin was sweeter than any human voice I ever heard. Unwilling as I was to be disturbed at dinner —the food spoiling on the table!—I could not but acknowledge that, as Ernest said, it was the hand of a master which held that bow. A moment, listening, we paused; then again ascended. Sweeter and sweeter grew the music, until, just as we reached the uppermost stair, all at once it ceased.

"He has heard us! But, never mind, he can't escape us."

Ernest rushed forward. He threw the door wide open. He entered the room.

"Coursault! Philip! Hallo! Why—there's no one there!"

There did not seem to be. I followed pretty close upon my enthusiastic nephew's heels. The room was empty.

"He's in hiding. Come, you rogue, where are you? We know you're here, Philip. Do you think I don't know your touch, and that queer song of yours? Come out, you beggar! Why, wherever can he be?"

Yes, where? My drawing-room contains no screen, no cupboard. Not an article of furniture behind which even a child could hide. Ernest, in his impetuous way, scoured round the room. It was empty. I confess that I was puzzled. We both of us stared round and round the room as though staring would resolve the mystery. Rouse was standing in the doorway. He, apparently, had taken French leave, and followed us upstairs. He spoke.

"There wasn't no one in the room when I came up just now. It was the same with me. I heard the fiddling most distinct as I was coming up the stairs; when I reached the landing it stopped. I made sure that whoever it was had heard me, and I should find him in the room; but when I opened the door there wasn't no one there. You see, sir, although it didn't sound as though it was, it must have been in the street."

"In the street, you idiot! Do you think I'm deaf?"

I mildly interposed—

"But, my dear fellow, there is the violin in its case upon the table. It doesn't look to me as if the case had even been opened."

Ernest made a dash at it. He opened the lid. He took out the fiddle. As he did so he gave a start which was quite dramatic. He stared at it as though he had never seen such a thing as a fiddle before.

"It's Coursault's violin!"

His exclamation startled me. Coursault's violin! It re-minded me of Mr. Box's remark to Mr. Cox, "Have you a strawberry mark on your left arm?" "No." "Then you are—*you are* my long-lost brother." The recognition was too opportune.

"Come, Ernest! Ernest! don't strain the thing too far. You recognise it, I presume, by the catgut and the bridge."

Ernest paid no heed to my admittedly feeble attempt at chaff. I am no great hand at badinage. He continued to hold the fiddle in front of him with both his hands, glar-ing at it as if it were a ghost

"It's Coursault's violin. I thought I knew it when I saw it first I know it now. It's Philip's!"

"How do you know it's Philip's?"

He did not directly answer me. Placing the fiddle very carefully upon the table, he stood for a moment in appar-ent agitation.

"Uncle, there is some mystery. Don't laugh at me!" I daresay I was smiling. "Something has happened to Cour-sault."

"From the character you have given the man the thing is very possible, and *still* there may be no mystery."

"Some time ago Coursault wrote the words of a little song, which he set to music. The thing was in commem-oration of certain pleasant days which he and I had spent

together. I am nearly certain that no one ever heard of
its existence except we two. He called it 'Where the Willows cast their Shade.' It is that which we have just heard
played."

"'Where the Willows cast their Shade'—rather a curious title for a song; but, even in titles, curiosities seem to
be the mode. Are you sure it was the same?"

"Am I sure! It was the quaintest thing—like all he
wrote, even the merest trifles, peculiarly characteristic. Is
it not strange that I should hear Coursault's song, whose
very existence was known only to him and to me, played
on Coursault's violin?"

I stared.

"Do you mean to say that the man has been in this
room, and at our approach, to use your own phrase, vanished into air?"

Ernest became preternaturally grave; he is the funniest
lad.

"Uncle, strange things have happened."

"They have. As witness my being disturbed in the middle of my dinner. How on earth do you know that that
three-and-sixpenny affair is Coursault's violin?"

"That is easily solved. We will go to the shop at which
you bought it, and ascertain from whom they got it."

We went, there and then, with the dinner not half-eat-
en. Rouse must have had doubts about my sanity. I have
declared, not once, but a hundred times, that not for the
Queen of England would I be disturbed at dinner. Yet, before we had even eaten the entrée, that young man—whom
I had invited to dinner—dragged me from my own house
on a dirty night, and put me into a hansom, and drove me
through the slums of London in search of a rag-shop. As
the vehicle rattled over the stones I reflected upon what
could be brought about by the expenditure of such a sum
as three-and-sixpence—the rule of a lifetime shattered at
a blow! The cabman could not find the street. I did not
know its name; how I originally chanced on it is more than

I can say. I am not in the *habit* of wandering in the pur-
lieus of Lisson Grove. We went poking out of one hole and
into another. I should think we must have penetrated at
least half a dozen when, just as I really believe the cabman
was on the point of insulting us, we lighted, not only on
the street, but on the shop as well.

The lady was in—the *same* lady. A little dirtier, perhaps, but still the same. My nephew conducted the nego-
tiations.

"We have called about a violin which this gentleman
purchased here this afternoon."

The lady stared at us with a watery, a gin-and-watery, eye.

"Could you tell me from whom you got it?"

The lady's response was oracular.

"Perhaps I could, and perhaps I couldn't."

"The fact is that I have reason to believe that it belonged to a friend of mine, whose whereabouts I am very
anxious to discover."

"That don't make no odds to me."

"But it makes considerable odds to me. Such odds that
I am willing to give half a sovereign if you will tell me
from whom you got it. If, for instance, he was a stranger
to you, could you describe his appearance?"

"Well, I could, and that's sacred truth. Good reason I
have to remember him."

"Indeed?"

Ernest's tone was sympathetic

"'Cause I gave more for that there fiddle than what I
sold it for."

"I should think that you are hardly in the habit of doing that, are you?"

Perhaps this time there was the suspicion of a sarcastic
intonation.

"I ain't. I shouldn't make much of a living if I was,
should I? I don't mind saying it now I've sold the thing,
but that there fiddle ain't all there."

"Do you mean that part of it is missing?"

"No, I don't. I don't believe in ghostesses, nor none of them there rubbishes, but if there ain't a ghost about that there fiddle, I never heard of one."

I glanced at Ernest; Ernest glanced at me. The lady continued.

"It's got a trick of playing tunes all by itself, when there ain't no one there to play 'em."

"No one there to play them! Of course, you're joking."

"I ain't joking. I ain't a joking sort." (To do her justice, I am bound to own that she didn't look as though she were.) "The very first night it played a tune, and it's played the same tune every blessed night since it's been in the shop."

"The same tune—always the same? Would you know it if you heard it?"

"I ought to. I've heard it often enough, Lord knows; and I ain't over and above anxious to hear it again."

"Is this it?"

Ernest whistled a little air. It was the same which we had heard being played as we were ascending the stairs. Quite an uncomfortable change took place in the lady's bearing. Hardly had Ernest whistled a couple of notes than, with a sort of groan, she shrank back against the wall.

"That's it! Stop it! It gives me creeps and crawlers!"

"Now, tell me, from what sort of person did you purchase the violin?"

"A little chap, about up to your shoulder—the queerest-looking little chap ever I see. He had long black hair, and big eyes—ah, as big as bull's-eye lanterns!—and that there wild, they made him look stark mad. He was that there thin—anybody could see he hadn't had a square meal for a month of Sundays. He says, 'What'll you give me for my fiddle?' I wondered if it was a swap that he was after. 'Do you mean how much money?' I says. 'Yes,' he says; 'how much money?' 'I'll give you five bob,' I says. 'Five bob!—for my fiddle!' He gives a kind of laugh, though it wasn't the sort of laugh what did you good to hear, not by no manner of means. 'I'll take it,' he says. So, after all, she hadn't given so much more for the thing than she had sold it for. "I was took back. Course I see it was worth more than five bob. But it wasn't my business to tell him so—'ardly! I hands him the pieces. 'Let me play a last tune upon my fiddle,' he says. He picks it up, and he plays that same tune which you've just now whistled. He could play, he could! Then he kisses the fiddle and he goes away."

The lady paused; we stood silent.

"I puts the fiddle on that shelf just where you're standing. That night I woke up sudden. I couldn't make out what it was had woke me. Then I heard a noise. First I thought it was cats. But it wasn't no cats; it was someone fiddling, right in the shop! 'Well,' I says, 'blame their impudence, if someone ain't busted in.' So I comes downstairs without my shoes and stockings on, and I stands outside the door what leads into the shop, and I listens. If it wasn't the same tune the little chap had played! 'If this ain't good,' I says to myself. 'Blow me if he ain't come back after his fiddle! I'll fiddle him!' I has the lamp in my hand, and I opens the door sudden, and I goes in."

The lady paused.

"You may believe me or you mayn't, but there wasn't no one there—ne'er a one. I couldn't make it out, I tell you that. As I was going forward I all but steps upon the fiddle and the bow what's a lying on the floor. 'Now then,' I says; 'where's the party as put you there?' Believe me, or believe me not, there wasn't a creature in the place. It ain't a large shop, you see, and I routs in every corner. I looks at the window and the door. The shutters was up, and the door was locked and bolted just as I left it I thought it queer; but I thought it queerer when the same thing comes the next night, and the next, and the next. It preys upon my mind so, not being used to nor yet partial to ghostesses and such-like rubbishes, that I says to myself, I'll get rid of the thing, even if I does it at a loss."

As we were going away I said to Ernest—

"Rather a curious story that of the lady's."

Ernest was sitting back in the cab. He seemed to be lost in reflecting.

"Very." There was a momentary silence. "I told you it was Coursault's violin. That was Philip, the queer little man with the long black hair and the great big eyes. I used to half fear sometimes that in those big eyes genius was struggling with insanity; he was at times so strange. 'Starved for a month of Sundays'—Philip! What a wrench to have parted with his violin—how bitterly he must have been amused by her offer of five shillings. He played his last tune and kissed it—Philip!"

We dismissed the cabman at the corner of the square. The night had become fine. We walked together towards my house. We were distant from it, perhaps, twenty yards, when Ernest, pausing, laid his hand upon my arm.

"Listen!" There is little traffic in the square at night. All was still. "He is playing!"

For a second or two I did not grasp my nephew's meaning. But, as I strained my ears to catch the slightest sound, I understood it better, for I caught the sound of a fiddle. It was very faint, so faint as to be scarcely audible. But it was unmistakable.

"Come," said Ernest; "let us go nearer."

We approached the house. In front of it we paused. Beyond doubt the music came from within, and from an upper room; the same quaint melody which we had heard before, played by a master's hand.

"I wonder why he always plays that tune?"

I was unable to supply the information. Frankly, I was becoming a little bewildered. With the lady at the rag-shop, I had no faith in "ghostesses and such-like rubbishes," but the thing was getting curious.

I opened the front door with my latchkey. An unusual spectacle greeted us as we entered the hall. All the maids were grouped together in a little crowd, guarded, as it were, by the stalwart Rouse. There was no necessity to ask the cause—it was the music in the drawing-room. Rouse, however, seemed to think that an explanation was required.

"It's not my fault, sir; I couldn't get them to stop in the kitchen. They seem to think that there's a spirit, sir, upstairs. The playing has been going on for half an hour and more."

"Don't let me have any nonsense. I'm ashamed of you. Are you afraid of a fiddle?"

The cook ventured on a meek remonstrance.

"It isn't the fiddle, sir; it's the fiddler."

I drove them down; Rouse, in his sheepishness, almost treading on the women's petticoats. Then I turned to Ernest.

"I, like the lady we have just been interviewing, am not partial to ghosts. With your permission, this time I will lead the way upstairs."

I led the way, Ernest following closely after. The music continued—always the same quaint air. It was pretty; but the player must have found that the absence of variety became a trifle monotonous. On this occasion, even when we reached the landing, there was no cessation. The fiddler still fiddled.

"Apparently we have managed to remain unheard. Now for your eccentric friend."

With a quick movement I opened the drawing-room door. Ernest and I entered almost side by side. For an instant, after our entrance, the playing continued. I saw that the violin was raised, I saw that the bow was being drawn across the strings. But who held the violin, and who handled the bow, there was no evidence—visual evidence—to prove. If we could trust our eyes, the room was empty. All at once, before we could say a word, or offer any sort of interposition, the playing ceased. The violin and the bow were placed upon the table—not dropped, but laid carefully down. And all was still.

II

The next day there was a small party on the river. The party consisted of three: an old gentleman—a complacent old gentleman, who carried his complacence so far as to allow himself to be cast for the rôle of "gooseberry"; a young gentleman, his nephew; and, not to put too fine a point on it, a young lady. This young lady's name was Minnie— Minnie West. There is reason to suspect that she was the cause of the party.

We started—it is probably unnecessary to observe that I was the complacent old gentleman—from Hurley, and we paddled up the stream—that is to say, Ernest paddled, the young lady steered, and I looked on. We kept it up some time, this paddling; but at last Ernest drew the boat into the shore. We landed—a hamper and ourselves. We lunched under the shade of the trees.

While we lunched Ernest persisted—persisted is the word—in conversing on a subject which was scarcely appropriate either to the occasion or the scene—the subject of his lost friend and his phantom violin. One does not wish to dwell on morbid subjects when one is lunching by the crystal waters; but Ernest, apparently, did not see it; and, oddly enough, what he did not see, it seemed that Miss West could not see either. When we had finished, and done justice to the fare, the young gentleman asked a question.

"Do you know why I have brought you here?"

Really the question did not need an answer. The reply was evident. The spot was charming. Sufficient shade above, mossy verdure underneath, and all around us, except upon the river side, tall bracken, which completely obscured us from the vulgar gaze. Ernest supplied an answer of his own.

"Do you remember that air which we heard played upon the violin? Do you remember that I told you it was a song of Coursault's, which he called, 'Where the Willows cast

their Shade'? I told you, too, that it was written to com-
memorate some pleasant days which we had spent together. Those pleasant days were spent upon the river, and the
pleasantest of all those pleasant days were spent where we
are now."

"Ernest!"

As she called upon the young man's name the lady gave
a little shudder. It must be allowed that his manner was
distinctly somber.

"It was a favourite place with him. He used to rave
about it in that raving way of his. He used to say that here
he would like to die and be buried. He came here often
when he was alone, and it was here he wrote that song. You
see it is here that the willows cast their shade."

He raised his hand with a gesture which was distinctly
gruesome. Looking up I noticed, for the first time, that
the trees above us were willow trees.

"I wonder why it is that the violin always plays that
song?"

And there came an echo from the young lady—

"I wonder!"

As she echoed the young gentleman's interrogation she
leaned back against the tree—a willow tree—and put her
hand behind her to pluck the bracken. She had to stretch
out some distance to do this. Suddenly she withdrew her
hand with a half-stifled exclamation.

"What's the matter?" inquired the younger gentleman.

He wore quite an appearance of concern, being still in
that stage in which a tight shoe upon the lady's foot would
give him corns. Most transitory stage—too sweet to last!

"I—I thought I touched something."

She looked startled. She put her hand behind her rather
more gingerly than she had done before. Instantly she
sprang to her feet in a state of most unmistakable dismay.

"Ernest, there is someone there! I touched his hand."

She stood, trembling all over, a pretty picture of distress—in tan shoes and a white piqué gown.

"What do you mean?" cried Ernest

"You are dreaming," murmured I.

We rose together. But he was the quicker. Going behind the willow tree, he parted the bracken with his hands.

"There is, by George! What are you doing there, sir? Are you drunk? Why—" He stooped down. "Good God! He's dead!"

Suddenly, with a loud cry, he fell upon his knees.

"It's Coursault!" . . .

It was. Lying dead among the bracken—"Where the Willows cast their Shade."

We thought at first that he had been the victim of foul play. But subsequent medical examination showed that he had died of aneurism of the heart, brought on by want of nourishment—in other words, starvation—and physical exhaustion. He was nothing else but skin and bone, and it appeared that he had walked from London—it almost seemed without taking rest or food upon his way, for the identical five shillings were found in his pockets for which he had sold his violin.

The supposition was that when he had sold his violin, and played on it his last tune, he had started, possibly in some spirit of half-madness, for the identical spot which that tune commemorated, and had reached it but to die.

On the previous evening, after that final solo with which we had been favoured by the unseen musician I had placed the violin and the bow in the case, and the case upon the topmost bookshelf in my library. When I came home from that river party an accident had happened. The case had fallen from the book-shelf to the floor. In falling, the lid had opened—the violin had tumbled out. The result was that the instrument, which must have struck with surprising force against some piece of furniture, had been shivered into splinters. These we collected, and with the bow, which was also broken, we placed in Philip Coursault's coffin. The dead man and his fiddle were lowered together into the gave.

"FROM THE SMALLER ORGAN RAVED UP A PANDEMONIUM OF . . . GHOULISH
EXECRATIONS."

The Canonic Curse
Arthur E. McFarlane
(1902)

At the request of my friend, Bruce Carrington, Jr., and the lady soon to become his wife, I herewith unreservedly give to the public the detailed account of their recent amazing and horrible experience. The sensational guesses and wildly distorted half-truths appearing unceasingly in certain New York yellow journals have made this course a bitter necessity. As to the matter contained in the narrative—and the plain baldness of my style should make it sufficiently evident that whatever of the "flesh-creeping" enters into it, enters only because I have been unable to exclude it—I own as I set it down that I find myself ready to doubt my own sanity. That the "devil-bought" soul of a Flemish kapellmeister should be able to reach out from the Middle Ages and set a dead hand upon a Harvard graduate in the first year of the twentieth century is, I confess, something wholly impossible and incredible. Indeed, only the fact that for years I have known Carrington for one of the most cool-headed and least credulous of young New Yorkers could induce me to have anything to do with his story at all.

I

From the time his organ studies introduced him to it, Carrington had made medieval music his hobby. Throughout his law course at Harvard he was constantly ransacking

both the college and the Boston library for everything
bearing upon the subject; and every bar written by the old
monkish composers seemed to have an irresistible fascination for him. In fact, when he graduated and entered the
office of his father's firm, it is probable that he was more
familiar with canons and fugues, counterpoint and Gregorian chants than he was with Coke and Blackstone. And
that summer of 1901 he had definitely made up his mind
to spend his holidays among the famous musical libraries
of Belgium and Northern Italy, when a letter from his
chum Keppel suddenly turned his eyes from the Continent
and sent him to Canada instead. Keppel was working up
his "Ph.D." in the great Parisian library, the Bibliothèque
Internationale, and the postscript of the letter read:—

> "By the way, old man, if you're still as big an
> old-music crank as ever, something I came on
> the other day ought to interest you mightily.
> It seems that when Louis XIV. took Liege in
> 1659 and rifled the abbey, he sent the whole
> choir library over to his Sulpician favorites
> in Quebec, and there's nothing to show that
> it was ever returned. Is any such collection
> known to you? If not, why don't you go and
> look it up?"

It certainly was *not* known to Carrington, nor in his
knowledge to any other "old-music crank." It was the beginning of the June hot spell; the law business was dead,
and the Carrington mansion on Madison Avenue a seven-
times heated furnace. On the following Monday the young
fellow was off for Canada.

From the beginning the Sulpician fathers were kindness
itself. "They were most highly honored that M. Carrington
should have come all the way from New York to see their
library. They believed it did contain a large number of
old musical manuscripts, though they had never done

anything toward sorting and arranging them. But, most unfortunately, their father superior was just at that time on a visit to their brethren in Montreal, and—they regretted it exceedingly—they could not admit him to their library without his authority. He might return almost any day. Could not M. Carrington wait? And if he could, would he not help himself to pass the time by making use of their organs? In the outside chapel attached to their foundation they had two which the musicians of the city had been pleased to praise not a little. Until the father superior should return, M. Carrington must look upon them as his own."

He accepted their kindly and novel hospitality as freely as it was proffered, and for the next few days he was in and out of the little chapel again and again. The big oriel organ was a revelation of swelling strength and billowy harmonies. And the smaller one, perched high in the loft opposite, made up in sweetness what it lacked in power. The young New Yorker and Father Laurence, the Sulpician organist, were soon the best of friends. Often in the afternoon when vespers were over the latter would take the larger instrument, and Carrington the other, and for a long hour they would play in unison, or in a kind of antiphonal, musical conversation.

Thus it was that when, one evening, Carrington entered the chapel and found the big organ rolling its melodious tide through the dusky aisles, he slipped quietly upstairs in the darkness, and joined him on the smaller instrument. He had never heard the father play so brilliantly before. In turn they set variations on each other's themes, and then as challengingly improvised on each other's variations; and every moment Carrington found it harder to follow the flying fingers of the old Sulpician. At last, outmastered royally, he struck a wailing discord of unconditional surrender, and stopped playing. From the obscurity of the other loft he was answered by a startled shriek of mingled fright and amusement. He ran wonderingly downstairs.

His antiphonist descended in a panic. Even in the chapel gloom she was a vision of soft and radiant beauty.

With one voice they broke into the same explanation: each had mistaken the other for Father Laurence. She, too, together with three or four other musicians of the city, enjoyed the freedom of the organs. She, too, had often played against the skill of the reverend organist! They both went into a common burst of badly smothered laughter, though all the time the girl was biting her lips in an attempt to sober herself to a proper decorum.

When they turned a minute later they found Father Laurence himself standing in the doorway behind them; and, if anything, he was enjoying the situation more than either of them. But he came hastily to the rescue and introduced them. "Mlle. La Shelle, permit me to present M. Carrington, a famous musical scholar of New York. Monsieur, mademoiselle is the daughter of our neighbor, Colonel La Shelle, who, though he is not of our faith, is our very dear friend. The Colonel is, like yourself, an American, a distinguished engineer of New Orleans. But for five years now the harbor work he is doing for us has made him our fellow-citizen, and we could well wish to keep him forever." He pointed over the greensward. "Between his mansion and our chapel there is, as you see, neither hedge nor wall, and mademoiselle honors us by permitting our brotherhood to provide her with a second music-room!"

They chatted with the smiling father for a few minutes longer; then, with Miss La Shelle's permission, Carrington walked with her across the lawn to the lamp-lit corner of her father's long French veranda.

II

When, an hour afterward, the young fellow took his leave the world was changed for him. If ever a man had recognized the "one woman" at the first meeting of the eyes, it was true of him. And with the girl, too, the feeling was no less intense and overwhelming. It seemed to them that somehow they had known each other from the beginning of things. When they parted they gazed into each other's eyes in a kind of mutual wonderment. And that night Carrington dreamed that they were again in the chapel organ-lofts building up together a world of glorious harmonies. And when Eloise La Shelle awakened all space and time was antiphonal of the young New Yorker.

There were, too, happily enough, bonds between Carrington and the old Colonel. For not only did they smoke the same tobacco, but the old gentleman's hobby, applied psychology—especially that strange gate of the science which opens upon spiritism, mental telepathy, occultism and the like—had been something which, in his Harvard course, had taken a grip of Carrington only less strong than the fascination of his old music. When he called again on the following evening the two men talked on the cool veranda for hours after the girl had left them, and they parted with the frank hand-grasp of sudden but thorough comradeship. It made the position of the lovers almost idyllic. Carrington called again the next day and the next. And when at the end of the week the forgotten father superior returned, and a notification that the young fellow's request for the freedom of the library had been granted suddenly recalled him to his original business in Quebec, he was filled with the most melancholy regret that the worthy father could not have prolonged his stay in Montreal for the remainder of the year.

But he had not been fifteen minutes in the low-roofed north wing of the old monastery library before he changed his mind. If the hours away from Eloise La Shelle could be anywhere endurable it would be in that treasure-house to which he had now the key. Any other collection in America was the merest pigeonhole of parchment beside it. There was shelf on shelf weighed down with ponderous volumes, twice the size of any modern quarto, pricelessly bound in stamped and gilded leather, ribbed and bossed, escutcheoned and brass-clamped. And when Carrington opened them their gorgeously illuminated title pages almost kept him from going further into their wealth of fugues and masses, canons, chants and counterpoint. As for the smaller volumes and unbound manuscripts, they were piled together, thick with dust, in hundreds. Morning after morning the young man ran his eyes along the uncouth, red-lined staves with their huge, square black notes, and turned over the yellow pages, dog-eared and finger-marked four hundred years ago. And, by the kind leave of the superior, almost every afternoon he brought a new armful of his treasure-trove to try over, often with Miss La Shelle beside him, on one of the chapel organs.

On Friday of that week he came upon a manuscript which drew his attention in a moment. It had been folded and doubled on itself, wrapped in parchment somewhat heavier than the common sort, and curiously bound with thongs like many knotted bowstrings. On the back of it was seared a rude but unmistakable devil's head, and the whole was sealed with the huge wafer of the prince-bishop of Liege. The father superior was once more generous and Carrington was given permission to open it. He carried it out into the chapel to Eloise, cut one of the thongs, slit the end of the parchment wrapper, and drew it forth.

It was a canon, one of that ingenious kind which the old monkish composers termed per tonos on account of their manner of modulating to the key of the note above, with each repetition rising gradually in a sort of frenzy until the circuit of keys is completed. And it was evident at a glance that it was not ordinary music. "Try it," said the young fellow.

The girl hesitated.

"I believe somebody's afraid of that horrific Satan's head."

She laughed, though not in a way that concealed her uneasy aversion, and began to play. She had not finished the first phrase before she stopped with a little shiver.

"You'll say it's my nerves, but really there *is* something uncanny about it. It acts on me like a ghost story. Do put the thing back and get something else."

Carrington chuckled delightedly, and took her place before it at the organ. The composition seemed to be a kind of blasphemy in music! It had all the stateliness of the mass, yet behind that lurked a burden strangely sardonic and sacrilegious. It might well have been written under the influence of some soul-depraving drug. And, what was incredible, if it had been, the baleful power which gave it birth still hung about it! Carrington might laugh crazily, and play on, but he could feel a cold sweat gathering on his forehead. A thick tent and curtain of oppression seemed slowly to draw in about him. Miss La Shelle's troubled protests came to him thin and far on the other side of it. And when at last he had finished the canon, and once more looked up, it struck him as strange that if she had been all the time so close to him she had not touched him! But other than to acknowledge that the music had affected him as it had affected her he said nothing, and in irritation at his own weakness tried to put the matter aside.

III

Carrington took dinner with the La Shelles that evening. Eloise had been nervously telling her father of their eerie experience of the afternoon, and the old student of applied psychology was still chuckling hugely over it when the young man was announced. "Well, sir," he said bluffly, "I guess there's a pretty straight case of hypnotic suggestion against you. It evidently acted first through the visual image—I refer to the devil's head; then through the auditory image, for I suppose a musician can find anything in music he's looking for, and, more than all, you were affected through the fear-sensations already in the mind of another. I refer finally to the spook-hunting little goose opposite me. You are probably of an extremely nervous, and what the hypnotists call susceptive, temperament, sir!"

Carrington shook his head in smiling but decided negation. "No, Colonel, no. I'm afraid I can't support you in that at all. When a youngster I was a confirmed sleepwalker, and on one occasion, being violently awakened, was given a shock which brought on brain-fever; indeed, I own that the specialists in charge warned my people that any repetition of such a shock might easily prove fatal. But you could hardly cite that as a fair or normal instance. And since then I have had absolutely no experience which would not go as evidence that I am of an extremely phlegmatic and unsusceptible temperament. I can read all the ghost stories in the calendar without turning a hair. I have attended spiritualistic séances a dozen times, and invariably came away disappointed and contemptuous. And I have been the only one of twenty Harvard freshmen to completely resist the power of a famous mesmerist."

The Colonel bit his mustache. "Yet you say that you did actually experience certain sensations of the uncanny while playing this—this banshee music?"

"Yes," said Carrington doggedly, "I did!"

"And you deny my hypothesis of hypnotic suggestion?"

"I'm afraid I must."

"Very well!" and the old gentleman set his finger-tips hard together. "Then isn't it possible, now, for us to go straight ahead and put this thing to the proof? Considering that I am as wholly skeptical of all musical 'haunts' as this girl of mine here seems to be credulous of them, if I were to go over with you to that organ loft, and stand beside you while you played that canon, and you were then, under those altered conditions, to find yourself experiencing no peculiar or uncanny sensations whatever, would that change your opinion, sir?"

Carrington laughed. "It certainly would!"

Eloise was alarmed in a moment. "Now, father, you're not—"

"Yes, indeed, now, daughter, but I just am! When vespers are over, if Mr. Carrington is willing to try it, you may accompany us and see how in a ten-minute experiment a little modern science may shed a vast deal of new light on the ghostly and supernatural."

IV

An hour later they were all three crossing the lawn through the dusk. The empty chapel was in darkness. The girl stopped at the door. "Father, Mr. Carrington, I know how silly I must seem to you, but why could you not leave this experiment till to-morrow? You would at least have the daylight then."

Her lover hesitated irresolutely, but the Colonel laughed bluntly and ordered him forward. "Eloise," he said, "I give you up. You're no daughter of mine. We shall go on without you." He pushed Carrington ahead. They groped their way up the stairs to the smaller instrument. The young fellow lit the organ tapers, drew the devil's-head canon from the back of one of the old-fashioned carved music-racks and began to play. The old man stood beside him, leaning on the loft railing; by the uncertain light of the candles he was watching his face with the eyes of a nerve specialist. To the music itself he had no thought of giving any heed whatever.

But he did give heed to it. Something in the first bars went to his brain like a swift, monstrous and malignant anaesthetic. Startled into an astounded resistance he clenched his hands upon the rail behind him and gazed steadfastly at one of the candle flames. It grew smaller and smaller. The black darkness closed and intensified about it like a burning pain, and suddenly it seemed to the Colonel that the flame was his own soul. He tore his eyes from it, and fastened them upon the face of the young man. His lips were lifted in a grin of fear and horror. His hands played on as if he had no longer had any power over them, as if his wrists had been grasped by some infernal gymnotus, some frightfully compelling current from the pit. And as the candle flames contracted to glimmering pin-points, the lines of his head and shoulders were picked out in a bluish, prickling "witch-fire," in the phosphorescence of a hellish halo.

The old man's soul filled with the terrible feeling that his reason, his identity, his life were slowly going from him. The satanic music seemed to be coming at him from utter darkness. In a desperation of terror he fought against it. He could still get the sensation of his fingers galvanically closing and unclosing upon the railing. He writhed and put forth his strength like another Laocoon. He once more got his eyes open. Carrington's face shone out a white knot of terror and agony. He was still chained to his bench of torture. The music mocked and triumphed over them, mercilessly, infuriately. Heart and brain seemed pressed together by the weight of millions of tons. Upon the old man's ears burst the thunderous clangor of a thousand great discordant bells. The candle flames were now huge as the lanterns of lighthouses; then, swiftly and frightfully, they began to fall away till they were no larger than two blind and staring eyes. The music was fast approaching its outrageous end. The candles shrank and cowered lower and lower, and with the last horrible note went out. Shriek on shriek burst from Carrington's bloodless lips. The old man dropped fainting beside him.

The hysterical screams of the girl at the chapel door brought a hurrying company of gray-robed Sulpicians. When they were able partly to comprehend her, trembling and crossing themselves, they climbed into the organ-loft, and bore down the senseless forms of the Colonel and the young man.

V

By the following day the Colonel and his daughter were almost themselves again. But Carrington, lying in the La Shelle guest chamber, passed from a state of coma into a raging delirium. His father was instantly summoned from New York, and for a week he and the wretched conscience-smitten Colonel watched in turn beside him. But all went well. The fever gradually burned itself out. And at the end of the third week the young fellow, though weak as a baby, was on his way to recovery. Eloise was with him almost more than the trained nurse, and before his father left them their engagement was formally announced.

The fortnight which followed was full of quiet but no less rapturous happiness for both of them. The girl tended him with a doting solicitude almost maternal. He was to eat just so much. He was to go to bed at such an hour. And she withheld his mail for days after the doctor had assured her that he might have it with perfect safety; but one hot August evening after dinner when he was sitting on the veranda in his invalid's dressing-gown, looking rather wistfully at the setting sun, she suddenly took pity on him, and brought forth the big, variegated bundle of doubly post-marked envelopes. If she could have guessed the contents of almost the first she opened for him he would never have seen it. It was from his chum Keppel, and he was still working in the great Paris library. Carrington had not read a dozen lines before his face began to change. The letter ran as follows:—

"Dear Old Man:—I don't know whether or not you took my tip about running up to Quebec on a hunt for that old music from Liege. Maybe you've been there already, and come back in disgust. But if you haven't, I've dug up something this last week which ought to send you up there by the next train. I can't give you more than a hint of the thing, though I've already found a good-sized volume of old Flemish chronicles, consistory reports and the like bearing upon the case.

"But it seems that in the early part of the fifteenth century in Flanders some of the kapellmeisters got to setting words to their religious compositions which were anything but sacred. And the matter finally grew to be such a scandal that the prince-bishop stepped in and forbade ten of the worst offenders ever again to touch an organ or to write another line of music of any sort whatsoever. Well, as it happened, one of them, Domenico by name, had a good deal of true music in him for all its dubious outward complexion, and he went on composing in secret. And, as sometimes happens, too, he began to do his finest work under the adverse conditions.

"But he could hope to hear it played only by passing it over to another. And when at last he could hold out no longer he took his successor into his confidence and delivered to him everything he had completed. That individual played it with all the willingness in the world. And he took all the credit for the compositions, too; indeed, I don't see how he could well have done anything else. At any rate while his glory began to go forth through the whole country this Domenico became more and more forgotten. And that seemed in the end to send the man almost out of his mind with rage and envy. He wound up one night by taking the medieval way out of it, and offered his soul to the devil for a chance to get even. Next morning his successor received from him a canon which had the pleasant little attribute of being able to hand out a sudden quietus to any one who should play it through three times, and, to clinch it, to any one, too, who should wittingly destroy it. Those things make curious reading nowadays, don't they? However, the tradition finishes with most circumstantial gruesomeness.

Two nights later the man was found dead before his organ, his face distorted as if from
some fiendish torture. Domenico's hatred of
him, if not the real cause of it, was generally
known. He came under suspicion, was put on
the rack, and confessed.

"The consistory condemned him to be
broken on the wheel and flayed. And shortly
before his execution they branded him over
the heart with the 'devil's head.' To crown it
all, after his death they used the skin from
his breast to wrap his canon in, and tied it
up with the sinews of his wrists. Then finally
the bedeviled music was given the curse of the
prince-bishop and laid away by itself in the
choir library.

"Now, while you possibly may not feel inclined to accept the story in its entirety, there
probably was among that Liege music a canon
with some such tradition attached to it. And
if there was it is not altogether unlikely that
it is now in Quebec. At any rate, whether you
give yourself any worry over your side of it
or not, there's a regular second edition of the
'Faust Legend' in it for me."

Carrington looked long at the letter. The girl watched
him with eyelids aquiver with anxiety. "What was done
with that—that canon?" he asked at last. They had never
spoken of it since that hour of never-to-be-forgotten horror in the chapel.

"Father has it in his safe," she answered trembling. "But
you know you mustn't talk about that, dearest."

"Oh, it's all right now," he said. "It's only a matter—a
matter of what the impossible thing might have done. I'd
like to look at it again."

She was still refusing him when her father came out to them, and she left it to him. Carrington passed him over the letter.

He read it, let himself dazedly down into a chair, sat slowly licking his tongue about his lips, and then read it again. "But, good gracious, Carrington," he finally broke out, "this is America, and the year 1901! I have a telephone in my library. You can see the railroad station from the back of the garden. I can't—we're not—good heavens, sir!"

"Yes," said Carrington grimly, "it certainly is hard to reconcile such a tale with modern science and enlightenment."

"But it's asking me to believe in—what is it they called it—diabology or satanophany? Why, the words themselves have been all but dead for a hundred years!" He wiped the perspiration from under his mop of gray hair.

The young man smiled and put the argument aside. "Well, I suppose we can safely look at the thing again, anyway."

In an instant Eloise was again entreating him, but her father overbore her. "Why, daughter, he's already had the excitement of reading the letter. To handle the music can add nothing to it." He strode into the library, unlocked his safe, and brought out the satanic canon. They examined it for several minutes without speaking.

The grisly thongs which bound it, and the hideous outer covering, a sort of softer and more open fibered parchment, had in them now a new and more horrid power of repulsion. But the music when unfolded looked forth vacantly and harmlessly.

"And it's so simple," muttered Carrington breathlessly. "I can't see where— There aren't twenty bars of theme in the whole thing. It's only the repetitions in it that give it its length. I could play it now from memory without the slightest difficulty!"

"Oh, but dearest, you wouldn't, you surely—" Eloise, had just laid down Keppel's letter. She was white to the lips and trembled violently. "I want you to swear to me that you'll never even let yourself think of the thing again, let alone play it!"

He looked at her with wan humor. "Well, I guess, dear, I needn't promise not to play it again, anyway. It seems to be a case of 'three strokes and out,' you know, and it came near enough to getting me the second time."

He slipt his hand over hers. The Colonel rose with the canon, and carried it back into the library. Left alone with her lover the frightened girl cuddled into his breast, and to coax his mind from the subject of her fears she began to talk of a thousand trifles about the house. Across the greensward there came to them the last soft strains of vespers. Far away the heat had called up a thunderstorm; its growlings were becoming every moment more distinct. The girl ceased talking, and they sat long in silence. And when suddenly she realized that her weary-brained convalescent had let himself drop calmly off to sleep in her heart there was anything but reproach. She rose noiselessly, hung over him for a moment in blissful brooding and then tiptoed away to see that all was ready for him in his room.

VI

A few minutes later she returned. Carrington's chair was empty. She ran to the veranda steps and looked out. The heavy pall of thunder-clouds fast driving across the sky had brought down the darkness an hour before nightfall; but she could not mistake the figure passing uncertainly into the chapel door. He was walking in his sleep; that she divined, quaking. But whatever else was in her thought she dared not let the terror in her know. In an ague of shuddering she fled across the lawn, and stumbled weakly up the four stone steps. Carrington had already seated himself at the smaller organ. She started after him, then stopped. He had himself given full warning of what it would mean to awaken him in such a condition and in such surroundings while he was still weak from fever! And as she stood there, from the fingers of the somnambulist there came mockingly to her through the gloom the first demoniacal notes of the hell-born canon. . . .

For a long minute she was as if frozen in a thick ice of horror. Her heart stopped, her limbs were dead, her open lips and staring eyes were like those of a Medusa carved in stone. And when once more she felt that she could move, once more, instinctively, she started toward her lover. And once more she stopped, gasping. She could not. If he was to die, some other hand than hers must deal the blow. Her tortured thoughts flung themselves from side to side like creatures in a cage of fire. The devil-music leaped forward, faster and faster. Over them, as swiftly, the storm was closing. A long roll of thunder came in to the girl like the trumpet of the day of doom. She could hold herself motionless no longer.

With a choking cry she fled down the chapel. A flash of lightning lit her steps, and in a kind of frenzy she flung herself up the stairs to the great oriel organ. Then—it was to drown the hideous voice of the Moloch music, it was with the wild unreasoned hope of somehow awakening Carrington unharmed, it was her woman-musician's soul fleeing to sanctuary and calling in despair for the help of the All-Powerful—her fingers struck the first mighty, heaven-born chords of one of the immortal choruses of the Messiah.

In an instant the swift and ruthless, horribly exultant, trampling march of the canon stopped dead. It was as if a crucifix had been raised amid the devil's mass, as if some skeleton-and-demon dance of death had been banned and halted. From the smaller organ raved up a pandemonium of fiendish snarlings, ghoulish execrations, haggish shriekings, and then the whole Gehenna gathered itself into one raging fury of resistance. All the challenged powers of darkness seemed to rush together and pour from the canon as from the pit's mouth. The chapel was a-surge with such a chaos of wild, atrocious malevolency as, it well might seem, nothing in earth or heaven could stand against.

The girl felt herself choking, swooning. But again her desperate love fought down her weakness, and her fingers pressed the keys in one final cry of agonized appeal. In that proud martyr's ecstasy strength flooded back to her. The great organ shook itself free once more, and, finding its full diapason, high above all that screaming devil defiance of revilings and blasphemies rolled on giant-mouthed in its tremendous exorcism.

Then it was as if that old Sulpician chantry had been that great Sistine chapel of Michael Angelo which is walled about with his stupendous configuration of the Last Judgment, and all the hosts of heaven and hell had sprung to warring life. And the thunderstorm gave to the battling organs an awful chorus and accompaniment. The lightning, falling about the chapel in an almost unbroken flash, struck through the ground-glass windows to right and left of the somnambulist, and leaped and rioted about his blind face in shuddering flickers of unearthly green. But through the great stained oriel which looked upon the girl the heavenly fires came in glowing bursts of color and wrapped her in a mantle of hues divinely luminous. And the thunder with its dreadful fulminations seemed now like some colossally protecting friend. It was the voice of the legions she was invoking. Higher and higher pealed the trumpet-tongue of the great organ. The canon still gnashed its teeth like a thousand frenzied hell-hounds, but gradually its hideous exultation died away. Stronger and stronger came the great conquering chords of good; and then the mighty anthem rose to its tremendous apotheosis in that earth-awakening, heaven-soaring chorus of hallelujahs. . . .

The storm was passing. The canon's voice was now only a raucous paroxysm of frustrated rage. Into the baffled

ranks of evil the chorus swept like some celestial sol-
diery. The girl felt herself inspired, and in her hands every
Gabriel-note became a sword of flame to beat the vampire
music from her lover's soul. . . . His fingers faltered on the
keys. . . . In a last, impotent falsetto the canon altogether
ceased.

He was awakening. The girl called to him. He answered
her. In his voice was amazement, but no note of brain-
destroying terror, nor of demoniacal possession. The spell
had been utterly broken! She fled through the darkness
from her organ-loft to his, and gathered him to her bosom.
Then white and trembling they hurried together from the
chapel.

The La Shelle mansion was in an uproar.

The servants were running about in the rain, terrified.
One of the last fierce thunderbolts had struck the cupola
and torn its splintering course down into the library.
Apparently the steel of the safe had drawn it, and indeed
the whole charge of electric fluid seemed to have plunged
itself into the open strong-box. Of the Colonel's papers
nine-tenths were burned past all hope of recognition,
and of the devil's head canon only the great seal of the
prince-bishop remained.

The one man who a month ago could perhaps have furnished a duplicate of the manuscript has now only a
rapidly-fading nightmare memory of it. Other than the
statement he is preparing with the help of Colonel and
Miss La Shelle for the secretary of the Society of Psychical
Research, what is here written contains his final utterance
upon the subject.

The Soul of Mozart
W. E. P. FRENCH
(1902)

You are the stenographer? Very good. Nurse, you may go.
Take this, please, exactly as I dictate it. In the fall of
1891, I, Stephen Van Ingen, person of leisure and student of the violin, met at the Players' Club in New York a
very charming old man, music-mad like myself. It chanced
that we had studied under the same master at Munich,
though nearly thirty years apart; and common interests,
associations and traditions in things harmonic paved the
way to an acquaintance that ripened rapidly. His wife, a
handsome, stately gentlewoman of the ultra-conservative
type, was with him in the city, and, by his invitation, I
called upon her and spent two or three agreeable evenings
with them at their hotel. She was intensely race-proud,
absolutely tone-deaf, and cherished for all musicians,
including her husband, a wondering, tolerant pity. While
I never heard her say so in so many words, I feel sure
that she thoroughly acquiesced in the saying of the famous
Frenchman that "music is spoiled silence," and endorsed
that other bit of clever philistinism, "The piano is a very
much underestimated instrument: it has wondrously enhanced the value of silence." However, though I played,
and had had a maternal grandmother of no especial pre-
tension to birth, who had been a noted concert-singer, my
father's people were of a good Albany family; so the old
lady graciously overlooked the fact that my ancestress had

sung on the stage, as well as my own unfortunate tendency
to create friction between horsehair and catgut, and very
cordially joined in her husband's invitation to me to
visit them in their country home before the holidays. No
date was set, but late in November a bulky telegram was
brought me, which read:—

"Will you not come to us on the 1st? The musical sensation of your life and the century awaits you. Come by
the morning train. I have the symphony in C with the
fugue, and you shall play it on my pet Amati. We lunch
at one and dine at seven. There shall be a German dinner
in honor of the sensation, and we shall drink to it and to
her in Assmannhauser Auslese. The marvel will be in the
evening, but we shall have a harmonious afternoon. Bring
a large trunk and your Stradivarius, for you must make a
long stay."

Then followed a funny sentence in German, of which,
as well as of the name of the wonderful red Rhine wine,
the operator had made a sad mess; but I recognized at once
the choleric entreaty of our old music-master, a literal
translation being, "Dear Mr. God in Heaven! can I not
make you accelerate yourself?" I laughed over the memories evoked, and I was amused by the despatch. Who but a
musician, with a fine and lofty disregard for dirty money,
would send such a voluminous telegram? Yet, my heart
was warmed and touched by it, too; for the rare lavishness
seemed the grace-note of a beautiful old-fashioned hospitality, softening the vulgar rag-time of our brutal commer-
cialism; and I treated myself to the luxury of a comfortably courteous number of words in my acceptance by wire.

I endeavored to "accelerate myself," and a few morn-
ings later I took the train for the pretty colonial town on
the west shore of the Hudson, near which was my friend's
home. It was the first day of December, 1891, brilliant,
cold and clear. At the station my host met me, and I was
presently seated in a roomy sleigh of Russian make, drawn

by three fine horses hitched abreast, who covered in an hour the twelve miles of road through the hills that led to our destination.

"Beautiful beasts, aren't they?" said my friend, as he urged them a bit.

"They are matched and gaited to a semitone," I acquiesced. "Is the gray mare, as usual, the better horse?"

"Yes; she is thoroughbred; the others are trotting-stock, and when my lady takes a notion to run they are outclassed. Here is a level bit. See!" He spoke to the team and let them out. The mare at once took up a long smooth gallop and the horses trotted easily abreast of her, pulling evenly. The pace was very fast, but it was nothing to what they could do, as I soon learned. There was a shrill whistle, followed by a report like a pistol-shot from the long whip. The mare flung herself into her tremendous stride, and the gallant beasts beside her trotted their hardest, but she was pulling the sleigh. Another instant and they broke, and the three straining animals were in a mad run. It was very exciting and exhilarating, with a good spice of danger thrown in; but the bounding creature in the middle was leading and evidently enjoying herself, while her running-mates were straining every nerve to keep out of the way of the sleigh.

As the gait slackened, and they fell into a walk before a long hill-climb, I inquired as to the nature of the sensation promised in the telegram.

"There are two," said my host, patting the steaming horses with his whipstock—neither he nor I then dreaming of the others that fate was preparing for us. "The first is a great musician, the finest instrumentalist of our day. She is past-grand-mistress of the organ, the harp and the piano. In touch and technique she is without a peer, in expression and execution she is faultless, and she not only grasps but can convey the subtlest shades of meaning in the works of the great composers."

"Who and whence is this miracle?" I asked, as he paused.

"She is Aloysia Weber, of Munich, the great-great-grand-daughter of the woman of the same name who was Mozart's first love and whose sister he married. She is, also, a pupil of our old master, and it was at his house Mrs. Hasbrouck and I saw her first when we were abroad five years ago. Have I excited your curiosity?"

"You have indeed," I replied; "I am all ears."

"You will be all eyes, too, my boy," put in Mr. Hasbrouck, "and I predict a tumble for you, Mr. Brave Bachelor."

"'Forewarned is forearmed,'" quoth I, hanging on with both hands, as the sleigh, bounding from a "thank-you-ma'am," took a longer flight than usual.

When my host had reduced the gait to that of an ordinary express-train, my breath came back to me, and I made inquiry as to the second sensation.

"It is a marvel just as Aloysia is. She has not seen it yet, but I shall spring it on her this evening." He paused, then resumed thoughtfully: "It is queer how things sometimes happen in this strange muddle of a world—queer and uncanny. Last year, in Vienna, I attended an auction-sale of curios and bought, among other things, a very good bit of woodcarving, a small music-cabinet, on the door of which is a cleverly done Pan and pipes, the reeds at his feet twisted into the date '1756' and the vignette 'J. C. W. A. M.' Do you place the initials?"

"What a piece of luck!" I exclaimed—"Johannes Chrysostomos Wolfgang Amadeus Mozart, and the year of his birth. You must have paid a long price for it."

"No, I got it for a song. It was fearfully dirty, and so decrepit that I sent it to a shop in Albany to be set up. Thereby hangs the discovery. The cabinet-maker—an honest man—found a false back in it and tucked away therein a flat packet, sealed, initialed, and dated less than a month before Mozart's death. There were also a few lines on the wrapper, faint and shaky, and the writing was blistered here and there, as if with tears. Somehow, the words seem to have taken a strong hold on me. And, oh, the pity of it!—to think that the dying message and the love-song of one of the world's greatest masters of melody should have failed to reach the woman he worshiped." We were both silent a moment, then the dear old man, with a little catch in his voice, repeated in German the inscription from the wrapper, which, freely translated, was as follows:—

"Thou, best beloved and adored, to whom I gave my love and my idolatry, to thee I give this the last music that my hand shall ever write, and in it I have striven to put the soul-worship of thy lover and a hope that shall outlive death. No one hath seen this score, save Goethe only, and the words he hath written to my poor song shall reach thee by another means with information how thou mayest—"

There, as he told me, the writing ceased.

For a little time there were no sounds other than the rhythmical hoof-beats, the jangle of the bells and the steady swish of the runners. Then my companion voiced my own thought:

"They were meant for his wife's sister. When the end is near, a man's thoughts fly back to his first love. A century ago! Perhaps she has heard in that other land we guess so much about the music we shall hear to-night and the words we shall never hear, played on instruments we know not of and sung by voices immortally sweet."

We were skimming up an avenue of sugar-maples, and before us was the big, hip-roofed, much-verandaed old house, so overgrown with ivy that the rough gray stone of its walls was but little in evidence.

Mrs. Hasbrouck met and welcomed me in the spacious hall where the cheerful glow from a huge fire of chestnut logs fell with loving benison on Flemish oak and Spanish leather, and flickered in rosy content from the copper sides of a tall, slim, cylindrical vessel with an absurdly long handle that stood half buried in the glowing wood-embers. There was a delicious and alluring smell in the air, which I presently perceived came from the bubbling contents of

the copper pot, and my mental analysis of the ingredients
had just begun, when my host advanced toward the fire,
rubbing his hands and quoting:—

> "'Nose! Nose! Nose! Nose!
>   And what gave thee that jolly red nose?
>   Cinnament and ginger, nutmeg and cloves,
>   And they gave me my jolly red nose.'"

"I hope you like mulled Burgundy, old fellow, and that
the long drive has created a 'right spot' for it?"

I assented eagerly; and he, still talking, and suiting
the action to the word, finished a very interesting bit of
cookery:

"This recipe was revealed to me by the shade of Bac-
chus in a vision. You bring a quart of Burgundy, a little
sugar, a twist of lemon-peel and a couple of wineglassfuls
of spiced rum to a boil; rub a red-hot poker over a bit of
clean stick to get off the ashes, and plunge it, thus, to the
bottom of the brew, which burns off the excess of alcohol
in this pretty violet flame and is, besides, 'mellerin' to the
organ.' Then you pour the heated liquid into these three
tall thin tumblers, in each of which, you perceive, is a
small piece of roasted apple and a scrap of toast; hand the
glasses, muffled in napkins, to your victims; and drink, as
I do to you, dear guest—a welcome as warm as the wine."

I long to dwell on these dear, generous, hospitable people and their ideal home, wherein everything was for use,
comfort and beauty, and nothing for show; but I have my
story to tell and the time is short. Miss Weber, I learned,
had been summoned to New York to confer with her manager, but would return that afternoon.

After luncheon, Mr. Hasbrouck and I sneaked off to
the music-room, a large octagon in a tower wing, walls
and ceiling paneled in lustrous white walnut, the shadow-
boxes of perhaps a dozen pictures (a spirited Orpheus
holding spell-bound with his lyre a fawn and a panther,

an exquisite Sappho, and several portraits of the famous composers) sunk flush with the wood, and little other ornament, save an oriel-window in stained glass on either side of the great organ whose pipes towered to the lofty ceiling. There I was shown the marvelous manuscript so long lost to the world, and there my host and I amused ourselves with sonata, aria and scherzo until it was time for him to start for the station to meet Miss Weber. We had hardly begun to play, when there was a soft thud against one of the windows and the insistent cry of a cat demanding to be let in. Mr. Hasbrouck laughed, said, "I might have known Wolfgang would insist on joining us," rose, and raised the sash. The cat marched sedately in, and leaping to the top of a music-stool, crouched there, surveying us gravely and calmly. A superb beast, dignified and irresponsive, with a coat like that of a silver-tip bear—black as jet, but sprinkled all over with snow-white hairs somewhat longer than the soft, close coat of inky fur, making the animal look as though he had been lightly powdered. I don't like cats, but this one was extraordinarily large and curiously beautiful. His gray hairs, I presumed, indicated extreme age, and I inquired if he was not the Methuselah of his race.

"No," responded my host, picking up his violin; "he is only about five years old, and, barring his size, he looks just as he did when we got him as a kitten in Salzburg. We named him Wolfgang partly because he came from Mozart's birthplace; partly because, while he was still a round puffball playing with strings, he would leave his milk to listen to music, and would yowl like a little black demon over persistent false notes or a discord. Play a little Chopin or Bach, then a bar or two of Mozart, and see what happens."

I began a favorite passage of mine from the delicious Eleventh Nocturne, covertly watching the cat. He was evidently pleased, his eyelids opening and closing softly, his tail slightly tremulous, and the deepest purr I have

ever heard coming out of him. I changed suddenly to the
selection from the mass we had been playing, and my host
joined in. The purring ceased, the vibrant tail was still,
and the unwinking eyes watched us intently. The animal
seemed not to breathe, and appeared to listen in every
hair.

Mr. Hasbrouck is an exceedingly good violinist, so I
was much surprised when, after a particularly difficult
passage, which he had rendered with great accuracy and
brilliance, his bowing suddenly became jerky, then lagged,
and, finally, there was the jar of a false note.

The effect on our small audience was immediate and
electrical. He sprang to his feet with a quick snarl; his
eyes, which a moment before had been narrow onyx
ellipses in disks of tourmaline, were balls of tawny, smol-
dering fire ringed with emerald; his tail was a club: his
ears were flattened against his head; one spiteful paw was
raised with every claw showing; and through his sharp,
bared teeth he spat and hissed at us. We both ceased playing, and Mr. Hasbrouck spoke kindly and soothingly to
the excited and angry animal; but he snarled again, leaped
to the floor and disappeared, in offended majesty, under
a divan, whence every blandishment to persuade him to
come out was met by sulky growls. The whole performance
was unusual and bizarre, and touched one's sense of the
ludicrous; but wonder, pity and an ill-defined uneasiness
were among my emotions, and, dominating all else, an
unmotived desire to hunt the thing out of the room.

My host's bow was going again, and softly, tenderly
there floated through the splendid room in delicate minors
a lovely little German lullaby. The low tones ceased, and
he turned to me with a half-laugh and an apologetic tone
in his voice.

"Poor old Wolfgang! I always play that after I have
teased him. Do you know, I sometimes wonder if Pytha-
goras did not make a shrewd guess at the truth in his
theory of the transmigration of souls."

"My dear sir," I remarked with some heat, "no human soul ever emitted such sounds or had such a temper as that cat. I will admit, if you choose, that he is possessed of a devil, and an uncommonly dangerous and vicious one. If I were blessed with a quadruped of like disposition, I should find means to induce it to rush violently down a steep place and perish in the sea." There was a peculiarly vindictive growl from the basement of the divan, as I finished.

"Take care!" cautioned the old gentleman. "He knows, as well as a deaf person, when he is being discussed; but there is no real harm in him.—It is just the musical temperament," he added dryly.

We played until time to start for the station, when, being left to mv own devices, I had a pleasant chat with Mrs. Hasbrouck, and retired to the library to write a letter. Later, I went to my room, and had hardly begun to dress for dinner, when the sleigh arrived. A stud, escaping from my fingers with the total depravity inherent in its kind, concealed itself with such malicious intelligence that the resultant game of hide-and-seek considerably delayed me. As I descended the stairs, a master-hand was extemporizing exquisitely on the harp. Miss Weber was alone in the music-room; and I stood for a moment in the doorway, drinking in the delicious harmony and watching eagerly the gracious picture she made standing by the most graceful of all instruments. She was in the full, strong light of the high organ-lamps, I in the shadow of the arched doorway. I caught my breath at her loveliness. She was a tall woman, deep-bosomed, round-throated, full-armed, brunette-skinned. Her hair, a deep brownish-red, was loosely puffed around her face in the manner of the charming Potocka of the Berlin gallery. Her eyes, a shade or two darker, but unmistakably reddish, were long and deeply lashed. Her mouth, large, generous, full-lipped, was richly colored and charming in contour. What her other features were, I don't know or care. Beautiful hair, eyes and mouth make a beautiful woman, and she had the added bounties of coloring and outline. Ravishingly sweet as was the theme she was extemporizing, and strongly though it moved me, I realized, with a sudden startled tightening about the heart, that there might be a more imperious passion than music.

It occurred to me finally that I had no business to lurk in the semidarkness of the archway glaring at that sumptuous symphony in red and creamy flesh-tones—I forgot to say that her dinner-gown was red—so I pulled myself together and came forward. Her hands fell from the strings, and she advanced to meet me with pleasant directness, saying in quaintly slow, painstaking English, burred with a pretty German accent, "This is Mr. Van Ingen, iss it not?"—adding, as I admitted my identity and expressed my pleasure at meeting her, "I feel that I know you yet—no, *already*—through our so kind hosts who have told much to me of yourself and of your playing."

I bowed my thanks, and, as I did so, I became conscious of a pair of coldly intent eyes watching me from behind Miss Weber. They were those of that infernal cat, seated on the trail of her gown and as close to her as he could get. "Scat!" I cried, but the brute never stirred, and the beautiful woman, making a caressing movement of her hand toward him, said kindly, "Ah, never mind; he does not trouble me. Wolfgang and I are good friends." Then in German: "Are we not, thou ink-spot?" The great black creature fawned at her, standing on his hind legs and rubbing his whiskered muzzle against her hand, while he purred like an electric fan. I hated to see the thing near her, and I was sick to kill it then and there.

Mr. and Mrs. Hasbrouck came in, and dinner was announced shortly after. It was a very good dinner, and the noble red wine in which we toasted one another and the kindly, quick-tempered old man who had taught three of us made it a jolly occasion.

Mr. Hasbrouck was plainly anxious to get back to the music-room, and before our cigars were fairly finished, he moved an adjournment thereto. As the ladies went on ahead of us, he came a little closer to me and whispered: "I am not going to give her the manuscript score till the night of the 5th, just a century after Mozart's death. We will make a centennial celebration of it." I acquiesced half-heartedly, for I was impatient to hear it, and, stepping quickly forward to pick up my hostess' handkerchief, trod on that ubiquitous and damnable cat, which let loose a most astounding squall and sought sanctuary in Miss Weber's arms, who comforted and petted the black devil. I thought she would never put it down, but she did at last, and began to play for us. It was, indeed, both sensation and marvel. I have heard nearly all the great players of the world, but never anything like her wonderful fingering. Her instrumentation was simply marvelous, her feeling perfect, her interpretation a revelation of harmony's deepest meaning. Then she sang to our violins, mainly the folk-songs of her fatherland; but, now and again, Elsa, Brunhilde and Isolde "made the common air blossom with melody." What a voice she had! Clear, deep, vibrant, full-volumed, soft as sleep, and with an added bell-like resonance that lingered in the room when the rounded white throat had ceased to swell with the bubbling notes.

But for Wolfgang, who hung about her like her shadow, it would have been an evening of unalloyed happiness. Looking back on it, I know it to have been the happiest but one, and the most wonderful but one, of all my life.

Before I fell asleep that night, I knew that I loved Aloysia Weber, loved her with all my heart and soul, as I had never cared for any other woman, and as I could never care again. When to a man of thirty-five whose life has been full and rounded, there comes love for a mature, beautiful woman in whom he fancies he will find nearly perfect comradeship, the subtle poison takes hold of brain and blood, of sense and senses, and becomes a part of the ego of the man. I loved her so.

The next three days were dreamland. We were much together, she and I; for Mr. Hasbrouck was away part of the time, and Mrs. Hasbrouck (God bless her!) invented duties and headaches and siestas until her conscience must have atrophied. Her good husband let the cat out of the bag one afternoon (when he should have been putting that other cat in a bag, and the bag through a hole in the ice), as the dear old lady, after yawning elaborately behind her fan, said, "John, I think the young people will excuse us if we take our nap."

"*Our* nap!" repeated her liege lord, in funnily aggrieved surprise. "Why, my dear, I never knew you to lie down in the afternoon. I have been trying to induce you to for forty years."

Aloysia blushed divinely, and said, in a deliciously quaint and embarrassed mixture of English and German, that she supposed she ought to rest too, and that perhaps she was keeping poor Mr. Van Ingen up.

"Nonsense, child!" exclaimed Mrs. Hasbrouck promptly. "It is a wicked waste of time for any one but old folks. Mr. Hasbrouck"—looking at him severely—"is pleased to be facetious. I *always* sleep between meals."

Mr. Hasbrouck endeavored to indulge in a pleasantry to the effect that the meals were dinner and breakfast, but his wife was too quick for him, and, with a muttered phrase that sounded like, "Was there ever anything so stupid as a man?" she took his arm and marched him off.

A silence hung for a few minutes between Aloysia and me. Then I went over to where she sat, her beautiful eyes troubled yet shyly tender, and told her that I loved her dearly, dearly, and asked her to be my wife. Was there ever another woman so frank and brave and sweet, so quick to give? She leaned toward me with a little tender sound, half sigh, half sob; and, kneeling, I held her close and heard her whisper in her own tongue: "I love thee. Thou hast all my heart." Ah! the dear familiar "thee" and "thou"! A moment before, I had been one of many. Now I was one only—hers—and the rest of the world shut out. The man who has never heard the woman he loves change for him from the plural to the singular pronoun has missed a joy than which life holds few sweeter.

Yes, we had known each other three days only, but there is no fixed period for the growth of love—

"The immortals know each other at first sight.
And love is of them."

How she played and sang to us that evening! And the beauty and the glory and the witchery of it all, the passionate softness of the organ tremolo, the ringing staccato of the harp, the piano's great crashing chords, the new caressing thrill in the dear voice, and the exultant happiness of the lovely woman, were for me, for me, for me—they were mine, all mine! The soul of my love was speaking to mine in the universal language—music, the soul's speech. And did my violin tell you, dear, of the love your lover could not put in words? You told me so, my sweet, my sweet, when you stole back for my goodnight kiss.

There was no shadow on my heart that night, for the black brute that I hated and feared was sick—sick unto death, I hoped. But the next day broke coldly damp, overcast, and gloomily still. A storm was brewing, and there was an eerie feeling in the air. I could not shake off the sense of oppression with which I awoke. The malign spell of the weather was upon us all, I found, when we gathered at breakfast. Ah! it was a miserable day, an accursed day, a day that smelled of evil and death and disaster. I wondered that the horror that lay hidden within it did not make the hours shriek with the birth-pang of the unthinkable thing they were to bring forth.

However, the household had pulled itself together somewhat by dinner, at which I noticed that every one

drank more wine than usual, and we sat at the table for
over two hours, the time being prolonged by an extraordinary and very heady punch that our host made for us out
of black coffee, burnt brandy and Burgundy.

It was nearly ten that evening when we entered the
music-room. Mr. Hasbrouck went at once to the cabinet,
and telling again, very rapidly, what he knew of its history, took out the manuscript and gave it to Aloysia. She
grew very white as she read the inscription, and gasped
out in German: "My God! my God! it is the lost music,
the score that Mozart wrote for my grandmother's grandmother, the words for which have been handed down for
five generations in the female line. I have them here. They
have never been sung. It is a tradition—a command—we
were to wait for this. And I am to sing them to-night—a
hundred years from the day when he died."

She hurried from the room, and when she returned
went straight to the great organ, with just one loving, imploring glance at me. She pulled the lever of the hydraulic
blower, spread the two manuscripts open on the rack and
began to play.

A noble prelude, pulsing, blood-stirring, heart-stilling,
the overture to the greatest masterpiece of melody ever
dreamed in a human brain. And then a song: a miracle
in words wedded to a miracle in sound; a thing so ineffa-
bly, unhumanly beautiful that we hushed our very breaths
to hear; a song of love and longing, of grief and joy, of
pain and parting, of loss and death; a thing weird, awful,
exquisite, throbbing through the great room, flooding the
whole house, drowning the howl of the storm that raged
without, filling the shuddering air with its mad, passionate protest, whispering of fear and of hope, sobbing with
the despair of a lost soul, and thundering in fierce, magnificent crescendo love's final triumph over time and fate
and death.

She ceased, stepped down from the platform, moved
over to one of the great bronze lamps, and stood, holding

its massive pillar in one slender hand, the other, with the manuscript in it, pressed to her bosom, her eyes wide with emotion and listening, waiting terror.

Merciful God! what was that cry outside, mingling with the shriek of the wind? The scream of a cat? The single German word, thrice repeated, that ended the song—"Come! come! come!"? Oh, horror beyond words to paint! that was it—the voice of a brute become articulate. Then the crash of glass, as the thin center of the oriel-window gave way under the impact of a heavy body, and the great cat hurled itself at the white throat of the woman I loved. She gave one agonized cry as the beast struck her, and reeled backward, dragging over as she fell the huge lamp that crushed out her sweet life. The cat had enough vitality left to bite me savagely as I tore it from her and killed it. My love died in my arms, and, though she could not speak, I know that she is still all mine, and that I shall have her soon; for they tell me I am dying from blood-poisoning from the bite. Well, let them think that if they choose, and that may be in part the cause, but a man may not live loving the dead as I love her.

They gave me the music and the words, and I burnt them both.

And now, before you call the nurse, give me my dear old violin and hold me up, for love is stronger than death and my sweet can hear me when I play.

The Flautist

J. H. YOXALL, M.P.

(1903)

"It's a rummy looking instrument, but a good 'un," Mr.
George Albert Greenup told himself, as he peered more
closely into the slum-shop window. "Seems to me I could
play a fair treat on that flute." He stood with his nose
against the smeary pane; his finger ends were creeping
with desire to fall upon the keys, and he stepped into the
little shop.

"How long's provision dealers sold German flutes, my
dear?" he said to the ruddy young slut behind the loaves
and margarine on the counter.

"Gawn!" she giggled. "Who're yer dearin' of?—It's
cheap, is that flute."

"Let's have a look at it, then." He reached into the window, unhooked the flute, and nearly dropped it; the thing
felt warm and flexible, almost alive.

"Funny!" He stared at it, and tried to bend it; but it
was rigid, of course. "I'll swear it kind of moved," he stammered; then he fitted his fingers to the keys and holes. He did
this nervously. "Somethin' queer about this flute, my dear."

He lifted it to his mouth, and blew. Dust, that had
gathered in the down-hung head of the instrument, came
eddying between his lips; but he spat, and blew again.
Sound floated out—pure, round, full, sweet, with somewhat of a violin's vibration in the tone. He blew a dozen
bars, and the woman listened rapturously.

217

"Gracious!" she cried, "y' can play!"

The wood of the flute was greenish walnut, and there were peculiar markings in the grain—scaly markings, almost serpentine; the levers were uncommon in shape, they were wriggly and twisted. He turned it round, and up and down, and stared at it more closely. "It's a rum 'un, this. Where's it come from?" he asked.

"Old furrin' gent's, what owed us for bread."

He played again, and the squalid little shop was sweet with melody. The slut and the flautist stared at each other in wonder. "It's a fair caution, miss!" said he. "How much?"

"Eight shillin', and I'm losin'—on'y yer plays it s' well."

It was Saturday afternoon, and the flautist's week's pay was in his pocket. "Give you six," he said.

"Seven," said she.

"Done!" and the flute was carried off.

Mr. George Albert Greenup was flautist in the band at the Alcazar Restaurant, Oxford Street. He played his new flute that night from seven till eleven. Half way through the menu of music came a pot-pourri of Savoyan airs, in which the flute is given a solo of eight-and-twenty bars. Half way through this solo Mr. George Albert Greenup became aware that the dining people had ceased talking, and had begun to listen. He ended with a tremolo that sent the listeners into a passion of applause, and the orchestra had to render the pot-pourri again. Again the flute solo received the tribute of rapture. "By Jiminy, Greenup! Didn't know you could play like that!" the pianist said, with a puzzled stare.

"Nor me," said George Albert Greenup, as he polished his flute. "But there! I never had a thing half fit to play on before. It's not much to look at, as you say. Only cost me ten bob. But it's a fair treat of a whistle."

Then a note was handed to the flautist.

"Come and see me Monday morning, eleven sharp, Queen's Hall. Bring your flute and scores.—Hugh Griffin."

The flautist went pale, then red. By George! Hugh Griffin, the famous concert manager! He must have been dining, and have heard that solo. "Hi, Number Eight! a B & S,—and quick," the flautist called to a waiter. . . . "Look at that, man," he said to the pianist, handing him the note.

"My fortune's made!" the flautist told himself that night as, at the end of the musical programme, he shut his new flute into the case from which he had ousted the old one, and hurried off to the "Three Feathers," in the Euston Road. "My fortune's made, boys—I'm going to be soloist at the Queen's Hall," he told his cronies at the Three Feathers. "Hi, Joe!" Potations all round must celebrate the triumph, and nothing less than six big brandies and soda could fitly celebrate it for George Albert Greenup himself.

It was *pede titubante* that he went, with merry drunken wavers, to his bed-sitting-room at the Crescent in Store Street, in the first hour of the Sunday morning. And there something happened to his flute.

He stood in the candle-light, and was polishing his new instrument lovingly, though he reeled as he stood. He put it back into the case, and shut the lid. But there seemed to be some obstruction; the case would not close. The lid shut down upon the head of the flute that seemed to protrude; the lid came down upon the flute-head in guillotine fashion, and he sickened at a pulpy resistance which his hands on the lid seemed to feel. "I've jolly well cut its head off!" he shivered, and he looked to see.

But no, the head did not protrude; the flute reposed on the tarnished purple velvet quite whole.

"I'm jolly well on again, that's it," he told himself as he stumbled into bed. It was not an unusual reflection.

All through closing-time on Sunday he practiced at Handel's "Soft, complaining flute" in "St. Cecilia's Day." The chance of his lifetime was to come on the morrow.

If he could then play well enough to please the Napoleon of concert managers, his fortune would be made; an engagement was certain for him, if not as soloist, at least as flautist in Griffin's famous band. There was no orchestral accompaniment to the knives and forks at the Alcazar Restaurant on Sundays, so that he was free to practice all that day, except for the hours he passed at the Three Feathers, boasting and toasting the victories to come. He was careful not to re-open the case when he got to his room that night: he sickened at the mere memory of that guillotiny, pulpy feeling of the night before. The flute had seemed alive, and he its butcher; he gave a shrug and a shiver at the thought.

"Fifteen pounds a week to begin with," Mr. Hugh Griffin told him, at half-past eleven the next morning, "Let me see. Be ready to play Mozart's Concerto for solo Flute and Orchestra in B, Wednesday afternoon. Rehearsal to-morrow. Chuck the Alcazar at once, can't you?" And the flautist went off to "chuck" the Alcazar.

"No Three Feathers to-night, my boy," he thought to himself when he got to Store Street, and commenced to practice; and, indeed, when at ten o'clock that night he went out, tired with long blowing at Mozart's very difficult score, he cheered his weariness with only three brandies-and-soda. "By George, this flute plays like heaven!" he said the next morning, as he practiced again; and at the rehearsal the tone of his playing, if not the technique of it. astonished the accompanying band. "A common-looking fellow, but he gets a rare tone!" the leader said to the first second violin. "Tips the elbow, I fancy," said the other, with his eyes on Mr. Greenup's face.

He tipped the elbow that night. The rehearsal had been a success for him, and he had five pounds in his pocket as an advance. All the cronies at the Three Feathers must quaff to his good fortune, and he himself must drink to each of them a piece of luck and merit as good.

He had left his flute on the top of the chest of drawers in his room at Store Street, and before he went to bed he took it out. As he did so he reeled, and the instrument seemed to give and bend in his hand. "By George!" He dropped it; it felt wriggly and warm. "Seeing snakes, eh?" He knew the symptoms, and could remember as many as nine or ten drinks that night.

Cautiously he touched the flute; it lay on the table askew. "Why, the thing's *bent!*" he exclaimed; it had a crook in its middle, the head made a wide angle with the tail. He tried to fit it into the case, but in vain.

"I'm drunk!" he shivered. Cold had come upon him, except to his feverish head. Dressed as he was, he snuggled into the blankets and lay there solemnly regarding his protruding boots. Then he blew the candle out and turned on his side to sleep.

But sleep he could not. The room was dark, but the soft accompaniment of darkness refused to come to his eyes. For an hour he lay, with his face towards the chest of drawers, and just at the moment when his eves began to close a light aroused them. It was greenish light, phosphorescent, flickering; something was burning on the chest-of-drawers!

In horror he stared. The flute had lifted itself from its purple bed; it was standing, it was shining; green light like a glowworm's suffused it, it was a viper, the mouth-hole was a malevolent emerald eye, green fangs flickered from the top of the head, where he knew a tightly-fitting cork must be!

He shuddered and groaned. Then he covered himself closely from the sight, and presently, half asphyxiated, he ceased to shudder and think, in sleep.

Broad daylight saluted him when he awoke. His mind seemed blurred; he hardly recollected anything of the evening and the night.

Suddenly he remembered that this was the day of the concert—*his* concert—the concerto day! He jumped out

of bed. "Why, I'm dressed!" he muttered. Then he recalled
his hallucinations in the dark, and he sprang at the flute.

"Must have been bad!" he muttered. The flute was lying across its bed of purple velvet. The flute was straight
enough; no bend in it now. "Never was one, of course!" he
told himself. And the cork tightly stopped the head, the
mouth-hole with its sharp edges looked anything but an
emerald eye. "Oh, I'll sign off drink a bit! No good goin'
on like this. What'll I do at the concert, else?"

What he did at the concert was matter for the critics'
praise. The concerto for solo flute and orchestra had never
been better rendered, the critics said. But this apprecia-
tion appeared on the Thursday morning, and George Albert Greenup did not read what the critics thought.

Another ten pounds in his pocket, and the snug bar
at the Three Feathers full of friends; it was not in mortal man to refuse to celebrate his success that Wednesday
night. "It ain't me, it's my flute," he confessed, when he
reached the maudlin stage. "I couldn't play like I played
thish afternoon, my boysh, if it washn't for my new flute."

The flute lay on the chest of drawers meanwhile, and
at two o'clock in the morning Mr. George Albert Greenup
became its neighbour again. "Lesh have a look at you, ole
shap . . . Good ole shap!" he addressed it, tenderly and
coaxingly, as though it might bite unless appeased. Yet the
flute lay in the case quite motionless and demure, and he
shut down the lid.

But the lid would not close; the instrument seemed to
have lengthened, its head stuck out, the lid went down
with that horrible guillotiny feeling again. Fierce anger
burned up in him at that, he cursed the awkward thing, he
took it by the ends and tried to push it into itself telescop-
ically, to shorten it to the length of the case. As he pushed,
the instrument bent in his hands; it was askew again, no
doubt about that, this time. Furious, he seized it at the
tail, and drunkenly he dashed it against the bevelled edge

of the chest of drawers: a shrill tremolo note of pain was heard, but he struck again and again.

Then fury seemed to seize the instrument itself. It seemed to writhe in his grasp, with a horrible scaly contraction against the skin of his palm. He cursed it, loosed it, and it seemed to spring at him; like a warm, flexible, snaky cord it clipped his throat and wrapped throttlingly around his neck. A rustle, a rattle, a thick breath, a triumphant hiss. The flautist gasped, and fell backward against the dingy bed.

"Suicide," the police surgeon said, next morning. "The fellow's hung himself, of course. Who cut him down? Where's the cord?"

"Not a bit o' cord anywhere, sir," the police sergeant said.

"Must be," the surgeon insisted. "Look again. Look on the landing."

"Can't find anything, sir," the policeman, returning, said. But the surgeon was not listening; he was holding the flute against the dead man's neck.

"Strange!" the police surgeon was thinking. "Same width as the mark on the throat! And bless my soul! the mark's blacker just where the keys would press!"

He dropped the flute as though it had stung him; it fell on the pillow and lay demure beside the dead.

The Pipers of Mallory

Theo. Douglas (Mrs. H. D. Everett)

(1917)

I

While my last letter was flying out to you in India, dear Margaret, and your reply flying back to me, a great deal has been happening.

My last letter was all about Jack, wasn't it?—how we met and fell in love and how he was under orders for the war, and so we had to be married in a desperate hurry—such a hurry that it shocked Aunt Winifred, glad as she was to get rid of me.

I told you what I was going to wear, and Jack says I made rather a nice-looking bride (he put it more strongly than that). He was, of course, in khaki, and looked dearer than ever, and half an hour or less turned me into Mrs. Frazer. We had only nine days for our honeymoon instead of the three weeks we hoped for, but they were nine lovely days. Then there was the dreadful going away; but, before that came about, the question had to be settled—the question you ask, my dear cousin—what was to become of me while Jack was away in France fighting those horrible Huns?

It was over this Jack and I had our first difference—not a serious difference, for we kissed and made it up at once—when I found out what he wanted me to do. He actually wished me to make my home with his mother in Scotland—fancy that—to bury myself for months and months in the wilds with a woman I did not know, who would be worse than Aunt Winifred twice over. I had never been free in my life, but always in leading-strings, and I made up my mind I would be free now, quite on my own, to make up for what I should suffer through Jack being away.

I didn't tell Jack that—about wanting to be emancipated, he would not have understood. I told him what was quite true—that I wanted to make my V.A.D. training of use, and do war work of sorts in a London hospital, like Violet Power. And my plan was that Violet and I should take a flat together, a tiny flat, which would cost next to nothing (I thought), near enough to her hospital to be convenient, a hospital which needed helpers, and would find work for me, too.

Jack did not like it. Dear fellow! He is one of the old-fashioned sort who thinks women should be hedged about and protected, and give themselves up to looking after their household concerns; but he gave in when he saw I was determined.

That was nearly at the end of our time together—our lovely time. He had planned to take me up to Mallory, to say good-bye at the end of his leave, but having to go off suddenly altered that. However, he made me promise I would go there alone as soon as he left, to pay my mother-in-law a long visit before I settled down with Violet in the flat. Over that I was obliged to yield (with some private reservation about the long), for, as you will understand, I could not say "No" to him just then.

Well, we parted, and it was a hard parting. He put me in the night train for the North, before he left to cross over to France. Peters, his mother's servant, was to meet me in Edinburgh and take care of me from there; you see, I could not get away from the "take care."

Now you will know from my letter, the "Jack" letter, that I had never seen Lady Heron. She is always more or less of an invalid, and bronchitis, or something like that, prevented her taking the long journey to be present at our wedding. Fancy having attacks of bronchitis, and yet living up there in the North! She has been a widow for many years, and Jack is her only son; there is a son by a former marriage, Jack's half-brother, who is now Lord Heron. The Frazers are poor in these days, but Jack's mother has an income of her own, though I do not think it is a large one. Mallory is the old family place—mind you pronounce it right—*Mal*-lory, and not the other way. I suppose Lady Heron would not live there if Heron married, but he is still a bachelor, and with the regiment somewhere in France. Jack does not say much about his half-brother. I fancy the two are not very good friends.

Peters was waiting for me on the Edinburgh station, and by that time I was feeling rather better, and able to take an interest in what was new. Breakfast was ready for me at an hotel, with no bill for it, as Peters paid everything. I was "her leddyship's guest," he said, and it was by Lady Heron's orders; he seemed quite hurt when I offered. A very good breakfast it was, and I was hungry, for I had been far too wretched to eat any dinner the night before. Then, after rest and refreshment, I had to sally forth again to a different station, Peters carrying my hand-luggage. And when we gained the street—that wonderful street with the Castle opposite, standing up grey against the morning sky—there was a skirl of wild music coming towards us, with the tramp of marching feet.

A skirl. That is the right word for bagpipes, as perhaps you know. I daresay you have heard them in India, as there are Scottish regiments there, but I had never heard them before. Their music may be barbaric—people say so; but there is something about it that fires the blood—that fired my blood, though I am only a Scotswoman married and not born. I could understand how it put spirit into the tired feet which were following, muddy from a long route march, as they kept time to the swing and beat of the brave tune. Jack belongs to a Highland regiment, of course, the same that Heron is in. And at the moment I felt prouder than ever to be Jack's wife.

"I suppose Lady Heron has a piper at Mallory, has she not?"

It was the first question I had put to Peters. I had the notion that a piper must be a necessary appendage to every Highland family of importance; Lady Heron would not of course detain a young man, but she might so employ some old retainer, past the age to be of service in the war. But the servant shook his head. He, too, is quite elderly—did I say?—and speaks broad Scotch, though his name might as well be English.

"No, mom," he answered, "we hef no piper at Mallory. Her leddyship does not like the pipes."

Not like the pipes! How odd of her, I thought. And upon this scrap of information the latent opposition which I had felt towards Jack's mother from the beginning swelled and took shape. How strange of a woman who had soldier sons—a son and a step-son—and who wrote as if she were proud of them and their calling; and of one who I knew from Jack was Highland bred to the backbone!

Throughout the journey north-west, now with great hills looming up through mist, now by the side of rushing streams, I was thinking of my mother-in-law, and how much easier it would have been to meet her for the first time if Jack had gone with me to Mallory. I was afraid of her, to tell the truth, and that made me brace myself beforehand to be defiant, picturing a great lady who would stand on her dignity, and think Jack might have done better for himself than in marrying me, an Englishwoman of no particular family and small fortune. She would condemn, she would dictate, she would want to interfere.

The day wore on; the train was not a fast one, and there were frequent stoppages, and every hour Peters would come to the window to know whether I wanted anything. But at last there came the station where we alighted for Mallory.

There was a car to meet us, and in less than half an hour Mallory came into view. Not the fine place I had been picturing to myself, only a moderate-sized country house, but possessing a tower with corner-turrets in the Scottish fashion, which gives it some distinction. The rest of the house is low, with thick walls of undoubted antiquity. The windows are small, but beyond them there are lovely views.

It was only a confused impression I derived from that first entrance—of a hall warm with firelight, decorated with heads of beasts, and skins and weapons, of a room beyond, also warm, and of a frail little lady rising from her chair at the window, and coming lamely across to greet me with an embrace and a kiss.

Such a frail little lady to be the mother of a great, strong man like Jack She, like the house, was not what I expected, but I was right in two particulars. She is *grande dame* to the finger-tips, and I am certain she views me critically.

II

On further acquaintance I like Lady Heron better than I expected, and I have been able to express myself somewhat enthusiastically in writing to Jack; this will please him. I would give a good deal to know what her letter—the long letter I saw her writing—said to him about me. She is kind to me, painstakingly kind, but still we are strangers to each other, and I think it likely we shall be strangers to the end. That she is fond of Jack ought to knit a bond between us, but somehow I strongly suspect it is the very thing which holds us apart.

She is always testing and appraising me, though not in the way I expected; she tells me little anecdotes of Jack's youth, and watches to see if I receive them with the enthusiasm I ought; she shows me some cherished pictures—stupid, old-fashioned photographs—of Jack as a baby, Jack as

a toddler learning to walk, and upwards at various stages
of his boyhood. It is plainly my duty to care about these,
but I don't particularly; they seem too far removed from
the Jack I know. The pictures bore me, and I shudder
inwardly when a new anecdote is presented. And, sitting
here in the chair of truth, I must confess it—I find Mallory dull.

My chief amusement is going out for rambles by myself, rambles Lady Heron is too lame to share; she can only
walk up and down the terrace with her stick by way of
exercise, and that at the sunniest time of the day. The surroundings here are certainly beautiful, and the Highland
people interest me. I talk to them when I have a chance,
and try to get accustomed to their way of speech. It was
from one of these Highlanders I found out the reason why
Lady Heron does not like the pipes.

I never put the question to her. I do not know why not,
as it would have been a simple thing to ask, but whenever
it came into my head, something happened to divert the
thought and keep the words unspoken. But that thrilling
pibroch heard in Edinburgh seemed to haunt me here at
Mallory, though not always the same tune. I dreamt of it
the first night I was here; it waked me from sleep, as a real
thing might have done but when I listened in the deep,
country stillness and the darkness of the unfamiliar room,
there was not a sound. And each time I walked in the
direction of Glen Fruin I heard it with my waking ears,
very faint and far in the distance, but I could be certain
it was there.

I went some way up the Glen on the third occasion,
hoping to get nearer to the sound, but it seemed to recede
as I approached; the preliminary skirl, and two or three
bars of a tune, as if the musician were practising, and
then a fault and silence. Presently my watch warned me I
should return, for Mallory is a punctual household, and
Lady Heron would be waiting tea. I was well on my way
home when I met an old shepherd I had spoken to before,

and, as I still heard the music at intervals, I bethought myself to ask him:

"Who is it about here who plays the pipes? Somebody is practising away there in the Glen."

Highland fashion, he met my question by another, and his shaggy brows drew together.

"You be the leddy Frazer, be you not?"

I was Mrs. Frazer, I told him.

"Eh, weel, ye are Frazer married, and so have a right to hear. 'Tisn't lucky for the Frazers when the pipes are sounding in Glen Fruin, but the Lord be thankit that they don't come lower down! I do not look to hear them mysel', being nobbut Steenson that was once Macgregor."

This was pretty well Greek to me.

"Why isn't it good for the Frazers?" I demanded.

"Ye've never heard the legend? Mebbe 'tis not for the likes of me to tell ye, but seeing as ye ask— Time gone by the chief of the Frazers had his pipers equal with the best, always seven of them in his tail, and callants growing up to take the place—and a proud place it was—of them as were short-winded or old. Glen Fruin was full of folk in those days, where there's nought now but a wheen ruins, or a square in the green to mark where walls have been. And custom was that Frazer's pipers should be chosen from the Glen Fruin folk.

"That was a time of battles, same as now, and the Frazers were up in arms. I don't mind the name of the battle, no, nor how long ago, but there was a great slaughter, and the Frazers fell to a man, and the pipers with their chief. It is said there was none to fill their places, for the callants had not been instructed, and the head of the clan was nobbut a wailing Cairn. And since that day the Frazers have had no pipers—the Frazers of Mallory. Mebbe that is why the dead men are not content, and when a Frazer is about to die they are heard piping in Glen Fruin."

I am putting down the old man's words as nearly as I remember them, but I daresay I spell them wrong. As I listened a cold shiver went down my spine and crept among the roots of my hair; if my hair had been undone I think it would have stood up with fright.

"Why, you don't mean to say," I stammered—"you don't mean to tell me that what I have been hearing is a ghost? A ghost in broad daylight and in the open air! And who is it who is going to die?"

"You needn't be afeared, my leddy, for him as is your own. There's a many Frazers at the war besides, and the pipers pipe the same for a death in bed. There's John Frazer near his end at the Mill, and mebbe 'tis for him. He has a son fighting, and Donald Frazer, farmer, has two more. Ye need na fear for the heads of the clan, or for their womenfolk, unless the pipers come right down to Mallory, and go round the house."

"Do they come as close as that?" I asked, shuddering.

"Ay, my leddy, that they do. And they are heard by all of the Frazer name, and sometimes by them as are not so called, but I never heard tell of their being seen. It is just a sound and no more, sometimes a lament on the pipes, sometimes a fine march for them as fall. And they go once round for a woman, and twice for the heir, and three times for the head of the clan. They went three times round the house when the late lord died, and there was many who heard them, together with my Leddy Heron hersel'. And ever since then she hasna been able to bear the pipes, the real pipes, and they are warned not to come nigh."

After that I wondered no more at what Peters had told me in Edinburgh. The faint, far-off skirling, which had sounded even while old Steenson was speaking, ceased as I hurried back, but Mallory looked a dark blot in the prospect, dismal as it had never seemed before. Was it because of this superstition that Lady Heron had grown old and grey before her time? It would be awful, I thought, to live here year in and year out, eternally listening for those notes of doom. What should I do, I, a married Frazer, if I heard them circling round the house, and if it meant that Jack—

I tell you frankly what was my first impression afterwards; some healthy scepticism came to my relief. An old man's story of impossible ghosts—where was the need to credit it?

Through that day and the next everything moved on velvet—the quiet, regular hours, the careful service, the slightly formal ways with an old-world atmosphere about them, which I found piquant and attractive when not in one of my impatient moods. And I was perhaps more patient, more inclined to be appreciative, because the weeks of my visit had nearly run out; very soon now I should be setting out to establish myself with Violet at the flat, in the midst of London and life.

I was softened, too, because Lady Heron appeared to recognise my right of choice as to what I would do in Jack's absence. All she said was:

"Your home is here, my dear, when you care to have it so. When you wish to come back to Mallory you have only to let me know."

Then I heard her sigh softly to herself, perhaps because she recognised that I did not care. I thanked her and said I would write, and she replied:

"I think I shall know without telling." An odd thing to say.

On the next evening, which was the last but one, we were sitting together in the half-light with the windows open, for although it was late October the weather was still warm. I was holding wool for Lady Heron to wind, and was so close in front of her and could clearly see her face, when, in the distance, and a mere thread of sound, but perfectly distinct, I heard the skirl of the pipes.

I do not think my hands trembled, held out stiffly with the skein, but hers did in the effort to wind. The thin, faint music came near, nearer, and then seemed to turn away. Not to the house; for all my cherished unbelief, I was thankful that it was not coming to the house.

Lady Heron had dropped her ball of wool, and now stooped to regain it.

"We will not wind any more now, my dear," she said. "I am obliged to you, but I shall have enough." And then she crossed the room and rang the bell, a hanging bell-pull, old-fashioned like all else at Mallory. Peters came quickly; was it only my fancy that he looked disturbed

"We will have the windows closed now and the lamp lit." Such was her commonplace order. I heard no more of the pipes that night, but next morning came the news that John Frazer, the tenant of the Mill, had passed away.

It was no doubt a coincidence, nothing more, but we may put it down as an odd one. That was the day before yesterday. I left early yesterday morning, Peters going with me as far as Edinburgh, and I have been busy writing, writing, all these hours in the train. What a packet you will have to wade through!

III

You have been good, dear Margaret, in liking my letters about the hospital work, although while I was so busy they could only be scraps. (And, what was worse, I am afraid my letters to poor old Jack in the trenches were scrappy too. Ungrateful, perhaps, for I have lived all this while on his scraps to me.)

But to go back to the hospital. You will be surprised to hear that I have had to give up my work there, which is a great disappointment. But everything has been horrid of late. I am alone in the flat. The beginning of the upset was that Violet turned horrid; wasn't it nasty of her, when we had been such chums? I told you about Captain Bridgwater, who used to come to see us after he left the hospital; he was cousin to some of Violet's people, and an old schoolfellow of Jack's. It seemed right and natural to be friends, as that was so I liked him in the beginning—really I liked him very much, and was pleased when he showed that he liked me. But Violet liked him in a different way, and expected a flirtation they had begun years before to have a serious meaning; she declares it would have meant something serious if it had not been for me. So we had a quarrel, and she said dreadful things, and I was indignant, as I had a right to be, and was not sorry when she packed her boxes and gave up her share of the flat, leaving me alone.

I was not sorry, but I was shaken by it, and it so happened that when Captain Bridgwater came in he found me crying. Then he was horrid, too, and said things—things that at first I did not understand, and that he had no business to say to Jack's wife, he who had been Jack's friend. I shall never speak to him again, you may be sure.

After this I went to the hospital, to my work as usual, but I did not feel a bit like myself. I had a fainting fit for the first time in my life, and they were a long while in bringing me to. Afterwards the doctor told me I should have to give up V.A.D.-ing. I am not strong enough.

I am wondering what I ought to do. Jack would not like me being here by myself. He only consented to the plan because Violet was joining me, and I do not know of anybody else. But nothing on earth will induce me to go back to Aunt Winifred.

I was interrupted there, and now where do you think I am continuing my letter? I am writing in the train, the Scotch express, and I am on my way to Mallory. There is a surprise for you, and a surprise for me, but I begin to think it is the best solution of the difficulty that could have been found. Lady Heron sent for me, and the queer thing is how she could have known or guessed. I begin to think my mother-in-law must be a bit of a witch.

Where I broke off above was when the servant came in to say a man named Peters had called and had brought a letter. It was a kind letter, so kind a letter that it made me cry, though that is saying little, as tears have been close to my eyes of late. The rigours of winter were past, Lady Heron wrote; the days were already lengthening into spring; a visit would give her the utmost pleasure, and she

fancied it might now suit me to come to her again. Peters
was her messenger instead of the post, and if I were willing
Peters would arrange my journey, and spare me all trouble
about it, as indeed he has done. And it was not necessary
for me to write. Peters would send her a wire, and a warm
welcome would await me.

So here I am travelling North. And I think you will
agree it has been a wise decision, and one that will please
Jack as things are. I shall post this to you in Edinburgh,
my dear, and write again from Mallory.

IV

Really, Margaret, I am happy to be here, much happier
than I was before. Lady Heron is so kind, and I think we
understand each other better than we did. I have a lovely
room on the south side of the house, and the air is far
milder than you would suppose. We never say anything
about the pipes, but I fancy they must have been heard
twice at least while I was in London, because two more of
the Frazers have fallen; sons of the people at the farm; and
another of the clan name died in hospital the week before
my return.

Alas! we have heard the pipes again, and I will tell you
how. They came at the edge of dusk, not what they call
here the murk of the night, but while there was still light
enough to see, had there been bodily presence to be seen.

Lady Heron likes me to play to her, and I was sitting at
the piano, recollecting old airs, and sometimes crooning a
bit of song half to myself, when it seemed as if my music
had an echo outside the house. My fingers fell from the
keys, and in another moment I was sure what it was, and
where.

It came with a sweep, swiftly, devouring space, heard
afar, and then immediately close, passing our window,
which looked out upon nothing—nothing, not a shadow
even, nor the print of a foot. The wild pibroch passed

by, but it went circling round the house, and, oh, it was coming back? We both sprang up and met in a close clasp together, each of us calling the other by name. "Mother!" I cried to her—the first time I have called her so, but it seemed rent from me without thought. It passed the second time, and now there was a cry with it, like a human voice in pain, and again it went circling through the air which had been still, but was rising with a gust of storm.

Twice for the heir! That was what the old man Steenson said, and, oh, me! Jack was the heir. There was a pause of seconds, and then it passed for the third time, the pibroch and the shriek. Afterwards there was a great silence. The wind which had swept with it fell also—if it were wind indeed; and we two women drew apart and looked at each other. Her face was ghastly, and I expect mine was no better.

"Cecily," she said, "you know!" And then, "Who told you?"

Soon afterwards Peters came in to light the lamps, and the old servant's hands so trembled as he performed his task that the glasses clashed and clattered—he who was usually noiseless. He, too, had heard; of that I made no doubt; he had heard even as we.

It was the sign for the head of the house. Lady Heron heard it just so before her husband died. There was some small comfort to us both in the belief that it came for Heron and not Jack. But that comfort did not last. The telegram from the War Office came two days after—"*Wounded and missing, believed killed*"—the intimation to Lady Heron about both her sons, Lieut.-Colonel Lord Heron, and Captain the Hon. John Frazer; not one alone, but both.

I cannot write about that time. A chink was left to us through which hope came, but one could hardly look at it in face of the awful doubt. And the sign for the head of the house would stand also for Jack, provided Heron had been the first to fall.

V

Looking back I cannot think how we endured the suspense. Counted by days the measure of it was not long,
but it seemed as if ages went by. We tried to comfort each
other; Lady Heron was an angel to me through all her own
pain; but for her I would have died.

I cannot write about it; you must take it for granted,
and I hurry on to the end. We were sitting together, we
two alone, as we were when the sign came. Lady Heron was
knitting, feverishly knitting at those socks for Jack which
she would not lay aside, little as either of us believed they
would be worn. We were together, as I said, when Peters
rushed into the room with another telegram on his silver
tray. (I wonder he remembered the tray.) Lady Heron tore
it open; it was addressed to her. *"Home slightly wounded.
With you and Cecily to-morrow.—Jack."*

My mind takes a leap from that moment to another
when he stood at the door. Lady Heron would not let
me go to the station because I had fainted again, and as
I might not, she would not either; she said it would be
unfair to take the advantage. Jack at the door, a figure in
soiled khaki, very pale, with his head bandaged and his
arm in a sling; Jack himself, alive and still to live. My
Jack; and I do not mind now, as once I did, that he is his
mother's Jack as well.

He has been through dreadful things. Heron fell—poor
Heron—and was left in No Man's Land, and Jack went
after him. At the utmost risk to himself he dragged out
his brother from under a pile of dead, and into the shelter
of a shell-crater. There they existed for three days under
incessant fire, all hope of them being abandoned; existed
by a miracle, for it was death to move. Heron was fearfully wounded, but Jack, wounded himself, managed so
to bandage him that the bleeding stopped; and then he
found some emergency rations on which they sustained life.
If there ever were a coldness between the brothers, as I
thought, it must have melted away in those dreadful hours.

On the fourth day our troops attacked again on the farther side of the wood, which diverted attention, and then Jack began the task—the difficult and painful task—of half-carrying, half-dragging Heron to where he could be helped, as his only chance of life. All this time Jack was wounded himself, in the head and on the shoulder and side, but the burst of shrapnel which shattered his arm did not happen till they were close to our own lines. By this Heron was wounded again, but in any case Jack thinks he could not have survived; the doctor at the dressing-station said so. Heron died there, but not till some hours later, and Jack was with him to the last.

So the pipers were right and not wrong when they bewailed the head of the house who had fallen. What it meant to Jack I did not consider then, and it came on me with a shock of surprise when Peters, some time later, addressed him as "my lord."

But I think more—much more—of the fact that he has been recommended for the Cross.

Drake's Drum

ARTHUR MACHEN

(1919)

"Take my drum to England, hang et by the shore,
  Strike et when your powder's runnin' low;
If the Dons sight Devon, I'll quit the port o' Heaven,
  An' drum them up the Channel as we drummed them
    long ago."

Sir Henry Newbolt.

We wake sometimes from dreams uttering strange phrases,
murmuring incredible things. At the moment of waking,
for some ineffable instant of time, the words we speak, or
perhaps think we speak, seem to us full of illumination. To
everyone who speculates at all as to the heights and depths
of the soul there comes at very rare moments—there are
not, perhaps, more than half-a-dozen such experiences
given to any man's lifetime—the sense of the true world
which lies beyond this dark place of images and shadows;
a world that is full of light and glory, a world where all
our dim desires are interpreted and fulfilled. It is as if
we stood amongst shadows before a black curtain, as if
for one moment a fold were caught back and we saw that
which we can never utter: but never deny.

In dreams and waking and in waking dreams most of
us, I suppose, penetrate into this other world, the world
beyond the black curtain. But we are not suffered to make
any report of it; the secret, it seems, must be kept fast.
And that is one of the reasons why I am usually inclined

to disbelieve most stories of the communicating spirits of the dead. Their messages are, to my judgment, altogether too lucid, too comfortably and easily and clearly set forth. There is no obscurity in the interpretation of their sentences, no impression as of a great gulf of the spirit which has been traversed with the utmost difficulty. And if we, still in the flesh, cannot utter to ourselves our own visions, it scarcely seems likely that those who have passed beyond the flaming ramparts of the world should be able to chatter to us so easily and colloquially of the regions of their dwelling.

The speech of that far land, if any speech there be, will, I think, be delivered rather in sensible images than in logical and grammatical utterance. And it is only the unspiritual who can discern nothing of the spirit in things audibly or visibly presented to our senses.

Here is the true story of such a presentation.

On the eleventh of last November the Armistice between the Allies and the German Empire was signed. This meant that the incredible had happened. A few months before all the world had been in terror of a Power that seemed capable of fighting all the world. Now; in a moment; as if by enchantment; that Power had ceased to exist. The Armistice terms were, most justly and wisely, rigorous, and on November 21st it was appointed that practically the whole German Fleet should surrender to the British. I said that the whole event was incredible, and so true is this that the British Navy could scarcely believe that the surrender would be accomplished peacefully. Sailors are generous men to all, but more especially to other sailors. There is a brotherhood of the deep, which surpasses the bounds of nations, and our Navy could not believe that the German sailors would give up their ships without fighting; even though the fight might be a hopeless one for them. Consequently, on the morning of November 21st, 1918, the British Navy awaited the enemy in a state of mind that is

hard to describe. The surrender of the German fleet, they
all knew, had been demanded and granted; but at the last
moment, our men thought, the unutterable disgrace must
boil in the veins of those German sailors, and the guns of
their great ships must speak their final word of fire before
they sank beneath the water. Every preparation was made
for the fight. The ships were cleared. The men were at "action stations." Naval discipline was at its strictest. Every
man on board every ship knew his place to an inch, his
duty to the most minute detail. The King's ships had made
them ready for battle; it is hard for a landsman to realize
the awful and inexorable import of such an array.

The Fleet steamed to the appointed rendezvous; waited; and looked eastward. It was a misty morning with a
gentle breeze.

One of the ships was the *Royal Oak,* chiefly manned by
sailors of Devonshire. She was flying on that day a magnificent silk ensign, made for her by Devonshire ladies.
On her bridge, sixty feet above the top deck, was a group
of officers: Admiral Grant, Captain Maclachlan, of the
Royal Oak, the Commander, and others. It was soon after
9 o'clock in the morning when the German fleet appeared,
looming through the mist. Admiral Grant saw them and
waited; he could scarcely believe, he says, that they would
not instantly open fire.

Then the drum began to beat on the *Royal Oak.* The
sound was unmistakable; it was that of a small drum being
beaten "in rolls." At first, the officers on the bridge paid
little attention, if any, to the sound; so intent were they
on the approaching enemy. But when it became evident
that the Germans were not to show fight, Admiral Grant
turned to the Captain of the *Royal Oak,* and remarked on
the beating of the drum. The Captain said that he heard it,
but could not understand it, since the ship was cleared for
action, and every man on board was at his battle station.
The Commander also heard, but could not understand,

and sent messengers all over the ship to investigate. Twice
the messengers were sent about the ship, about all the
decks. They reported that every man was at his station. Yet
the drum continued to beat. Then the Commander himself made a special tour of investigation through the *Royal
Oak*. He, too, found that every man was at his station.

It must be noted, by the way, that if someone, playing a practical joke, had been beating a drum between
decks, the sound would have been inaudible to the officers on the bridge. Secondly, when a ship is cleared for
action, the members of the band have specially important
duties in connection with fire control apparatus assigned
to them. The band instruments are all stored away in the
band room, right aft, and below decks.

All the while the British fleet was closing round the
German fleet, coming to anchor in a square about it, so
that the German ships were hemmed in. And all the while
that this was being done, the noise of the drum was heard
at intervals, beating in rolls. All who heard it are convinced that it was no sound of flapping stays or any such
accident. The ear of the naval officer is attuned to all the
noises of his ship in fair weather and in foul; it makes no
mistakes. All who heard knew that they heard the rolling
of a drum.

At about 2 o'clock in the afternoon the German fleet
was enclosed and helpless, and the British ships dropped
anchor, some fifteen miles off the Firth of Forth. The
utter, irrevocable ruin and disgrace of the German Navy
were consummated. And at that moment the drum stopped
beating and was no more heard.

But those who had heard it, Admiral, Captain, Commander, other officers and men of all ratings held then and
hold now one belief as to that rolling music. They believe
that the sound they heard was that of "Drake's Drum"; the
audible manifestation of the spirit of the great sea-cap-
tain, present at this hour of the tremendous triumph of
Britain on the seas. This is the firm belief of them all.

It may be so. It may be that Drake did quit the port of Heaven in a ship of fire, and driving the Huns across the sea with the flame of his spirit, drummed them down to their pitiful and shameful doom.

The Music of Erich Zann

H. P. LOVECRAFT

(1922)

I have examined maps of the city with the greatest care, yet have never again found the Rue d'Auseil. These maps have not been modern maps alone, for I know that names change. I have, on the contrary, delved deeply into all the antiquities of the place; and have personally explored every region, of whatever name, which could possibly answer to the street I knew as the Rue d'Auseil. But despite all I have done it remains an humiliating fact that I cannot find the house, the street, or even the locality, where, during the last months of my impoverished life as a student of metaphysics at the university, I heard the music of Erich Zann.

That my memory is broken, I do not wonder; for my health, physical and mental, was gravely disturbed throughout the period of my residence in the Rue d'Auseil, and I recall that I took none of my few acquaintances there. But that I cannot find the place again is both singular and perplexing; for it was within a half-hour's walk of the university and was distinguished by peculiarities which could hardly be forgotten by anyone who had been there. I have never met a person who has seen the Rue d'Auseil.

The Rue d'Auseil lay across a dark river bordered by precipitous brick blear-windowed warehouses and spanned by a ponderous bridge of dark stone. It was always shadowy along that river, as if the smoke of neighbouring factories

shut out the sun perpetually. The river was also odorous
with evil stenches which I have never smelled elsewhere,
and which may some day help me to find it, since I should
recognise them at once. Beyond the bridge were narrow
cobbled streets with rails; and then came the ascent, at
first gradual, but incredibly steep as the Rue d'Auseil was
reached.

I have never seen another street as narrow and steep
as the Rue d'Auseil. It was almost a cliff, closed to all
vehicles, consisting in several places of flights of steps,
and ending at the top in a lofty ivied wall. Its paving was
irregular, sometimes stone slabs, sometimes cobblestones,
and sometimes bare earth with struggling greenish-grey
vegetation. The houses were tall, peaked-roofed, incredibly old, and crazily leaning backward, forward, and side-
wise. Occasionally an opposite pair, both leaning forward,
almost met across the street like an arch; and certainly
they kept most of the light from the ground below. There
were a few overhead bridges from house to house across
the street.

The inhabitants of that street impressed me peculiarly.
At first I thought it was because they were all silent and
reticent; but later decided it was because they were all
very old. I do not know how I came to live on such a
street, but I was not myself when I moved there. I had
been living in many poor places, always evicted for want
of money; until at last I came upon that tottering house
in the Rue d'Auseil, kept by the paralytic Blandot. It was
the third house from the top of the street, and by far the
tallest of them all.

My room was on the fifth story; the only inhabited
room there, since the house was almost empty. On the
night I arrived I heard strange music from the peaked garret overhead, and the next day asked old Blandot about
it. He told me it was an old German viol-player, a strange
dumb man who signed his name as Erich Zann, and who
played evenings in a cheap theatre orchestra; adding that

Zann's desire to play in the night after his return from the theatre was the reason he had chosen this lofty and isolated garret room, whose single gable window was the only point on the street from which one could look over the terminating wall at the declivity and panorama beyond.

Thereafter I heard Zann every night, and although he kept me awake, I was haunted by the weirdness of his music. Knowing little of the art myself, I was yet certain that none of his harmonies had any relation to music I had heard before; and concluded that he was a composer of highly original genius. The longer I listened, the more I was fascinated, until after a week I resolved to make the old man's acquaintance.

One night, as he was returning from his work, I intercepted Zann in the hallway and told him that I would like to know him and be with him when he played. He was a small, lean, bent person, with shabby clothes, blue eyes, grotesque, satyr-like face, and nearly bald head; and at my first words seemed both angered and frightened. My obvious friendliness, however, finally melted him; and he grudgingly motioned to me to follow him up the dark, creaking, and rickety attic stairs. His room, one of only two in the steeply pitched garret, was on the west side, toward the high wall that formed the upper end of the street. Its size was very great, and seemed the greater because of its extraordinary bareness and neglect. Of furniture there was only a narrow iron bedstead, a dingy washstand, a small table, a large bookcase, an iron music-rack, and three old-fashioned chairs. Sheets of music were piled in disorder about the floor. The walls were of bare boards, and had probably never known plaster; whilst the abundance of dust and cobwebs made the place seem more deserted than inhabited. Evidently Erich Zann's world of beauty lay in some far cosmos of the imagination.

Motioning me to sit down, the dumb man closed the door, turned the large wooden bolt, and lighted a candle to augment the one he had brought with him. He now

removed his viol from its moth-eaten covering, and taking
it, seated himself in the least uncomfortable of the chairs.
He did not employ the music-rack, but offering no choice
and playing from memory, enchanted me for over an hour
with strains I had never heard before; strains which must
have been of his own devising. To describe their exact nature is impossible for one unversed in music. They were
a kind of fugue, with recurrent passages of the most cap-
tivating quality, but to me were notable for the absence
of any of the weird notes I had overheard from my room
below on other occasions.

Those haunting notes I had remembered, and had often
hummed and whistled inaccurately to myself; so when the
player at length laid down his bow I asked him if he would
render some of them. As I began my request the wrinkled
satyr-like face lost the bored placidity it had possessed
during the playing, and seemed to shew the same curious
mixture of anger and fright which I had noticed when first
I accosted the old man. For a moment I was inclined to use
persuasion, regarding rather lightly the whims of senility;
and even tried to awaken my host's weirder mood by whist-
ling a few of the strains to which I had listened the night
before. But I did not pursue this course for more than
a moment; for when the dumb musician recognised the
whistled air his face grew suddenly distorted with an expression wholly beyond analysis, and his long, cold, bony
right hand reached out to stop my mouth and silence the
crude imitation. As he did this he further demonstrated
his eccentricity by casting a startled glance toward the
lone curtained window, as if fearful of some intruder—
a glance doubly absurd, since the garret stood high and
inaccessible above all the adjacent roofs, this window being the only point on the steep street, as the concierge
had told me, from which one could see over the wall at the
summit.

The old man's glance brought Blandot's remark to my mind, and with a certain capriciousness I felt a wish to look out over the wide and dizzying panorama of moonlit roofs and city lights beyond the hill-top, which of all the dwellers in the Rue d'Auseil only this crabbed musician could see. I moved toward the window and would have drawn aside the nondescript curtains, when with a frightened rage even greater than before the dumb lodger was upon me again; this time motioning with his head toward the door as he nervously strove to drag me thither with both hands. Now thoroughly disgusted with my host, I ordered him to release me, and told him I would go at once. His clutch relaxed, and as he saw my disgust and offence his own anger seemed to subside. He tightened his relaxing grip, but this time in a friendly manner; forcing me into a chair, then with an appearance of wistfulness crossing to the littered table, where he wrote many words with a pencil in the laboured French of a foreigner.

The note which he finally handed me was an appeal for tolerance and forgiveness. Zann said that he was old, lonely, and afflicted with strange fears and nervous disorders connected with his music and with other things. He had enjoyed my listening to his music, and wished I would come again and not mind his eccentricities. But he could not play to another his weird harmonies, and could not bear hearing them from another; nor could he bear having anything in his room touched by another. He had not known until our hallway conversation that I could overhear his playing in my room, and now asked me if I would arrange with Blandot to take a lower room where I could not hear him in the night. He would, he wrote, defray the difference in rent.

As I sat deciphering the execrable French I felt more lenient toward the old man. He was a victim of physical and nervous suffering, as was I; and my metaphysical studies had taught me kindness. In the silence there came a

slight sound from the window—the shutter must have
rattled in the night-wind—and for some reason I started
almost as violently as did Erich Zann. So when I had finished reading I shook my host by the hand, and departed
as a friend. The next day Blandot gave me a more expensive room on the third floor, between the apartments of an
aged money-lender and the room of a respectable uphol-
sterer. There was no one on the fourth floor.

It was not long before I found that Zann's eagerness
for my company was not as great as it had seemed while
he was persuading me to move down from the fifth story.
He did not ask me to call on him, and when I did call he
appeared uneasy and played listlessly. This was always at
night—in the day he slept and would admit no one. My
liking for him did not grow, though the attic room and the
weird music seemed to hold an odd fascination for me. I
had a curious desire to look out of that window, over the
wall and down the unseen slope at the glittering roofs and
spires which must lie outspread there. Once I went up to
the garret during theatre hours, when Zann was away, but
the door was locked.

What I did succeed in doing was to overhear the noc-
turnal playing of the dumb old man. At first I would tiptoe
up to my old fifth floor, then I grew bold enough to climb
the last creaking staircase to the peaked garret. There in
the narrow hall, outside the bolted door with the covered
keyhole, I often heard sounds which filled me with an in-
definable dread—the dread of vague wonder and brooding
mystery. It was not that the sounds were hideous, for they
were not; but that they held vibrations suggesting nothing
on this globe of earth, and that at certain intervals they
assumed a symphonic quality which I could hardly con-
ceive as produced by one player. Certainly, Erich Zann was
a genius of wild power. As the weeks passed, the playing
grew wilder, whilst the old musician acquired an increas-
ing haggardness and furtiveness pitiful to behold. He now

refused to admit me at any time, and shunned me whenever we met on the stairs.

Then one night as I listened at the door I heard the shrieking viol swell into a chaotic babel of sound; a pandemonium which would have led me to doubt my own shaking sanity had there not come from behind that barred portal a piteous proof that the horror was real—the awful, inarticulate cry which only a mute can utter, and which rises only in moments of the most terrible fear or anguish. I knocked repeatedly at the door, but received no response. Afterward I waited in the black hallway, shivering with cold and fear, till I heard the poor musician's feeble effort to rise from the floor by the aid of a chair. Believing him just conscious after a fainting fit, I renewed my rapping, at the same time calling out my name reassuringly. I heard Zann stumble to the window and close both shutter and sash, then stumble to the door, which he falteringly unfastened to admit me. This time his delight at having me present was real; for his distorted face gleamed with relief while he clutched at my coat as a child clutches at its mother's skirts.

Shaking pathetically, the old man forced me into a chair whilst he sank into another, beside which his viol and bow lay carelessly on the floor. He sat for some time inactive, nodding oddly, but having a paradoxical suggestion of intense and frightened listening. Subsequently he seemed to be satisfied, and crossing to a chair by the table wrote a brief note, handed it to me, and returned to the table, where he began to write rapidly and incessantly. The note implored me in the name of mercy, and for the sake of my own curiosity, to wait where I was while he prepared a full account in German of all the marvels and terrors which beset him. I waited, and the dumb man's pencil flew.

It was perhaps an hour later, while I still waited and while the old musician's feverishly written sheets still continued

to pile up, that I saw Zann start as from the hint of a horrible shock. Unmistakably he was looking at the curtained
window and listening shudderingly. Then I half fancied I
heard a sound myself; though it was not a horrible sound,
but rather an exquisitely low and infinitely distant musical note, suggesting a player in one of the neighbouring
houses, or in some abode beyond the lofty wall over which
I had never been able to look. Upon Zann the effect was
terrible, for dropping his pencil suddenly he rose, seized
his viol, and commenced to rend the night with the wildest playing I had ever heard from his bow save when listening at the barred door.

It would be useless to describe the playing of Erich
Zann on that dreadful night. It was more horrible than
anything I had ever overheard, because I could now see
the expression of his face, and could realise that this time
the motive was stark fear. He was trying to make a noise;
to ward something off or drown something out—what, I
could not imagine, awesome though I felt it must be. The
playing grew fantastic, delirious, and hysterical, yet kept
to the last the qualities of supreme genius which I knew
this strange old man possessed. I recognised the air—it
was a wild Hungarian dance popular in the theatres, and
I reflected for a moment that this was the first time I had
ever heard Zann play the work of another composer.

Louder and louder, wilder and wilder, mounted the
shrieking and whining of that desperate viol. The player
was dripping with an uncanny perspiration and twisted
like a monkey, always looking frantically at the curtained
window. In his frenzied strains I could almost see shadowy satyrs and Bacchanals dancing and whirling insanely
through seething abysses of clouds and smoke and lightning. And then I thought I heard a shriller, steadier note
that was not from the viol; a calm, deliberate, purposeful,
mocking note from far away in the west.

At this juncture the shutter began to rattle in a howling
night-wind which had sprung up outside as if in answer

to the mad playing within. Zann's screaming viol now outdid itself, emitting sounds I had never thought a viol could emit. The shutter rattled more loudly, unfastened, and commenced slamming against the window. Then the glass broke shiveringly under the persistent impacts, and the chill wind rushed in, making the candles sputter and rustling the sheets of paper on the table where Zann had begun to write out his horrible secret. I looked at Zann, and saw that he was past conscious observation. His blue eyes were bulging, glassy, and sightless, and the frantic playing had become a blind, mechanical, unrecognisable orgy that no pen could even suggest.

A sudden gust, stronger than the others, caught up the manuscript and bore it toward the window. I followed the flying sheets in desperation, but they were gone before I reached the demolished panes. Then I remembered my old wish to gaze from this window, the only window in the Rue d'Auseil from which one might see the slope beyond the wall, and the city outspread beneath. It was very dark, but the city's lights always burned, and I expected to see them there amidst the rain and wind. Yet when I looked from that highest of all gable windows, looked while the candles sputtered and the insane viol howled with the night-wind, I saw no city spread below, and no friendly lights gleaming from remembered streets, but only the blackness of space illimitable; unimagined space alive with motion and music, and having no semblance to anything on earth. And as I stood there looking in terror, the wind blew out both the candles in that ancient peaked garret, leaving me in savage and impenetrable darkness with chaos and pandemonium before me, and the daemon madness of that night-baying viol behind me.

I staggered back in the dark, without the means of striking a light, crashing against the table, overturning a chair, and finally groping my way to the place where the blackness screamed with shocking music. To save myself and Erich Zann I could at least try, whatever the powers opposed to me. Once I thought some chill thing brushed me, and I screamed, but my scream could not be heard above that hideous viol. Suddenly out of the blackness the madly sawing bow struck me, and I knew I was close to the player. I felt ahead, touched the back of Zann's chair, and then found and shook his shoulder in an effort to bring him to his senses.

He did not respond, and still the viol shrieked on without slackening. I moved my hand to his head, whose mechanical nodding I was able to stop, and shouted in his ear that we must both flee from the unknown things of the night. But he neither answered me nor abated the frenzy of his unutterable music, while all through the garret strange currents of wind seemed to dance in the darkness and babel. When my hand touched his ear I shuddered, though I knew not why—knew not why till I felt of the still face; the ice-cold, stiffened, unbreathing face whose glassy eyes bulged uselessly into the void. And then, by some miracle finding the door and the large wooden bolt, I plunged wildly away from that glassy-eyed thing in the dark, and from the ghoulish howling of that accursed viol whose fury increased even as I plunged.

Leaping, floating, flying down those endless stairs through the dark house; racing mindlessly out into the narrow, steep, and ancient street of steps and tottering houses; clattering down steps and over cobbles to the lower streets and the putrid canyon-walled river; panting across the great dark bridge to the broader, healthier streets and boulevards we know; all these are terrible impressions that linger with me. And I recall that there was no wind, and that the moon was out, and that all the lights of the city twinkled.

Despite my most careful searches and investigations, I have never since been able to find the Rue d'Auseil. But I am not wholly sorry; either for this or for the loss in undreamable abysses of the closely written sheets which alone could have explained the music of Erich Zann.

Symphonic Death

Fred R. Farrow, Jr.

(1928)

The four great kettle-drums stood shrouded in their soiled covers. Bass viols stood and leaned at queer angles against, the back wall. Cellos and tubas sprawled upon the floor. The conductor's desk, littered with manuscript, seemed a gaunt sign-post in the midst of a wilderness of chairs and orchestra trappings.

Most of the lights had. been turned off, and in the feeble light that remained the theater looked dingy and forbidding. Great, ugly carvings frowned down upon the stage. The faded drapes swayed silently in the draft, seeming to wave at an invisible audience.

Philip Schmitt, the youthful conductor, and Hanforth, his concertmaster, walked up the center aisle, their footsteps echoing hollowly on the marble floor back of the parquet circle.

Schmitt was nervously talking, ". . . and according to his will, we must play the fourth movement of the *Fate Symphony* at sight. Not one of us, not even I, the conductor, has seen the score. I tell you, Hanforth, it seems uncanny.

"Think of the last thirty-two bars of the *Marche Exotique*. God, what awful harmony! Terrible ninths for double-basses and bassoons and those infernally shrieking chromatics for first fiddles! There's more than power behind that music. I seem to feel old Scheel right back of me when I conduct it."

Hans Scheel was the former conductor of the orchestra. He had taken the organization, then only a group of fair amateurs, and by his unflagging energy and genius had built it into the artistic ensemble of a perfect symphony orchestra of one hundred and ten men. He loved it with all the fervor of a genius for his brain child, and resented the slightest criticism of its playing, or of his own compositions.

Belonging to the modern school of composition, Scheel had many critics who attacked him and his works. The chief one of these was Emil Brandenburg. Like Scheel he was arrogant to the nth degree, and although they had never come to blows, many hard battles had been fought verbally.

One night after the concert, Brandenburg had knocked at Scheel's dressing-room, and after being admitted he began, as was his custom, to pick apart, piece by piece, one of the conductor's favorite numbers.

Said he, "It's a lot of claptrap—so much orchestral bookkeeping. Twenty years from now no one will remember any of it. Modern harmony—bah! Modern discord, I call it!"

Scheel had stood looking at him with his burning eyes. He pronounced, almost like a curse, these words: "You fool! Dare you mock me and my works? In life I can defend my art, but after death it must, for the world, stand alone. However, if you continue, I will crush you, even from the grave, along with any other unworthy upstart who attempts to fill my position when I am gone."

This had silenced Brandenburg for the time, and one week later Scheel died, leaving the *Fate Symphony* and specifying in his will that the final movement was to be played without rehearsal. It was significant, too, that the score for this number, the *Scherzo Fantastique,* was written in red ink.

Hanforth and young Schmitt walked silently across the street to a tiny restaurant. They sat down at their favorite table in the back, and Schmitt nervously lighted a cigarette.

He had been concertmaster of the orchestra for five years, and had distinguished himself at this post. Now that he was conductor his youthful shoulders seemed to bend under the responsibility of leading one hundred and ten men through symphonic mazes. He lacked the self-confidence which time alone could give him.

"I don't know whether you will believe it or not, Hanforth, but whenever I conduct I seem to feel his sneering, domineering personality, just as he was in life."

"Well, I don't take any stock in that, but I wish we didn't have to play that scherzo at sight. The rest of the symphony is difficult enough, even after rehearsal."

Schmitt pushed his blond hair back from his brow and said, "Well, it's just got to go all right, or if it doesn't I'm afraid to think. There's something uncanny about it all. I keep remembering what Scheel told Brandenburg just before he died. Furthermore, Hanforth, you never read the program of the *Fate Symphony.*"

He shivered and went on: "The story is that of a young man who knows that there is hereditary madness in his family. In time he goes quite mad himself. The *Marche Exotique* depicts him being taken to the asylum, and the finale paints his ravings in a padded cell."

"What a horrible subject to write a symphony upon!" exclaimed Hanforth.

"Yes, and Scheel could write. He was like these artists who draw impressionistic sketches—all lines and queer distorted angles. I would rather take a sound thrashing than go through with tonight's program. The men themselves are uneasy. They have scented something, and it wouldn't take much to make them walk out."

"You can't really blame them for not liking to play such difficult stuff by sight, without having rehearsed it at all."

"No, but everything must go right; it's just got to."

The two men sipped their coffee in silence. Schmitt called for the check, paid it, and climbing into a taxicab, went to his hotel to dress for the evening.

Eight o'clock. Fifteen minutes more and the concert would be under way.

Expensive limousines carrying bejeweled women and men in top-hats drove up to the front entrance.

The musicians themselves began to arrive. Already quite a number were tuning up on the stage, each individual adding his bit to the dissonance of an orchestra before playing.

Eight-ten. Philip Schmitt arrived at the stage door. He looked pale but determined. The doorman took his coat and hat, and Schmitt nervously adjusted his tie in front of a small mirror back-stage. Precisely at 8:15 he opened the door at the left wing, and walked to the conductor's desk. A storm of applause greeted him.

There was the score of the accursed symphony under that of Moussorgsky's *Night on Bald Mountain,* the opening number on the program. There in the right balcony box sat Brandenburg, smug, sneering and complacent as ever. Schmitt tapped his stand for order, and the players ceased their tuning.

Turning slightly to the left, to the first violins, he began to conduct the eerie triplets of the first bars of Moussorgsky's composition. At the fifth bar he turned to the flutes, which shrieked the approach of the spirits.

All well. The spirits gathered, danced, and were dispersed by the tolling of the bell at midnight, and the number was brought to a close amidst whole-hearted applause from the audience.

Schmitt waited a minute or so to enable the men to tune and get their breath. Then they began with a grumble from double-basses that shook the floor. This was answered by a plaintive strain for oboes and clarinets; then an upward sweep for cellos, and a harp cadenza. He gave the violas their cue after the harp, and the symphony was under way. First violins announced the terror motif of the young man doubting his own sanity. This was answered by the bassoons, which seemed to mock. Again the terror motif, this time more pronounced. The movement ended with a sad strain for English horn and viola.

The second movement was much similar to the first, the terror and doubt motives being developed with awful certainty. Schmitt then began to feel it. He had tried to concentrate on his reading and to be oblivious to all other influences. Now, however, he knew absolutely that he was not alone on the conductor's platform. Another presence was there, invisible and malevolent.

He glanced toward Brandenburg in the box. His sneering look had been replaced by one of awe not unmixed with fear.

They began the *Marche Exotique*. The great orchestra groaned in horrible dissonance. Silvery glissades from the celesta were crushed by the ominous rhythm of double-basses.

Schmitt seemed in the grip of something intangible yet all-powerful. This, then, was to test his worthiness. Well, he would give them all he had. The number concluded with the cellos and the bass viols seeming to descend a giant staircase into the infernal regions accompanied by the terrible despair motif from first and second violins.

Brandenburg's face now bore a look of fear. He, too, had sensed it, remembering the fateful words of Scheel, "I will crush you even from the grave."

Hard-headed and stubborn though he was, he began to be afraid. He wondered what the concluding movement would bring forth. He nervously hitched his chair around in the box where he sat alone, and fearfully looked behind the faded draperies. The sneer gradually replaced itself on his face. He was a fool to take any stock in dead men's curses! He swore softly under his breath, as a child talks to itself in the dark for comfort.

The scherzo was under way.

Philip Schmitt was pale. His knees trembled. He glanced at the horrid array of red notes on the score before him. Red! The color of madness! He felt like shouting, but continued to beat time as though in the grip of some invisible power. He seemed to feel old Scheel's eyes burning into his back.

Violins laughed horribly. Flutes and clarinets shrieked in awful glee. The orchestra seemed to be running away, yet under it all the hand of the master had bound them together in perfect counterpoint.

The audience looked on and listened, spellbound with the awful miracle that was being wrought.

Suddenly, after a loud cymbal crash, the lights went out; the whole house was in darkness save for the small lights on the music stands.

Some few detected a bluish glow around the conductor's desk. Brandenburg was one, and he observed it with stark terror clutching at his heart. He seemed to see the words written in letters of fire: "I will crush you even from the grave." His eyes bulged. His reason seemed to totter. The orchestra was groaning like a giant in pain. Through it all crept the madness motif—seven shrill little notes for oboe. Above the grumble of double-basses, above the moaning of the violins, the madness theme stood out and seemed to triumph in the downfall of a human soul.

The blue glow around the conductor's desk grew more intense. Brandenburg, his face horribly contorted with fear, saw Schmitt reel and fall. He attempted to rise, but in his place was a shadowy form, beating time. The form grew in distinctness, and the features became those of Hans Scheel. There he stood, his eyes flashing fire, his huge forehead bulging under his scant locks. No, there could be no doubt.

A shriek tore through the air from the balcony box, followed by another and another, and the sound of people wildly stampeding toward the exits.

The lights went on. Ushers ran upon the stage to quiet the crowd. Over the rail of the balcony box there hung something that had been human but which now leered, with bulging eyes and distorted features. From its mouth came strange, meaningless sounds. Suddenly it recovered itself, climbed over the rail and fell to the stage below.

The orchestra stopped playing. Schmitt sat on the edge of his platform, head in hands, shaken but sane.

At the side of the stage, physicians were doing all they could to ease the last moments of a thing that gibbered horribly and glared with the light of madness in its protruding eyes.

The Chords of Chaos
L. A. Lewis
(1929)

"Have you ever heard of astral music?"

Rex Eustace replaced his pipe in his mouth, leaned back and looked at me interrogatively. We had just finished dinner, and were taking our coffee on the terrace in the cool of the evening.

It was not the first time that we had touched upon the supernatural. Many a night in our dug-out "over there" mutual interest had led our thoughts along the same path, the light of one flickering candle casting its elusive shadows on walls of damp earth lending a spice of reality to the topic.

But back home in my friend's pretty, old-fashioned garden, with the dark uncertainties of war at an end and a hundred trivialities of daily amusement to occupy our minds, I wondered what train of thought had prompted this sudden question.

"I'm not sure," I replied cautiously; "What exactly do you mean?"

"I mean music which belongs to the spirit-world and can be reproduced by a medium during a state of trance."

"I have heard of that," I said, "but have never seen it done. Have you?"

"Yes. Quite recently," he answered.

I became interested. Spiritualism is a subject of which I know little, but it is a fascinating study.

"I have a neighbour," he continued, "a Mr. Julian West-enhanger, who is a medium. He will sit down at the piano, make his mind a blank, and play the harmonies that come to him from beyond the barrier. The thing is absolutely genuine. He really plays the most wonderful stuff, quite unlike anything else which I have heard. Nearly sent me into a trance myself the other day when I was listening to it. On regaining consciousness he can recall nothing. It's most weird."

"I should like to hear him," I said quietly.

"You will have the opportunity," Eustace declared. "He is well known as a musician, and has been asked to give an organ recital in St. Mary's Church to-morrow night after Evensong."

"Yes. But I mean the spirit-music."

My friend looked at me quizzically for a moment. Then his gaze travelled vacantly to the sky as though he were considering some problem.

"I don't know him very well," he observed at last, "because he has only come to the place during the war, and I have been away as we both know: but, if you really care to meet him, I see no reason why we should not drop in for an hour right away. What d'you think?"

"Certainly," I responded, rising to my feet.

And with that one word I ignorantly committed myself to the most painful, ghastly, and grotesquely incredible adventure of my life—a thing made the more *bizarre* by its setting of peaceful security in the little country town.

Mr. Westenhanger was at home, and we were promptly shown into his drawing-room. I walked over towards the French windows and glanced casually about me. One can frequently read something of a man's character in the objects with which he surrounds himself. To my disappointment, however, this room presented no features of especial interest. In all respects it was commonplace. I do not mean drab or ugly, but just average—the kind of reception room one would find in a dozen small country houses. There were the usual rosewood chairs, the usual landscape pictures on a pale blue wallpaper, a chintz-covered sofa, and various other pieces of strictly conventional furniture. A vase of lilies, standing on the piano, diffused a sweet though rather heavy perfume.

I began to regret that my friend had told me nothing of the man himself.

"At all events," I thought, "he is not a genius of the long-haired tribe,"—a deduction which was verified as our host made his appearance.

In no way did Westenhanger give the impression of an artist except in his slender hands with the long, sensitive fingers of the musician. Of medium height, with rather close-cropped hair, and neatly attired in a grey suit, he also fell very short of my ideal Spiritualist.

Eustace rose, and said in formal introduction: "This is my friend Mr. Steer—one of the overseas crowd. He is staying with me for a week to celebrate Peace."

I bowed and extended my hand.

"You see," I remarked, "I am a great lover of music. That is why I asked Eustace to bring me round."

For an instant a look of pleasure crossed his face, but, as his hand gripped mine, the expression seemed to change. What emotion it depicted I am powerless to describe; but the effect upon me as I met his eyes was most peculiar. I experienced simultaneously a feeling of exultation and loathing, which vanished as swiftly as it had arisen.

You may think that, having heard of him as an occultist, I was, unconsciously, on the look-out for something abnormal, but I am not usually imaginative, and the queer sensation puzzled me. If I had given any sign, however, of what I felt bound to consider a ridiculous fancy, neither Eustace nor Westenhanger himself appeared to have noticed it. The latter leaned one elbow on the piano and courteously motioned me to a chair.

"You play yourself, Mr. Steer?" he inquired. I was obliged to confess my claims were limited to admiring the performance of others, and the conversation drifted for a while over many diverse subjects.

Presently Westenhanger seated himself at the piano and began to play from memory. Some of the pieces were unfamiliar, and others the best-known triumphs of famous composers. The whole production was an aesthetic banquet, so faultless was his technique and so soulful the rendering. I was lost in the pleading accompaniment of Tosti's "Parted" when he turned abruptly from the instrument.

"You will take a glass of port, won't you?" He said in the most matter-of-fact tone. It was more of a command than a question, and before either of us could reply he had rung the bell. Brought back to reality by his sudden change of demeanour, I began to fear that we should be denied the real object of our visit when Rex broke the silence.

"Steer, like myself, is interested in the supernatural," he ventured, "and I took the liberty of mentioning to him your mediumistic powers. I am sure he would like you to give us some astral music if it will not trouble you too much."

The way in which he spoke amused me slightly. It seemed by far too casual a tone for such a matter, and I felt a little apprehensive lest it should be taken as the irreverent banter of a sceptic.

Our host made no answer until the servant had placed a decanter with three glasses upon a side table, and the door was once more closed.

I was becoming quite excited, like a schoolboy immersed in a blood-curdling ghost story, while he poured out the red wine and handed each of us a glass.

At last he turned towards me thoughtfully. "It is a thing I very rarely do at anyone's request," he affirmed. "Do you really wish me to?"

"Yes," I answered briefly.

"Very well. You shall hear it. But, remember, I have no idea what I am about to play, and shall remember nothing of it afterwards—so please ask me no questions."

That was all, and there had been no great difficulty in persuading him. I took a sip of port, exchanged a glance with Eustace, and leaned forward to listen.

Once more Westenhanger took his place at the piano and, closing his eyes, let his head sink forward upon his breast. For the space of several minutes there was absolute silence. He seemed instantly to have fallen asleep. Then his lean, white fingers began to wander over the ivories with a strange, half-conscious caress, and the first rippling notes of an unknown music rang out in the stillness.

Even with those first trembling bars I held my breath. It was as though a primeval voice were speaking out of the unborn darkness of eternity. Without rhyme or rhythm the sound rolled forth, now low and plaintive, nor rising to an exultant crescendo in waves of unearthly melody, alluring though foreign to the human ear. To this day I wonder whether an instrument made by man could have produced those sounds, or whether, rendered receptive by some unseen influence, I heard them in spirit alone. Whatever their origin, to me they were real; and as I closed my eyes, the more readily to absorb their wild cadence, they conjured up vague, formless pictures chasing each other across an opaque veil.

Astounding as it may seem, scarcely a moment could have elapsed since the medium had entered into his trance, but already I was forgetting time, place, everything in a kind of hypnotic sleep. How long this condition lasted I do not know. The scented air seemed to grow denser and still more dense, a green mist surrounded me, and ears were filled with a reverberating roar. Fainter and less distinct came those musical waves, and some dormant inner consciousness called into being a dream that was not a dream—the memory of a long-forgotten life.

I stood alone on the outskirts of a great multitude
thronged in the moonlit courtyard of a temple. On three
sides rose massive walls of hewn stone, their castellated
summits dimly outlined against the starry sky; and in
front, the temple itself, a vast pile wrought in black marble with towering minarets, its base half hidden in a pool
inky shadow. There was something terrifying in its looming majesty—a callous, indestructible pride.

The brilliant moon immediately overhead poured down
a cold white light upon the sea of upturned faces from
which came the murmur of a thousand tongues. Each motionless figure was bareheaded, and clad in flowing robes
of some dark material. My own dress was the same, a long,
purple garment embroidered with serpents of black and
gold, and fastened on the left shoulder with a single metal
clasp.

I looked down at my feet. They were encased in sandals
of raw hide; and, strangely enough, there seemed to me
nothing unusual in this attire. It was as though I knew
no other and had worn it all my days. My eyes lifted, and
once more I gazed round the packed assembly.

All were waiting even as I waited—but for what? Dimly
I remembered that it was the performance of some mystic
rite, but of its nature I was profoundly ignorant: nor was
there a sign within the whole spectacle, save for a restless
motion which now began to stir the feet of the crowd.

Presently I felt a hand upon my shoulder, and became
aware of another standing by me, the clear light revealing
his bearded face.

"Greeting to thee," I whispered in a language long dead,
though one which I spoke with natural ease.

"Greeting," he answered softly: and, by some freak of
double consciousness, I knew him for the past self of my
friend Eustace. Evidently we have been age-long associ-
ates, and in my dream-memory, trusted comrades-in-arms
even as in the present life. One bend in the eternal spiral
of evolution, and the conditions were repeated.

"Tell me then," I said, addressing him by his ancient name, though that I have now forgotten, "to what ceremony are we bidden—thou and I?"

"It is the night of our father Chaos," he replied, "of him that bred the Earth in fire-mist: yet of the manner of his worship I too am without knowledge. Once in ten score years this festival is held, nor is its nature told to any, save to the priests alone; for some say that no man of the people shall leave these walls alive!"

At these words a chill crept over my body, a thrill of expectant fear and a sense of dread stirred my heart. With a shudder I turned to look behind me, and, as I did so, the mutter of voices grew in volume. There came the shuffle of many sandals upon stone, like waves on a shingle beach, and the mob surged outwards to the sides of the court, so that we were jostled this way and that.

With a resonant clang two gates of bronze swung back, and as a lane opened through their midst, a great cry went up to the echoing heights: "They come! They come!"

Then stillness fell again as the babel of tongues gave place to the tramp of a marching column.

Through those twin gates they entered—a sinuous procession of white-robed priests each bearing upon his brow a tiny lamp like a diadem of flame, and at their head strode a stately leader, his vestments glittering with a maze of jewels. As he went, those in the foremost ranks bowed themselves to the ground.

By reason of our stature, my companion and I were able to see a him over the heads of the throng, and it was with an inward shock that I saw in him the soul of Julian Westenhanger—yet still I dreamed.

Speechless the column moved on until it came to the temple steps, where it halted in a half circle, the high priest solemnly ascending until he stood within the gloom of the portal. Not another sound could be heard as, in a dirge-like chant, he addressed the tremendous gathering:

"Give ear, O people of Atlantis—ye that have come up from the four points of the heavens to make obeisance to the Father of Life. Ye are the dust, the fragments of his creation. How then shall ye exalt yourselves to tyrannise the world that gave you birth? Humble yourselves, things of vileness, that your Father may see in you repentance. Haste ye, slaves of vanity, to make your sacrifice; for Chaos, the Lawless, the Ungoverned, knoweth not delay."

He ceased, and withdrew into the dark interior followed by the file of priests, while, in echo of his words rolled up the muffled answer:

"We make our sacrifice."

Little did they guess by what means the Black Powers would take their toll.

One and all bowed themselves low, hushed and awestruck, awaiting some manifestation yet untold.

It came.

A burst of thunderous music boomed through the columns of the temple, a volume of bass chords from some tremendous organ. Out of the inmost recesses it poured forth to fill the quivering air, until the whole huge fabric of the temple throbbed with its mighty utterance. Its effect upon the audience was instant and notable. Some swayed dizzily as they stood, some fell upon their knees, while others prostrated themselves as though overcome.

For my own part I felt that my reason was tottering. The mass of sound—it seemed almost tangible—hammered in my ear-drums with a sensation of acute physical pain; and all the time those it stupendous notes increased in power until they broke and mingled in one terrific paean flinging its echoes infinitely into space.

All about me the wonderful, unholy music pealed out, whirling in a tempest irresistible, and my senses withered like shrivelled grass. Dazed and half blind, I sought vainly for some pathway of escape, but the monstrous walls mocked me, and the crowd, a maelstrom of formless spectres to my distorted vision, pressed close around.

Then came the fearful climax.

Somewhere within that temple of sin the unseen instrument crashed into hideous discord, causing an anguish no human tongue could describe. My whole frame was racked with the agony of it, and the last shreds of self-control swept away in blind, brutal insanity.

Within one flash of time the court became a ghastly scene of carnage, men and women rending each other in a frenzy of diabolic hate, and beating their own heads against the granite floor. In tortured fury I clawed and struck at my companion, snarling like a beast—my one passionate desire to kill—to kill! His arms gripped me with superhuman strength, his teeth were grinding at my throat . . . and in that appalling moment I regained consciousness.

Eustace was crouched near to me upon the carpet, his eyes reflecting my own unutterable horror; and Westenhanger lay spread-eagled upon the keyboard sunk in deep oblivion.

Mutely we staggered out into the twilight.

All that night I lay awake, tired out in mind and body, but unable to sleep for the poignant remembrance of that dreadful nightmare. Time after time my thoughts travelled back over every detail of the sinister drama which had become part of my waking life, until no vestige of doubt remained that it was true. Not a single word had Eustace exchanged with me upon the subject, for each knew what the other had seen.

Had we not stood together through the ordeal up to the consummation of all things—victims of the black magicians in old Atlantis? Both had awakened with the same loss of energy, the same indelible terror of the spirit, and, try as I would, I could not put aside the premonition that oppressed me.

The story was not complete. The curtain had yet to rise for the last act. And somewhere, locked in the fathomless heart of nature, existed that foul combination of sound waves which could turn the whole human race into a race of maniacs.

In the morning I felt no relief. My head ached, my limbs were heavy, and I was shadowed with uneasiness. Eustace noticed it but himself looked thoroughly over-wrought.

"It is the effect of last night," he explained; but said no more. On that Sunday nothing could restore our vitality or our contentment. We tried to read, to play bowls, even to weed the garden, but our listless melancholy only increased.

About five in the afternoon Rex found me in my room staring out of the window, and appeared anxious to unburden himself of something.

"Are you coming with me to the evening service?" he inquired after a pause.

"If you wish me to," I returned. I did not ask the name of the church. It would be St. Mary's, I felt sure.

"Very well," he said briefly; "I will be ready in half an hour."

At six we were in our places for the celebration of Even-song.

It was a fine building containing a great deal of beautiful carving and some very noteworthy stained glass. The size, I thought, was; sufficient to hold a congregation of about six hundred; and, to judge by the way the pews were filling, quite that number would be present, many, no doubt, having come more for the concluding organ recital than to join in the divine service.

The architecture of oaken roof-beams, the magnificent reredos and the stone columns, all occupied a large part of my attention. I am no great churchman, and always prefer a church when it is empty, from the artistic point of view.

Some time before the benediction I had found West-enhanger sitting in a front pew, just below the pulpit. To render the service short, no sermon was given, and I do not think I was the only one glad of this as the time for his part drew near. Despite my recent, awful experience at his house, the consequences of which I could not yet shake off, I found myself looking forward to a new exhibition of his skill.

At last the blessing was given, priest and choir were gone, and quietly Westenhanger left his seat. It was noticeable that, of the whole congregation, not one man, woman, or child moved, and I could not help smiling as I remembered the words: "A prophet is not without honour—"

And then came the greatest artistic treat I have ever known.

If this man could handle the piano, his execution on the richest of all instruments was nothing less than superb. Oblivious to my surroundings, I listened in ecstasy as he played from Mozart, Mendelssohn and Elgar indiscriminately, each piece with more feeling, if possible, than the last.

But suddenly something took place which called me back to earth from the sublime. The key-note of his music was changing as he drifted on into a fresh composition. The seductive charm of his touch remained, but something cold had crept in like the voice of a condemned soul; and as I listened to its evil grandeur, a frightful conviction stabbed through my heart. In a trance, or with the full consciousness of a hellish purpose, he was playing once more the music of my dream.

With a rush that undefined fear which had hung over me took form. Another moment, and the awful Chords of Chaos would hurl destruction upon hundreds of innocent victims. Panic-stricken I turned to seek the help of Eustace. He had risen and was standing motionless in the aisle. I tried to follow, but a supernatural power had paralysed my limbs, so that I could only watch, wondering childishly what he would do. Then I saw that he held something in his right hand—something which glittered. A man behind me in the next pew had evidently seen it as well, for, with an inarticulate cry, he sprang forward.

It was too late.

There came a muffled report, a spurt of flame, and half way through a bar the music stopped.

As the horrified congregation leaped to its feet, Julian Westenhanger fell dead at the base of the organ.

There is little more to tell.

I cannot bear to linger upon the sad conclusion. The silent horror of the onlookers, the arrest, the trial, the verdict—all is a lurid dream of yesterday: for what Bishop, or what stern-faced jury would hear this testimony and believe?

Among many of its kind in the grassy churchyard of St. Mary's stands a tombstone, inscribed: "JULIAN WESTENHANGER . . . REQUIESCAT IN PACE."

In the northern shadow of the belfry, beyond the pale of consecrated ground, is a nameless grave. Some say it is that of one who desecrated the House of God by the Unforgivable Sin.

Let me pray that two souls find justice before a Higher Judge.

CoachwhipBooks.com

LIGHT SPIRITS

Horrific Specters, Comedic Shades, and Criminous Phantasms in Vintage Periodical Ghost Stories

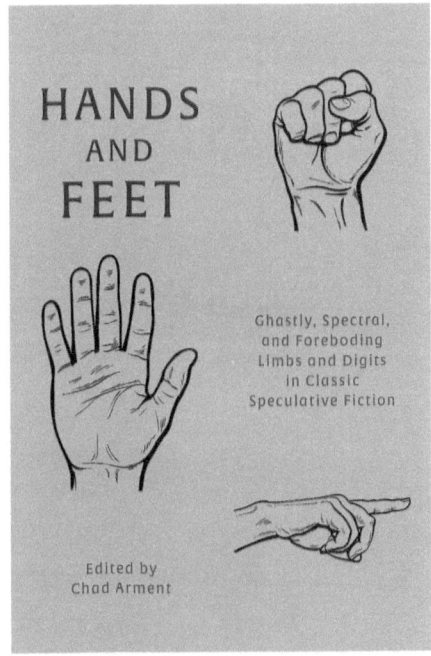

HANDS
AND
FEET

Ghastly, Spectral, and Foreboding Limbs and Digits in Classic Speculative Fiction

Edited by
Chad Arment

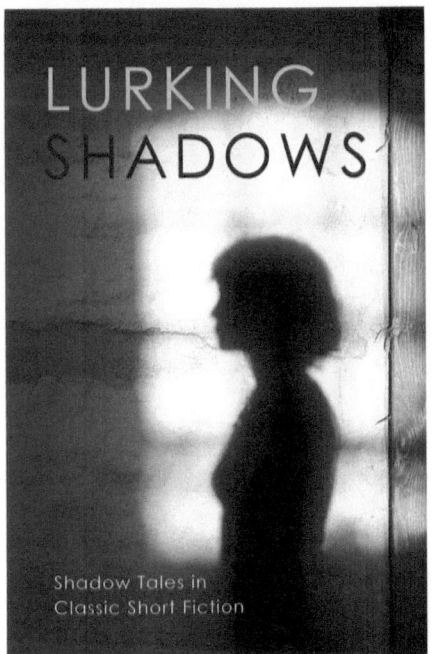

LURKING SHADOWS

Shadow Tales in Classic Short Fiction

UNCANNY OF PLACE

CITIES, STREETS, SHOPS, AND SPACES
IN CLASSIC SPECULATIVE FICTION

Also Available

BLACK SPIRITS AND WHITE
RALPH ADAMS CRAM

TALES OF THE SUPERNATURAL
JAMES PLATT

SHADOWS GOTHIC AND GROTESQUE

STRANGE HAUNTS

STORIES BY
F. MARION CRAWFORD &
H. B. MARRIOTT WATSON

ANCIENT HAUNTS

The Stoneground Ghost Tales
by E. G. Swain

Tedious Brief Tales
of Granta and Gramarye
by Arthur Gray

LONELY HAUNTS

Also Available

CoachwhipBooks.com

HAUNTS & HORRORS

STRANGE & SUPERNATURAL FICTION BY M. P. SHIEL

ROAMING THE DARK

STORIES BY RICHARD MIDDLETON AND BARRY PAIN

FANTASIES OF SCIENCE, ROMANCE, AND THE WEIRD

Volume 2

ROBERT W. CHAMBERS

FANTASIES OF SCIENCE, ROMANCE, AND THE WEIRD

Volume 1

ROBERT W. CHAMBERS

Also Available

CoachwhipBooks.com

CARNACKI: GHOST FINDER
WILLIAM HOPE HODGSON

JOHN BELL: GHOST EXPOSER
L. T. MEADE AND ROBERT EUSTACE

SUPERNATURAL DETECTIVES

SHIELA CRERER
ELLA M. SCRYMSOUR

LUNA BARTENDALE &
THE UNDYING MONSTER
JESSIE DOUGLAS KERRUISH

SUPERNATURAL DETECTIVES

EXPERIENCES OF FLAXMAN LOW
E. AND H. HERON

SOME EXPERIENCES OF LORD SYFRET
ARABELLA KENEALY

SUPERNATURAL DETECTIVES

AYLMER VANCE
ALICE AND CLAUDE ASKEW

THE METHODS OF MORRIS KLAW
SAX ROHMER

SUPERNATURAL DETECTIVES

Also Available

FLORA CURIOSA
CRYPTOBOTANY, MYSTERIOUS FUNGI,
SENTIENT TREES, AND DEADLY PLANTS IN
CLASSIC SCIENCE FICTION AND FANTASY

BOTANICA DELIRA
MORE STORIES OF STRANGE,
UNDISCOVERED, AND MURDEROUS
VEGETATION

HORTUS
DIABOLICUS
*Further Twisting Tales of
Menacing Flora and
Malignant Fungi*

Edited by Chad Arment

ARBORIS MYSTERIUS
STORIES OF THE UNCANNY AND UNDESCRIBED
FROM THE BOTANICAL KINGDOM

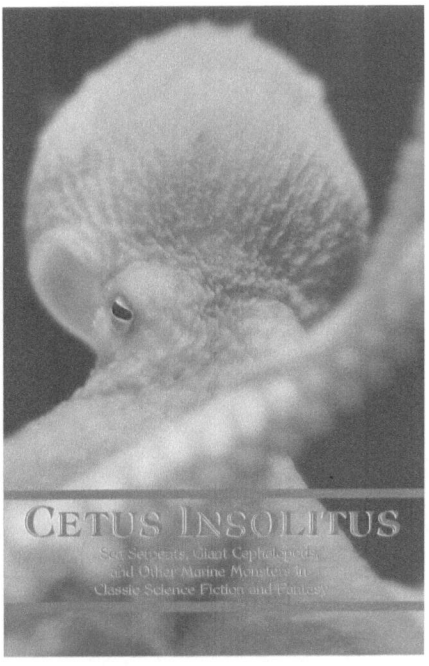

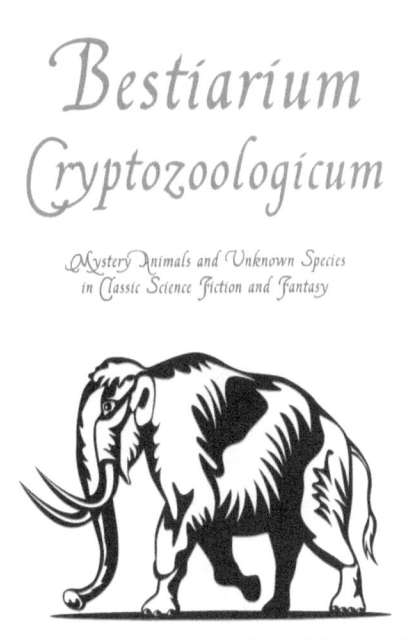

www.ingramcontent.com/pod-product-compliance
Lightning Source LLC
Chambersburg PA
CBHW030353020726
47493CB00003B/802